Published by: New Era Books
2569 Pitkin Ave
Brooklyn, New York 11208
Newerabooks.net
347-651-6366

This is a work of fiction. Names, characters, places and incidents either are a product of the author's imagination or are used fictitiously, and any resemblance to actual persons, living or dead, business establishments, events, or locales is entirely coincidental.

ISBN: *978-0-9844071-5-6*

Editor: Lavonia Miller
Cover designed by: HOT BOOK COVERS

First Print March 2016

Printed in the United States

Web site: www.newerabooks.net
www.newerapublication@aol.com

DEDICATION PAGE

This book is dedicated to Ms. Gwendolyn Johnson, Patricia Lloyd, and Helen Lloyd. Thank you from the bottom of my heart.

ACKNOWLEDGEMENTS

First I would like to thank God for the gift of storytelling. I would like to acknowledge those whose books I used for references:

David Goldberg's - America Afiame

James McPherson's – Battle Cry of Freedom

Cormac O'Brien's – Secret Lives of the Civil War

I want to thank Malik, Ronnie "Snobs" Melson, Maxine Miller, Dr, Kevin Ellis, Charles Belim and Craig Williams for their invaluable help. Thanks Easy, Matt, Chop and my partner Mario "Chi Town" Shields, President of the Wordsmith Fan Club. My inspiration comes from Rasheed, Dilisa, Diamond, Tyrell, Dominique, Douglas, Destiny, Jasmine, Benia, Ben, Noah, Miles, Asa, Da-Da Donteyah and a special thanks to Clarence Robinson. You rescued a faltered ship. Thank you, Bobby Dozier for your artwork and Reginald Ussery for your photo work. Also thanks to Douglas Jones and my Washington Regional P.R. Directors Jarrelle Elliot, Mike Wells and Jason Poole. My team is strong and God is good. To all my fans in the Bop, I'm still with you in the struggle. Thanks for your support.

ABOUT THE AUTHOR

Douglas Lloyd is a native Washingtonian and a gifted athlete. Lloyd attended Delaware State University, Howard University in Washington, D.C., and graduated from the University of Wisconsin –Stevens – Point with a BS in Human Resource Management.

Nicknamed the Woodsmith, Lloyd has embarked on writing a 5 book series of novels based around his hobby, the study of Civil War Era America. He is currently battling cancer, and a portion of the proceeds from all his books are donated to the Prostate Cancer Society and Tom Joyner's Historically Black College and Universities.

Lloyd encourages fans to contact him on his publisher's website to comment, blog, or enter the Civil War Era History contest and win a cash prize. To order Book 1, "Jo Ann – She rose from the ashes" or soon to be released, Zack – From Harvest to Hero: book 2 in the Douglas Unleashed series. Go to newerabooks.net.

PROLOGUE - 1845

On the border of the south, on the eastern shore of Md., in a ramshackle, ill lit, dirt floored shack; at the edge of the plantation, a drama was unfolding.

"Alice, get off your knees and fetch me some hot water," snapped Nadine, the midwife.

"If God heard you by now, he's busy. It's been twelve hours," she yelled!

She turned her attention back to the sweat drenched, tattered straw bed. The floor of the shack was black dirt. April, the mother to be, arched her back, reared upward, and tried once more to summon up some strength. The baby's head stretched her womb past the limit. The infant was fighting for her right to live, despite all odds. The fight being waged by eerie candle light.

"Push girl! Push for your life." Pleaded Nadine; the wisdom lines on her ebony face showing thru.

"It's going to kill us both! We gonna die," shouted April. She screamed, arched her back upward, and out slipped this big headed, 7 pound baby girl, all slippery and slimy with afterbirth. Nadine wrapped the half torn towel around the infant. Alice asked, "Is it alive? Boy, girl, what?"

This infant child had come blasting her way into the world with no idea about the trails she would blaze. No idea about the famous name she would create for herself. She had no idea about the dangerous, prejudiced, topsy-turvy, world she had arrived in with such a big splash, despite such heavy odds stacked against her.

Not 50 feet away outside of the shack, the father to be, Jasper Douglass, rippling muscles, jet black complexion, 6ft, 4 inches, 215 pounds of energy, paced. He was jerky and nervous as a June bug.

"Got to go to the outhouse," Jasper said.

"Again," one friend asked?

“Yeah, again,” he muttered, as he disappeared into the night. Five minutes later, Aprils' screams were upstaged by howls, and tussling sounds coming from the outhouse area.

"What the hell is that?” Screeched one of the other four men that were gathered outside the shack with Jasper.

Jasper, who always had a kind word for everyone, or a helping hand to give, had stepped out after relieving himself, and was so intent on getting back to the broken down shack, that he stepped completely unaware into 8 inches of cold, hard steel that went right thru his chest.

"Oh God," screamed Jasper, "who the?" Before he could bellow the rest of the words out, the shock and surprise registered, he collapsed and in a short term, he had nine stab wounds and several boot marks on his body and face, the result of being caught off guard. The screams and howls happened at just about the same instant. A new life was being welcomed into the world and a tragic death was happening, all on this emotional, gut wrenching night.

As Jasper was rolling around on the cool, briny thorn bush covered ground, leaking bright red, he whimpered, "Oh God, take care of my baby. Let it know some kinda way that I loved him." He gurgled, coughed up some more blood, and knew he would be dead in five minutes or less. He was the victim of a planned, well executed, damn near perfect murder. But damn near, ain't perfect and Jaspers last words eked out of his mouth! As his eye rolled up in his head, he whispered harshly. "Somebody's gonna pay for this." "Somebody's... got... to... pay...

FIVE YEARS LATER...1850, JULY

CHAPTER ONE

The year was a good one so far for the Grand Harvest Plantation of Dorchester County, MD. It was located on the Eastern Shore, with 100 acres of prime Tobacco farm land founded originally by the Douglass family. The plantation had grown and started to prosper because of two major reasons:

1) John Jay Douglass, the master and grandson of the founder of Grand Harvest. He was a calculating, shrewd businessman that trusted absolutely no one, and took care of every detail that had anything to do with a dollar Personally.

2) He was a good judge of human flesh, and breeding stock and very rarely made a mistake when it came to spending his money on labor and breeders for his tobacco farm.

He was not a harsh or callous man. He treated the slaves that he owned a little less disrespectful, a little less unrelenting, a little more like human beings;

not cattle or property. As a result, he had less runaways and less incidents of slaves found drowned mysteriously in the Sycamore Creek. He had almost no lynching by overseers, and very few amputations. (Feet cut off) (Arms amputated at the elbow for disrespect) (Tongues cut out for talking back.) Also, there was not much withholding of food or rations. Most important for the slaves, Sunday was always a day off. Church and rest the order of the day with some great sex on the side. Amen!!! From April, until October, the weather was usually nice and mostly around 60 to 80 degrees. The fire barrel would keep you warm from October until March, so freezing was not an option either.

The Douglass family consisted of Master John, forty years old in 1850, wife "Lizzy" Elizabeth also forty years old, son "Zack", Zachery, twenty two, and daughters June, twenty, and Willow, six the baby an "accident" nobody saw coming.

The overseer of the plantation was Irish Brutus McCoy. "Count them there bales again boy," snapped Brutus, forgetting just that fast, that he had just counted the first two rows of 10, five minutes ago. "Damn it," he cried, "Mr. John said somebody with pencil and paper learning was supposed to come this morning. Hell I can't keep up with all this damn tobacco." His body odor, his bad breath and his stinking clothes were constantly at war with each other, and he looked like a red headed Rhino if you caught a glimpse of Brutus from the side. He was smirking to himself and fantasizing humping on little Sarah, one of the slave girls, when this sorry excuse for a man slipped on his gimpy leg, and barked to high heaven, "Ain't I told y'all stop unloading two bales at a time. Shit, I can't hardly keep the count straight now!" It was easy to understand why his wife took the 3 young guns and ran off. Brutus was dumb as a brick and his redneck disease was contagious. The last time Brutus leaped from the frying pan into the fire was almost fatal. (Flash Back)

"What the hell are you breathing so hard for Brutus?" Inquired John.

"Master John that goddamn preacher man made me shoot him", Brutus confessed.

"Are you crazy?" Yelled John. "Why in the world did you shoot Rev? Damn it Brutus, is the man dead?"

"I don't think so. Leastways, last time I saw him, he was leaking red from the chest and screaming like a wounded cat," Brutus replied. "I only plugged him twice before I jumped out of the window." Master John bribed Judge Landry to get Brutus off, this time.

Brutus' loyalty was amazing. He worked hard, drank like a fish, and labored for room and board. For that John forgave most of the stupid things he did that blew up in his face. Screwing Rev. Jamison's cross eyed, acne faced, nappy headed wife was just one of them. At 35 his IQ was well below average. So was 2/3's of the men in Dorchester County. Slavery thrives here. There are thousands of Brutus McCoy's.

The Douglass family and Master John in particular are also unusual for their tradition of passing their family name on to the slaves. All of the Douglass' slaves last name is the given Christian name of Douglass. This includes some sixty three people. There is a running joke in the county. People swear to God you can't tell the masters kids from the slaves children. They say Master John is the father of about twenty of them. Of course they never say it to his face. At 6'3, 220 lbs solid, he has a fighting history throughout the county. Master John is a good match for almost any man that steps in front of him. His courage is almost never challenged, and he is never known to back away from some work. His right hand is legendary. His shooting skills are talked about for two or three counties distance, and many wear reminders of his temper when it finally boils over. Once it tops over, you best get out of the way. He's like the bull in the china shop.

"Happy birthday sweet meat," Lizzy said, in her southern drawl. She was glad that John had turned 40.

“Maybe now I can get some sleep at night," she joked. "Now that you're an old man, maybe my husband will stop ravaging me every night."

To be truthful, John only ravaged his beloved Lizzy when he had too much "Devils Brew," moonshine right from his own still. Give credit where its due, John had done a masterful job after taking over the plantation when his pop got sick. Grand Harvest has been in the Douglass' hands since 1765. Indians, smallpox nor measles couldn't drive the Douglass' away. His granddad planted tobacco, harvested it himself, and carried it to the market in Baltimore. Now slave labor collects that and his Overseer, Brutus makes sure it is collected.

Although Johns view of slavery is somewhat liberal, he knows without slave labor the plantation would not run. But still there are times when he wonders. "Does God really think working another man sun up to sun down for no pay is okay? The big guy (God) is going to see me in Hell come Judgment Day." Have mercy on my soul in the afterlife," he pleaded.

ONE EVENING, IN THE TOWN OF PRINCESS ANNE...

"Stop Zack, you're going to kill the man. I said stop it!" Yelled John. He pulled his son Zachery off the bleeding and battered Jerry Wilson. "Zack" was 22 now. His 6'2", 190 lb frame was mostly muscle. His hazel eyes and brown hair were the cause of many of Zack's fights over the last 15 years or so. It was said quietly, but constantly throughout the county that Zack looked eerily like a slave that disappeared from Grand Harvest some 20 years back by the name of Cyrus.

"Damn it didn't I tell you keep your hands off of other people, boy," John said angrily. "Put some of that brains into your school work boy. If you did I wouldn't have such a hard time trying to get you in that damned Navy Academy. It's bad enough you try to screw everything with a heartbeat around here. Hell boy, there are slave girls that talk about that damn birth mark on your ass cheek."

"You got a nerve Dad," roared Zack. "They think every other sambo born to our darkies belong to you. I probably got 40 brothers and 20 sisters," he spat right back.

"Careful with your mouth boy," John warned. "I can still hit a Nat at 20 yards with this pea shooter. Don't tempt me."

The argument cooled down and Zack and his dad hugged and made up. Still unwilling to admit like father, like son. Zack was waiting to go to his appointment at the Naval Academy in Annapolis. Although he had never piloted a boat before, he fell in love with them at the age of ten. He studied everything he could find. At 11 he announced, "I'm going to be the best sailor ever when I grow up." His Parents both smiled and said, "Okay."

When Zack was old enough he started helping his dad make his deliveries. Each time he learned a valuable lesson. Now at age 22 he still asked questions.

"Zack hurry," John shouted. "Keep up with me. I told Mr. James 12:00pm Sharp!"

"This is close enough," Zack replied. "58 bales is just as good as 60. Let's just go with these. We can bring him the other 2 next trip."

"58 is not 60," John said emphatically. We shook hands on 60 bales of tobacco, 60 James will get. You will know it is 58, I'll know its' 58 and "God" knows it's 58. That's the only thing that matters in this bit of business," John explained. "Your granddad says a man is as good as his word, and no piece of paper or silver tongue can change that son," said John.

Zack thought that thru as they were making good on Mr. James delivery. Another question popped up in his head. He looked his father in the eyes and asked,

"Man says all men are created equal, that our niggers don't have a soul like us. So they don't count as much in God's eyes. If that is so why do they cry when you sell their babies? Why they go to church and pray on Sunday, just like we do? What "God" are they praying to? When did he make us chief over what they can and can't do?"

John laughed and answered, "Well Zack, my mom was smarter than most. Your mom is smart too, but they are women son. Women think different, getting to heaven is first on their list, things that matter most. But us men we gotta provide and survive first. So we gotta ask, who would "God" rather have doing the supervising? Us that's the same color and look just like him, or them that need help thinking things thru? Besides God didn't put them here to think, just work."

LATER THAT EVENING...

John was thinking about going to the dance at his friends Ronald Stroman's house that evening. While choosing between his blue denim suit, and his jacket made of suede, on the other side of his brain he was tossing around figures for the tobacco tally for the month. His mind suddenly halted, he flashed back on a scene years ago when he was nine. He was watching his dad win a big hand at the poker table. After the hand was over he flipped the cards over that his dad played. There was a 5, 6,9,10 and 7. His opponents hand read a pair of 5's, a 6, 2 and an ace. John was amazed.

He quickly caught up with his dad, he inquired, "Pop you did not even have a pair. How could you keep betting their hands? Did you cheat?" Master John looked right in his dads eyes trying to read the truth in his answer like his mom taught him to do.

His dad smiled and replied, "Robert blinks twice when he has a good hand, then tilts his head to the left. Nelson tips his hat twice then looks to the floor.

Robert leans back, smiles a little and folds his hands together. Henry stays quiet as a mouse. In cards just like life you read everybody, pay attention to everything. You listen with your eyes and your ears. Your gut will tell you the rest. Go with your gut, those butterflies that you feel are like an answer machine. They will always give you the answer. You just have to know what it says."

John nodded as acknowledgement of the lesson. One of thousands he would file and remember as a thoughtful family lesson. Pulled back to the present and out of his memory, John wiped the sweat from his brow. He ran his fingers down the scar on the left side of his face. He winced at the memory of the childhood accident that cause it. He loved these talks with Zack now. They were enemies for too many years before now. There was bitterness and hate between them for too long.

CHAPTER TWO

"Zack" Jo Ann giggled, with her gapped toothed smile lighting up the Meadow. "Show me that trick again. I love this pony. Jezebel is just my size. She don't bite or kick." Zack, Master Johns son, but a carbon copy of the slave named Cyrus, patted the pony.

He said, "Here Jo Ann. You give Jezebel a carrot treat. You and Kelly spoil the poor horse to death." Kelly, a slave girl, was Willow and Jo Ann's babysitter. Secretly she was the love of the moment for Zack.

"Zack, stop teasing Jo Ann," said Kelly.

Zack replied, "If you two treated me as good as that horse, I'd walk around on my knees all day and night." He whispered to Kelly, "Id carry you off to California and marry you if I was that horse." Kelly had no idea where California was, but she knew a white man and 'a nigra girl wasn't supposed to go there together.

"I'm going to put a baby in you if it's the last thing I do," Zack promised. Kelly blushed and smiled. Jo

Ann blurted out, "I heard you Zack. I won't tell. I can keep a secret!" Of course she would tell Willow 30 seconds after she saw her today.

Zack was thinking about all the other slave girls that knew about the birth mark on his left butt cheek. Of course, his girlfriend, Catherine, 'Cat' for short had no idea.

"Marry me Cat," Zack would beg, praying each day that she said no. The relief of his 6'2", 190 lb frame would be obvious every time she would say, “We are not ready. Let’s wait." You could hear him crack a smile, and stop trembling, in the next state.

Later that evening, the family was gathered at the Stroman’s birthday party for their daughter. June 5'9", hours glass figure, pretty hazel eyes, dimpled chin and wavy brown hair was holding court. Her blue gown revealed just enough cleavage.

"My goodness June," said one of the 5 young men vying for her attention. "Your smile can light up this whole house. You look stunning."

"Why Eddie,” beamed the brown haired bombshell, “I hadn’t realized you kept up with my birthdays. Thank you so much for the Filly. Of course you know I have to send her back to you awhile.

Daddy says, "it's not proper for such an expensive gift to be given to a young lady unless she is your fiancée or wife." June smiled coyly, and sighed. She is selfish and beautiful, I am tempted to marry you just to Keep the horse.

"How did you know Carol and I were born on the same day? This is the third present I have gotten at my best friend's birthday party. It makes no sense at all," beaming a smile that would light up the black lagoon.

Eddie pleaded "Just keep her. She is just right for you."

June agreed, "I know, but I couldn't possibly do that. People would talk."

Eddie argued, "No I'll make sure everyone knows there were no strings attached, that we are not a couple or anything like that. I promise."

June replied, "Well let me think on it. I'll let you know later tonight." And with that, the deal for a $1,000 horse was sealed as a gift, no strings attached. June had won again!

At 20 she was always the life of the party. She had her coming out 3 years prior and everyone expected by now she would be married, have two or three children and be working on establishing her own little kingdom: A plantation, 100 acres, tobacco, cotton, wealthy husband and many slaves, the whole nine yards. When that did not happen right away people just assumed she was waiting for the wealthiest boy to cross her path. After a year went by the rumors started flying. One was, she was waiting for one of the richer families from Baltimore to invite her for a tour of the cities eligible. When year two rolled around, people started gossiping. "Who have you seen June dating? What boy is keeping her company? What is Lizzy saying? Surely, her mom wants her married and starting a family by now?" In truth June was beautiful, intelligent and understanding, She just couldn't figure out, and did not have the foggiest idea how to find a woman to please her. Yes that's right, a woman. June was gay as X-Mas and did not have a clue how to express it.

In the 1850's woman did not even consider such things. June thought she was mentally ill. Her heart would do triple time around a beautiful woman. Around a handsome, eligible man she would hardly take a look. She was horrified, and scared out of her mind to even begin to talk to her mom about these feelings. Her father would have probably beat half the skin off of her body if she told him. So here she is twenty, beautiful, and stuck, miserable enough to be thinking of suicide because the slave girl who was her playmate growing up, is now a young woman.

Sally May Douglass has a long, beautiful neck, round doe like eyes, bushy frizzy hair grown short, June is crazy about her. Sally may be a slave girl with nothing to look forward to. But to June she is, a princess that she dreams erotic thoughts about every night. She would gladly slit her wrist in six places if she could just spend one night with her. The fact that they grew up together learning to read, write, sew, and dress makes it all the better. At 14 the time came for them to separate because there is an unspoken color barrier in the county. June was miserable and hurt. She made excuses to her mom for another year about why her and Sally May should continue to play and be friends. Then the other mothers began to gossip and "Lizzy" cut the friends off. She told June, " She would give her Sally May as a gift when she got married and was ready to start her own household."

Lastly, there was Willow, the unexpected bundle of joy that came along some fourteen years after June. Everyone's spoiled brat! The apple of the families' eye. At six she runs the house. Her every want and need is cause for a major change of plans for the day. The slave children adore her because she gets right down in the dirt and plays with them. She would just as soon eat out of the pot of chitlins that was cooking, as off the table with roast chicken, gravy and mashed potatoes. Strangely, she has [ratty dark brown hair, full lips and round, doe eyes (brown). Her nose is rather full. She is kind of full bodied, bordering on plump. She and the slave girl Jo Ann are like twins they are together all the time. Her mom is teaching both of them to read, write and count, even though there is a law against teaching blacks to do any of these things. Since Jo Ann never knew her daddy, (he was killed on the night of her birth) she often is seen with Willow and her father John. They sit on the front porch of the main house. They listen to a story, or learn some family history. Rumor has it she (Jo Ann) may even be Willows blood sister !!

"Darn it. Not again," shouted Willow.

"Yeah again," teased Jo Ann.

“That’s not fair,” shouted Willow.

"Why, just tell me why not? Asked Jo Ann.

Six year old Willow pulled up the tablet slung it across the room and stood up over top of five year old Jo Ann. She pointed her finger at the broken up tablet and said, "I'm the one that goes to school. I'm the one that has to sit in that classroom every cotton pickin day. You aren't supposed to just wait for me to get home, you sit around and ask me stuff, and all of a sudden you know more than I do."

Willow paused. She thought for a few seconds and said, “You aren't even older than me. How come you know so much? Do you people have some kind of magic spell or something? You are smarter than anybody I know," Willow pouted.

Jo Ann smiled. She knew that Willow was paying her a compliment. She just hadn't figured out how to take it apart, an make sense of it yet. Jo Ann was a truly different child than most. Only 5, she was born on the same night someone murdered her father. It seems from that moment on she has been a super talented, extraordinary young lady.

"Why did God make some people dark and some people white?" Willow questioned Elizabeth, her spirited mom. Before Lizzy could think this one all the way through, Willow piggybacked that question with another one. "Why are some people slave’s and some people free, if all men are created equal?” Lizzy wondered at that one. As the light bulb switched on and Lizzy was getting ready with a brilliant reply, Willow asked, "Where do babies come from mama, If the story you told me about the stork and the babies in the basket is only a joke. I didn't laugh. I don't think that's funny Mama," said Willow.

"Willow will drive you to drinking," John said.

"Willow will make you get grey hair early," replied Lizzy.

"Willow will make you hide from her until, she can find out what she wants to know," cautioned John.

"I ain't no country hick with an accent. Y'all act like I'm a country South Carolina geeche, you think I can't learn how to talk," mumbled Willow.

Jo Ann is old enough to help her mom with the house chores at main house. John and Elizabeth prefer that she does, not work like other slave children. Willow loves her so much, and they are so close in age and temperament, that the Douglass' just want her to be a playmate and best friends to Willow. Sometimes this causes jealousy and friction with the other families.

CHAPTER THREE

It is with this setting in 1850, in the town of Princess Anne, Dorchester County MD. The first strange happening occurred. It was the month of May. Among the sixty three people of color on the Grand Harvest Plantation there were twelve females between the ages of 10 and 20 years old. All were professed to be converted Christians. All attended the Christian Church service each Sunday. Some of the Africans secretly carried on the worshipping of gods and idols that they had worshipped in the African bushland. For the most part, the slaves had converted to Christ.

Right after Reverend Dooley's morning service the sky clouded up heavily. His blood shot droopy eyes peered thru the church between the long dead, bent over oak tree branches. He was grinning that crooked weird upside down question mark. He was sweating like a quarter horse running. Church was letting out and this pervert was sizing up the young, tender black meat, hurrying to get out of the coming downpour. They were taking the short cut back to the slave quarters.

His perverted eyes settled on Ella Jean, 18 year old almond eyes, with a honey nut complexion. Somewhere around 5ft tall, she tipped the scale close to 120lbs. He smiled, "Look at that tender booty". He slobbered saliva down the front of his stinking, sweat stained overalls, with the hole cut in the pocket. He could jack off in public and no one would know. He mumbled a couple of "Oh shits," while playing with himself, and tore off behind Ella as she set out at a fast walking pace.

She was about 25 yards into the woods when she heard the first noise. Some branches broke off a tree. This let her know she was not alone. It was raining hard, she figured more than one person would be trying to hurry up and get home. She was not alarmed. When she got about 15 yards deeper, she heard the noise get a lot closer to her.

"God damn," the giant yelled. He had tripped over some bushes, while trying to keep up with Ella. The noise echoed like a bullet through the woods. Ella called out, “Who dat?” She cupped her hand over her ear. "Who dat out yonder? You trying to make company with me?” Now she turned and hiked up her Sunday go to meeting dress, so she could put some distance between her and whoever or whatever was keeping her company. She now thought it could be a wolf or a dog with the rabies. As she rounded the next set of tress, suddenly something snatched her by the neck. He tackled her off of her feet. While holding a hand over her mouth, he put a bowie knife blade to her throat. She fought like there was no tomorrow!! She kicked, scratched, punched, and head-butted like a wild tiger. But 22 stab wounds were just too much. Blood was everywhere. When the last life leaked out of her, the man ripped what was left of her dress off. He mounted her while she was still twitching, and pumped until his seed came. He dragged her body deeper into the woods. He cut her breast off, her face up, her eyes out. He cut her vagina up. He spat, and pissed on her. He cursed her to every devil and pagan god he could think of. While the rain washed the blood from his face, it could not keep the stains and dirt from his clothes. He did not care. He was in another world. This was his fourth victim in two years. Each time it got more gruesome, and gory. Each time it got uglier. Who was this sick monster of a man? What was driving him? As he walked away from the carnage and wreckage he had just created, he kept muttering to himself, “God help me."

This was Princess Anne, Md. 1850. The town that the Douglass family called home. A killer was on the loose.

In the County of Dorchester, race relations always seemed to play an important, if not very prominent role in daily life for both whites, and blacks. Maryland was a state that had a lot of abolitionist, and religious Zealots that believed slavery was wrong on moral grounds. It had people that had been indentured in the county that they fled. They believed with all their heart, that it was wrong to hold another man in bondage. On the Eastern Shore the economy of the region, the money that kept the area afloat, came from two things, The Chesapeake Bay seafood industry and the tobacco farms, that dotted the region. It wove the fabric of the region together. Its society centered on, the southern traditions of plantation living. That meant coming out into society balls and for young white wives and mothers to be, old fashioned, southern dating, and marriage. It also was southern bred manners with dueling rights and a class system. Sometimes you would think the Eastern Shore wasn't really a part of the rest of the state. It was rapidly becoming industrialized. There were free blacks that were a visible part of the population, and a necessary part of the population. They were also part of the work force. Blacks that were still bound in slavery took every opportunity to run that they could get. They saw the dream of freedom as right around the corner, or just up the street. They tried harder than the slaves that were living further south. Southern slaves could not reach freedom as easily, so they suffered way worst when they were unsuccessful. Amputations, tongues cut out, and hangings were common punishment for running and getting caught.

Nat Turners uprising in 1831, had put the fear of God in a lot of these white families' heads. They now understood that they were the minority, totally outnumbered, and vulnerable to slaughter if the blacks bonded together, and rebelled! The fugitive slave society that formed in 1841 had helped to create an underground railroad, that led runaway slaves to freedom. A lot settled in Pennsylvania, around Philadelphia. A local woman off of one of the plantations, Ms. Harriet," Tubman was beginning to make a reputation for leading slaves to freedom. By 1850, the Fugitive Slave Act passed. It made it legal to hunt runaways, catch them and return them for money or bounty. You had to keep running all the way to the Canadian border to be safe. By then, a lot of blacks were settling in Upstate New York.

Dorchester County was a fire keg. Blacks were restless for freedom, but also scared because young, black woman were disappearing, raped, and murdered. Whites did not want to see their way of life change, so they pushed back hard. They wanted less say in their affairs by the Federal Government. There were quite whispers in congress about some Southern states pulling out the union and forming their own country with their own government, constitution, rules, and regulations. Rumors were flying, people were buzzing.

CHAPTER FOUR

It was an ordinary day in princess Anne by almost any standards. July 18th, the sun peeking out from behind a white puff of cloud. It hadn't rained for a week, so the dust settled on the road was dry and baked hard.

A small wagon coming from the east side of town was being pulled by a lop eared, spotted face mule. A little man maybe 5'3 " or so, wearing all black clothing and a bowler hat was pushing the way on. A corn cob piped jutted out the corner of his mouth. You could tell by his boots, not much coin had filled his pockets in a month of Sundays. A farmer maybe? Beside this gentleman with the ruddy complexion and four fingers on his left hand, sat one of the largest black men ever seen in these parts. The wagon stopped in front of Hank's general store. Hank peeping thru the front glass, moseying on out front to get a better look at the two strangers.

"Howdy stranger," said Hank calmly, he looked the black man up and down, while addressing the four fingered driver.

"Greetings brother" the driver answered equally calm.

"Names Hank, this here's my store. Reckon you might need some supplies. If you do, bring your boy on in and fill up your list. We take gold or paper. Make no never mind to me."

"Mighty white of you brother," the driver replied. We running a little short of some items. I was telling Tiny here we need to stop and restock our supplies. Let's take a look.

Once in the store the two strangers took their time and picked from a list they had written. They ran up a pretty sizeable tab of supplies. The supplies were totaled up and the last item rang up.

Tiny, looking like a baby elephant, voice sounding like a bass drum boomed, "I'll settle with gold," pulling out a sack from under his shirt. The pouch looked triple thick!

"Jesus" the white store owner bellowed."

"God Damn!" one customer shouted.

"Who in the hell is he?" Hank's wife barked loudly, tongue half hanging out. None had ever seen a sack of gold dust that large or that heavy. Now they started to realize it was the black man not the white man with the gold.

Reluctantly Hank inquired, " Uh, Mr. Tiny, what is it exactly you do sir? I didn't catch it."

"You didn't catch it cause I didn't say it pilgrim, " Tiny answered. "My gold spend here or not?" He asked.

"Yes sir" Hank answered quickly. He spread a smile on his face and told his wife to fix Mr. Tiny a cup of hot brewed coffee. While Tiny sipped coffee and ate biscuits, Ole Ned, (nobody even asked him his name) loaded the wagon alone. He struggled, lurched, and fell twice trying to load the supplies. The irony of a white man struggling with back breaking labor, while his black partner sipped coffee and ate biscuits was not lost on the towns people.

"That's disgusting," whined Old Lady Taylor. Mister Jameson," the barber hissed, " that should be against the law!" Jackson said. "I think it is. It got to be on the books somewhere."

Both Tiny and Ole Ned were exercising their God given rights. Tiny had goals to reach, and Ole Ned had to work hard to survive. It's the American way.

Tiny reminded every one of the future not many whites wanted to see. Black men as equals.

"I'm not rich, you know that Ned," explained Tiny.

"Yeah Tiny I know. But them white folks in town think you rich," replied Ole Ned.

"Listen, as long as people think you got money in this county that's power," explained Tiny some more to his only employee. "That's the reason that we put on that big show this morning," laughed Tiny. "When we need credit or run low on supplies, even go dead broke, no one will refuse to give us what we need."

"The thought of a black man with a pocket full of gold dust will set them folks to scheming how to separate this big dumb nigger from his money." Predicted Tiny. "By the time they realize we ain't never going to pay our bills that's due, we will be long gone to the next town."

Both men laughed, and kept on laughing at the greed that separates men from their money. Six weeks later they were gone.

CHAPTER FIVE

1858 was the turning point for the Grand Harvest plantation. The summer month of August was hot as an egg frying on tar. Richard Wesley, better known as Black Richard was now the leader of the slave side of the Douglass family. Richard was black as a berry, 6 '1 close to 200lbs and spoke 3 given dialects. He settled arguments and disagreements with his hands. He owned a sharp buck knife with a white ivory handle, and enough common sense that those with book learning respected his mind.

He yelled up at Homer, " Put your back in it boy. Stop acting like a woman and push." They were clearing a spot for a new cabin for the family. He yelled, "Jo Ann is stronger than you boys. Damn, there ain't one muscle between the both of you, except between your legs, that probably don't work either."

Richard was proud of the fact he was the family breeder. They picked him when they wanted to make babies to sell. Richards thinking was twisted enough, to think this was an honor. He wasn't even nurturing to the 3 babies he had already made with slave woman at Harvest. They meant no more to him than any of the other slave children.

He could often be heard shouting, “God don’t care about me. If he did why he got me working sun – up to sundown every damn day? Why my feet swollen? Why my hands blistered? Why my arms cut up? God need to give me a rest. I damn sure done earned it,” he hissed like a snake.

“He do care,” April would shout back.

“He don’t.” says Richard.

“He do.” Says April

“He don’t.” says Richard

“He do.” Says April

“Well you pray,” Richard would snarl. “I’m going to sleep. Every bone in my body is hurting.”

April was thankful someone was there to take up the slack after Jasper was murdered. April was still young and a goddess to look at, a dream to talk to, and still at age 32, she wanted freedom and the best things out of life for herself and her family.

Lizzy picked her to work in the main house because she was great at washing and ironing. She could sew better than most. She was not sassy or forward toward Master John. April stayed humble, and was not hell bent on expressing her opinion about everything. She was also old enough to understand the caste system of the plantation class. Lizzy did not see her as one to put arsenic in the food, or slit someone's throat. April was twelve years younger than Elizabeth. They were worlds apart in culture, but their idea about how to raise Lizzie's children often ran along the same lines. Both believed fervently in the one God, and fire and brimstone Christian religion. April was 36, and Lizzy was 48. April had been married to Richard for 2 years now. Even though she knew he had been brought to the plantation mainly to make babies, she still fell in love with "Black Richard." It had been a couple of years before they started seeing each other. Her mom, Hattie May, had been the main cook for over twenty years, so everyone was used to her being around the house. Lizzy made April, number 1 housekeeper. She also oversaw most of the clothes that were made. She had beautiful eyes, and a fabulous sense of fashion. Though she had no formal training or schooling, she was a fashion genius at 36 years old. The only hic – cup, the only blister to the picture was Lizzie's uneasy feeling whenever April (nickname Peach pie) was around Master John. April was unaware at first, but John damn near passed out whenever she came around. His eyes would get big, his heart would beat faster, his pants would grow a bulge the size of Mt. Rushmore. You could see the change come over him even if you were Ray Charles. He had it bad for Peach Pie.

Sex wasn't one of Lizzie's favorite past – times, and she knew John had strayed many times. She just didn't want neighbors saying Master John was in love with a darkie. That was embarrassing to her. The one time she tried to mention the subject to him, he had a few nips of shine, and after about one minute worth of conversation, he back handed her to the floor, and stalked out of the bedroom. Case closed, no more talk. Subject was never, ever mentioned again! After this, she really froze up when the thought of asking him why Willow and Jo Ann looked so much alike, ran across her mind. One was dark and one light, but both favored him.

When she looked at April, 5'0 " 115lbs, size 34 (c) breast, nice big legs, and butt round as a wagon wheel, she felt a little envy. When she put that together with that complexion that looked like blueberries, full luscious lips, and pretty brown eyes that were wide and round as deer lights, April had the full package.

"Master John," said April softly as she cleaned the desk in his study. "I ain't trying to be disrespectful, but I need to ask you a question?" April almost whispered the sentence. John barely heard her.

"Yeah what is it April," he replied, " you see that I'm busy." John was pretending to be writing a letter while covertly watching April clean up. He was fantasizing about her.

"Can you open the door a wee bit, so I can get me some fresh air? Dang if it ain't stuffy in here. I can't hardly breathe. I don't mean to bother you sir, but I sure need some fresh air. Or maybe I can just open the porch door some, and let the breeze come on in?"

John almost burst out laughing. He knew April was uncomfortable in the room with him all alone. He knew she was aware that he called her to come to the barn 3 or 4 times a month. He wasn't sure if she liked it or not. He just knew he did, and she did not want Lizzy to send her to the field. April did not think she could live thru the hot Sun, day after day, hour after hour, minute after minute. The thought made her sick on the Stomach.

John said, "Go ahead open the door," and smiled.

TWO WEEKS LATER...

Mary peeped through the hole in the fence. She was out of breath and sort of pale, from running across the meadow to chase some butterflies. She loved nature. “Gotcha,” she screamed, as she clasped her hands together to catch the butterfly. She opened her hand and looked on in wonder. She smiled then let the little insect fly quickly away. “Gotcha,” she giggled as another one settled in her sweaty palm. She could do this all day. Play among “God’s” creatures and have fun without hurting one of them. Sickly as a child, she is gentle as a lamb. Strangely shy for a slave girl, she was everyone’s favorite. Even Black Richard, her step dad, who is hard as a birch, treats Mary Like the Virgin Mary. This child is sweet, precious, and unlikely to live past her teen years.

“Why won’t they let me run and fall down and jump and have fun mama?” Whimpered Mary. “Jo Ann acts like I’m glass. I won’t break.” A tear rolled down her cheek and April ran her hand thru Mary’s hair. She said, “My precious, they just love you is all. No one wants to see you get hurt. No one wants you to go get sick again." "Ever," she sang, "Never, ever, ever."

CHAPTER SIX

Of course there was Jo Ann, the miracle baby. Born on the night papa Jasper was murdered, she was and continues to be the apple of everyone's eyes. At 13, she is a year older than Mary, but you would never know it. She is 2 inches taller, plump, light brown complexion. She is much lighter than any of her brothers and her sister. She doesn't resemble her mom, although April is a pretty black woman. Jo Ann is very talkative and imaginative. She asks question after question until satisfied. She wants badly to be treated as an equal on the plantation, but something inside of her automatically keeps telling her when to tone it down.

She is quickly absorbing Lizzie's lessons on reading, writing, and counting that she practices with Willow. She acts like she cannot do any of these things when she goes to town, or is around certain people. What she does not understand is why she has to act this way. They teach her the importance of living in a godly manner, but if God says we all are equal, "Why do I have to eat this way? Why can't I go to school with Willow? Why does mama cry at night sometimes? She acts like she is so tired she might drop dead one evening? Why can't I use the outhouse by the main rooms? It is almost a mile to come back here to go to the outhouse. Who is this Nat Turner everyone keeps whispering about?" "Not even mama or Miss Lizzy will tell me about him?" I like Master John a lot, but sometime he won't even look me in the eyes. Why is he like that to me if he is my friend? Jo Ann thoughts were many. These were just a few. All of us are Douglass'. "Are we really one big family, or does master loan us his name until we are given to some other white people? Sometimes I get dizzy with all the things that run in my head."

CHAPTER SEVEN

"I fought back Master John. I fought back," sobbed Nelly. "I gave that Irish monkey good as I got. He bit me. He kept biting and punching my face. Kept tearing at my clothes. I ain't done nothing to that stinking Brutus. I scratched him up good, Master John!"

Nelly was shaking and breathing hard. There was a long cut going up between her legs. It was right where her dress had been ripped. Her fingernails were broken where she had tried to defend herself. Nadine was there now, having been summoned by Jo Ann when all the commotion started. Not only was she the midwife, she was the family doctor for the slave population.

"Damn it let me see. Move out of the way. I need to look close," Nadine ordered. "Let me put a cloth on that eye girl. Hold still, lay back! That knot on your head going to need some sewing. Jo Ann! Run get my sewing box off the shelf. Hold your head back Nelly. I need for this blood to stop running from your nose. Wake up child! Wake up.

Don't you nod out on me. I knows you hurting, but Master John need to know your story. He need to hear who done this. You said Irish?" She snarled.

Master John had his Sharps rifle at his side, his German shepherd, Billy, on the other side panting and looking for someone to launch on. He had a notion to split Brutus McCoy's head to the white meat. As soon as Nelly said Irish John knew automatically Brutus was the one. Deep down for The past couple of years he kept wondering if Brutus was the killer that had been terrorizing the county.

"Goddamnit! I'm going to kill that bastard. I'm going to cut his nuts off and hang him from that oak tree out back," yelled John. He had lost it. Spit sweat, face turning red, he can't stop pacing, he lost it. Lord help Brutus McCoy, cause nobody else could save him from John.

The sheriff came and a posse looked high and low for Brutus. They looked everywhere in to the next county. Brutus had disappeared. After two weeks some more news about another event put Brutus on the backburner. Some even bigger news that lit up Dorchester County like a Roman, Candle.

In front of Hanks General store the four old timers sat around rocking in their chairs spitten tobacco in the dirt. Old Henry was writing on the piece of wood with his pocket knife.

"You heard about that damn fool Evangelist, John Brown? "Asked Jeremy."

"Yeah, said he killed more than 60 people," replied split Fingered Bill.

"Got them niggers all stirred up, and tried to kill everything in sight," barked Jeremy.

"You know these niggras outnumber us about 5 to 1. If they got a hankering to take over, we would be hard pressed to stop them! I don't know about you but I'm going to stop letting them come round the house. No nigger within 100 feet, ever. Got to keep your gun under your pillow at night too. Shit, they tried to take over the arsenal at Harpers Ferry. A black man with a gun ain't that some scary thought. My Julie Ann couldn't even get to sleep last night just thinking about it. Kept me up all damn night! bellowed Bill.

"They hung that fool Brown, so that should give them a warning," bragged Willie. "If you start something we will finish it. Kill you dead niggra," forgetting all about John Brown was a white man.

Willie who was just listening and shaking his foot up until now, looked up and said, "It's going to be changes round here. Mark my words God don't like ugly. God don't like slavery. How the hell can you love the lord and be for holding another man -in bondage? It's just starten yall, they just lighting the fire. In a short while God gonna come down on this land like a ton of bricks. Everybody hold your breath, you gonna feel what them slaves feel shortly!" Willie sat back and smiled.

CHAPTER
EIGHT

In August, 1858 as the weather got hotter, the blood began to boil in Dorchester County. People were still uptight about John Browns' Harpers Ferry Adventure, but mostly mad as hell at Brutus McCoy. The redneck former Overseer had everyone mad at him. They were still searching and wondering how he got away for so many years right under their very noses! All those girls! All the sick psycho amputations, and cutting breasts and nipples off! Humping on bodies that were dead, where was this sick fool hiding? How did he get out of the county, past everybody?

Twice a month or so, Jo Ann and Master John's son Zachery, would go off into the woods, spend some time in the clearing by the Sycamore Creek. They would hand wrestle, do close combat drills, and target practice with the Sharps rifle. Almost at the end of an exciting, but exhausting day, Jo Ann heard a loud rustle in the woods, an some branches crack. Thinking it might be a wild boar, she took off after the noise. She was full bent on firing her Sharps and showing Zack she was almost as good as him with the big powerful rifle. As she creped around the bend of a small path, she tried to slip quietly around a large boulder. She was startled out of her skin by a large man with his back to her. He was looking down in the creek bed trying to catch a fish. Suddenly she realized it was Brutus. He had not heard her sneak up on him. She watched him for a minute or two, her mind racing. If she took the time to run back to get Zack, Brutus could be gone. What to do? Sweat balls popping off her forehead, her heart was beating so hard she thought Brutus might hear it. She thought she might have a heart attack. She made up her mind. Trying to steady her shaking hand, she aimed her Sharps right at Brutus' legs. She squeezed off a shot and hit him right below the left kneecap, making him tip over into the creek bed. The dirt was too soft to get a good grip on to get up and run. She ran over to peer over the creek bed and saw the hate filled face of Brutus staring up into hers. If looks could kill, She would already be dead.

He had little strength left, but he kept saying, "help me," "help me get up." "Don't leave me like this you little black bitch." His idea was to grab her when she got close enough to crush the life out of her body, taking one more with him before he got dropped off in hell. He was going for sure with all the murders and rapes he had done. But something strange came over Jo Ann. Her body got warm all over. Something like hate rippled through her body, leaving her shaking, but feeling almost numb. She reached down into her waist band, and pulled out the bowie knife that Zack had taught her how to use so well over the years. With one quick, sharply executed cross cut, Jo Ann slit Brutus's throat from ear to ear, blood spurting like a water fountain. She followed that up with about 10 or 15 stab wounds to the body. By that time Zack had wandered up and found her working! Once he realized who it was that Jo Ann was working on, Zack grabbed his own Bowie knife from his belt. He ripped open Brutus pants, grabbed him by his penis and removed it with one or two good, sharp cuts. He started kicking him in his face. Forcing Brutus mouth open, he jammed it in his throat! Once they realized they could do no more damage, they dragged the body over to a fallen tree. They buried Brutus McCoy 4 feet deep under bushes, rocks, and anything else that they could find. It was certain that by night fall the wild animals would have him for supper. The vultures would have the leftovers for breakfast.

Jo Ann was a changed person from that moment on. Unlike most people, the close-up hand to hand bloodletting did not make her nervous or jittery. She was not upset and certainly was not sorry. She seemed to change in front of Zack's eyes. Gone was the little girl that he knew, loved, and protected like a little sister. He was confused only because he had no idea what, or who she had changed into.

She kept saying, "I'm fine, I wish I could kill him again." "Zack don't tell Master John, he won't understand." "You know what I am now. Only you know. We will take this to our grave, right Zack? You know what I am." Jo Ann was 13 years old, fresh from her very first kill.

CHAPTER NINE

SIX WEEKS LATER...

With the hiring of Luke Appleby, the new overseer, things changed rapidly around Grand Harvest. Luke was a lot less fascist, not brutal and not cruel. His only major concern was to get the work out of the way. He cared about the bottom line. He even made a deal with Master John, taking less salary so that at the end of the harvest season, he could get a lump sum bonus. He got it only if the pounds of tobacco brought to the market was more than last season, He even promised to cut the slave laborers in one of the deals. Promising to let them have their own cow to raise if they helped him get his bonus. That meant milk for the babies and who knows, maybe even the start of their own cow herd if things worked out. Luke Appleby was a big improvement. He was 5' 8' 160lbs, bow legged, ruddy complexion, with acne scars on his face. He looked more like a teenaged cowboy, than a 28 year old overseer. Master John had a good feeling about the youngster.

He liked his uncle Hartley, who was a life time friend, and trusted his gut, about giving the young gun a chance. At time the younger slaves took his kindness for weakness.

"Roscoe, I told you yesterday to move that boulder so the plow wouldn't get messed up," Luck said.

"Yes sir, I plum forgot," Roscoe replied. He was using his; I'm so old I forgot things routine.

"I be having so much to think about sometimes, with the baby being sick, some things just slip my mind. "I's sorry Mister Luke sir," he whined?

"Ok Roscoe," replied Luke. Don't let it happen again. "I hope your son is feeling better," he said, sincerely. Luke rode off to check another task.

"Nigger!" shouted Big Shirley. "I'm a break my foot off in your ass if you do that again." He got up in Roscoe's face nose to nose. "All them damn overseers that takes a whip to us for no reason, we finally get a man that's decent and you gonna slack on em. Remember those slashes on your back nigger," yelled Shirley. "Them white folks beats us for sport," remembered Shirley. "I been on this damn farm 32 years and this is the best white man we had. I'll snap your neck before you slacks on him again, " barked Shirley.

At 6'4", 225Lbs Shirley could back up his threat. Even though he had one eye and ½ right arm from a drunken Brutus with an axe, Shirley and three Other "old hands" were grateful to have a decent boss. They would kill their own before they let someone get him fired. If this was Uncle Tomming they didn't give a damn! They had enough of the cruel, ruthless bosses. Luke was decent and fair.

Toby weighed in, "don't forget Luke's wife Violet be bringing our young guns milk and bread from the big house kitchen. She don't have to do that. They "Gods" fearing, decent folk." Toby was a 40 year old slave born on Grand Harvest. "If Big Shirley don't snap your skinny neck, my sticker will cut your tongue out," Toby roared. "Now get over there and move that God damn rock."

The wife of Luke who Toby spoke about, Violet, was part Cherokee and part Crow Indian. Silky black hair, dark eyes, bronze looking skin, and beautiful hands and feet, she was stunning. Their two year old son, Tim, was a bundle of energy that had his mother's facial features and his dads Stocky body already. Everyone loved him. He was very talkative and friendly.

On this particular Thursday evening, Master John was in his study smoking a cigar and talking a few nips of shine when Lizzy burst right in.

"Damn it John," said Lizzy. I have asked you time and time again not to have a go at that shine in the middle of the day.

John replied, "I earned it." He smiled, started laughing and rose up. "Have you seen the tallies for this month? No I guess you haven't. You don't make the money, you just spend it. Well If you can wear some of it, I can drink some of it. So go somewhere and teach the girls 2+2 is 4 and leave me the hell alone." At that he took two steps toward Lizzy. It hit her like a ton of bricks.

"Damn it," shouted Lizzy. "That's it. That is what I been seeing all this time, and it just now hit me. When you stretch like that and rose your hands over your head, you look just like Jo Ann! She looks just like you! You Jo Ann papa. Damn it, John you been laying with April right under my nose all these years."

She set out for the kitchen, surprised everyone in there. She grabbed the longest butcher knife she could find, and bee-lined back to the Study. Yelling at the top of her voice she cried, " I'm going to cut your lying tongue out of your mouth. You slave loving, dirty, low down bas..."

Before the rest could dribble out of her mouth, the moonshine kicked in. John couldn't take another insult. He jumped up from the chair, threw the glass he was drinking from against the wall. He missed Lizzy's head by inches. He scared her half to death. He balled up his fist and stalked around the desk. He grabbed Lizzy by her head, and yanked her down to her knees. He then jerked her head and her memory back to June 5, 1845, 13 years ago, when he was going into town to the slave auction. He was going to buy a breeding buck for the plantation. He reminded her how he had to drag her with him. She did not want to see no man being sold at auction by another of color. How when they got to town, and the auction got started, he had his eye on this black, fine specimen of an African that turned out to be Jasper, Jo Ann's father. How the bidding got rough, the price got steeper, how he kept fingering the limited funds in his bankroll. How in an effort to get a few more dollars for the African that was built like a Greek god, the man at the auction block told the hired hand, to pull down his britches.

"Show these fine gentlemen what they are purchasing for their baby breeders." Then them, men yanked Jasper britches down. Lizzy who was sitting in the buck ford in revulsion at this human auction was stunned, mesmerized. She was staring in rapt, amazed attention. She broke out in a cold sweat at the big black penis that looked her in the face. She could not turn her eyes away. She was in lust! At that point in her life, she would have swallowed Jasper manhood whole, if only she could touch it. But Wait, the man was saying something. Oh no, John could not bid further. His money had run out. Budget exhausted, the man next to him was still bidding. Jasper was going to someone else. Suddenly out of nowhere a voice shouted, "Six hundred fifty dollars."

A stunned silence descended on the crowd. This was fifty dollars more than the highest bid. Who said that? What fool was this that would pay more than any slave had ever been brought for here at an auction? People looked around and all eyes landed on Lizzy. She sheepishly looked at John and pulled out her purse with her money in it. She had been saving for two years to buy a piano for the main house parlor. John was amazed. He was shocked, embarrassed, and could not believe his ears. Here was his wife bidding to buy a black for a record price. She said she did not even believe in one human purchasing another. It was wrong in the eyes of the Lord.

"Well hot damn! It looks like I'm not the only one in this family that likes dark meat," John said as he cracked a smile. "Remember that Lizzy." John yanked her hair back once again to bring her back to the present. "So yeah, I found out you fucked him a few times. I snuck out one night, caught him coming out of the outhouse, and put my blade in his chest. It is just co-incidence Jo Ann looks a little like me. I am not her daddy," bellowed John. She looked up in his eyes. Guilt was burning her up. Yes she had been having sex with Jasper every chance she got to sneak away and be with him.

After he was killed, her sex drive died off. "But damn it," Jo Ann is Johns' spitting image, and Willows twin. "What to believe?" Shouted Lizzy. "How can I tell? Is John, Jo Ann's daddy?" The yelling and noise had leaked to the yard. Willow and Jo Ann, who only occasionally socialized, now got together less often because they were no longer kids. They stood outside the window in shock.

At the same time Willow felt joy that Jo Ann might really be her blood sister. Jo Ann's blood ran cold inside of her. All she could think about was Master John ramming his bowie knife in her daddy's chest, at the same time she was coming into the world. She made a promise to herself and God. Before the week was out, she would cut the Masters throat and feed his tongue to the dogs!

CHAPTER
TEN

It was much harder to get to be alone with Master John than Jo Ann thought it would be. For three days she watched and waited for a chance to extract revenge. She was confused by the different feelings that kept running through her mind. She did not think that she loved Master John and she certainly had never thought of him as a father. But she did admire him and respected the fact that he treated her almost like Willow. The fact that she was black never seemed to bother him. He especially treated her mom different. It was almost like he had special feelings for her. Now that she found out he was, or might be, her real father, it made her understand a lot of things. She wasn't sure if she was a result of a rape by the master, a cheating love affair by her mom, or if Jasper was really her dad, and he may have gotten murdered for cheating with Willows mother. Maybe Jasper was Willows father too. How about them apples! (Smile) So whatever the truth, Master John had to go.

"You can't kill my daddy and I just let it go," Jo Ann said. "My brothers and sisters are different. They don't think like me, look like me, or act like me." Maybe they already know. That's why they don't acts as close to me as they do toward each other. Damn, I'm getting dizzy again with all this stuff running through my head.

She was lost in her thoughts while sitting in the stable. She used to go there to think when she wanted to be by herself. Master John walked up on her by surprise. She hadn't even heard him come into the stable. Jo Ann almost jumped out of her skin.

"Damn Meat Ball," his pet name for her, "What the hell are you doing out here by yourself this early in the morning?"

At that moment she knew she had to lay it all on the line. "Word round here is you killed my daddy. I'm trying to figure out if there is any truth to that?" She looked him right in the eyes. "Don't suppose you could help me out?" He looked right back in her eyes for about 30 seconds. Not cracking a smile, he said. "Don't suppose I can Meat Ball." "What Now?"

Inside, Jo Ann's heart was pounding. Her ears were beginning to ring. Things were getting kind of fuzzy in front of her. She kept blinking her eyes. She knew it was bad when her mouth got dry like a desert sun beating down on her. Master John was no better. He looked calm on the outside. Inside, he was like scrambled eggs. Legs Like jelly, he wanted his head to stop pounding. He wanted his hands to stop shaking and sweating. The bad part of the situation was, not two minutes had passed. It felt like two days. He wanted to walk over to her and hug her but his feet were stuck in place. They felt like lead weights.

Jo Ann pulled the .44 cal. Colt from behind her back. She knew the Master always kept it behind the hay bale she had been sitting on. She had grabbed it before she stood up to face him. She pointed, cocked the hammer back, and bam!! At 10 feet she couldn't miss... But she had. At the last second, something jerked her hand. (God?) (Voo Doo spirit?) (Guilt?)

They both stood stock still, looked each other in the eyes, and burst into tears, his in amazement that he was still breathing and hers in confusion at jerking her shot. All she had been thinking about was sending him to hell with half his head blown off. No one said a word.

She walked pass him out of the barn. Jo Ann mounted her master's horse and broke into a trot, than a gallop down the road. For his part he just stood there frozen to the spot. The stable boy, and the slave helpers, looked on in amazement!

Lizzy ran into the barn yelling, “What happened? What happened? John are you okay?” (In her deepest southern drawl.) When Lizzy was scared or startled, all those high society southern manners flew out of the window. She was back to regular old Elizabeth when frightened, and right now she was scared shitless. John just pushed past her and walked right out of the barn to the house. Things would never be the same.

CHAPTER ELEVEN

It was a fine October day on the plantation when April heard the whistle and the singing of the negroes hymn "Go Back Sweet Moses." Out the back of the big house, April looked. She sat her wash pail down on the kitchen floor, and calmed her jumpy, jittery nerves. April wiped the sweat from her face. She walked through the back door. The short path led to the outhouse. Harriet Tubman. April could not believe it. She had made it be known through the underground grapevine, that she was ready to try to get to freedom with her family. She didn't really believe she would ever have a shot at the title. It was just a dream to keep her going every day, so she wouldn't fall out losing her mind. Now she was so excited she could hardly talk. Ms. Tubman outlined the plan. She told April she would be back 5 hours after the sun went down. Ms. Tubman scooted off into the woods. Aprils' heart, mind, and body seemed to go in separate directions all at once. This was it. This is what she spent her last few years dreaming of. Her stomach was jumping with butterflies. Knots were locked in like cement. Her hopes and dreams for herself, and her family would finally come to pass. She was almost overcome with happiness, and anticipation. She would piss her pants if she didn't get a hold of herself.

Then it hit her like a ton of bricks. She had forgotten. Her heart sunk like the Titanic. Early this morning Luke had taken 10 slaves down to the plantation next to the Grand Harvest. They went to give a hand with some tree clearing. It was only about fifteen miles, but, it might as well have been the other side of the world. Richard, her husband, Homer and Willie, her oldest and youngest boys were among the 10 helping. They would not be back until tomorrow. Oh God, Ms. Truman would not risk holding the trip off until then. This was escape! Run to day light. Haul ass as fast as you could. This wasn't a walk in the park with your lover. When you make the plan you take that one chance at freedom, and you strike.

She couldn't ask Ms. Truman and the others to wait. Head spinning, she prayed, asked God for guidance. While on her knees she looked up a saw a big eagle soaring away from the plantation. Proud, flying free, squealing, two baby eagles following.

"Lead me mom," they seemed to be saying. "Where you go, I will follow." That did it. Richard would understand.

He would follow her with Homer and Willie. She had to try. She had to take her children Jo Ann, Mary and baby Jane to freedom. She was going to make it or die trying.

She walked back to the big house and ran into Lizzy coming out the back door. The look on her face said it all. The smile, the eyes, the look that said good bye. Lizzy stopped. She felt it too. She looked in Aprils' eyes. A tear trickled down her cheek as she thought of all they had shared. These two women of different color, who shared daughters by the same man. She knew in her heart, April was leaving. She knew in her heart she should tell John that an escape was in the air. But in her heart she knew slavery was wrong. People should live free. April deserved a chance for her and her family. Jo Ann was going to be somebody. She could feel it in her bones.

She touched Aprils hand, squeezed it, and softly said, "Remember us. Always remember Jo Ann has a sister who loves her." With a lump in her throat, she turned and quickly walked away without waiting for an answer, or a reply.

Now the stage was set. April was sure Lizzy would not say anything. There would be no snitching, no betrayal from the house. If something went wrong it would be her own kind that sold her out. The Judas would be black.

CHAPTER TWELVE

Five hours after dark, April tugged on Jo Ann's' blanket. Jo Ann was tossing and turning in anticipation of this journey.

"Jo Ann, Jo Ann," whispered April.

"I ain't sleep mama. I was just waiting on you. I'm so antsy; my eyes keep popping open by their self." The tattered straw mattress was itching her like mad. The smell of tired bodies hung heavy in the cabin.

"Me too," said April. "I been woke since we laid down." April had been praying and wishing upon a star for the last 2 hours. Her heart was beating like a drum. All she kept thinking about was Hattie, her mama, and how she never even thought about living free.

She wrapped her arms around herself and said, "chill bumps on this run. I got a nervous streak running up and down my spine, Jo. I is scared, but come hell or high water we going."

"Shhh, Mary going to hear you," replied Jo Ann. "It's bad enough we both scared enough to piss our britches. We never going to see freedoms door, if Jane and Mary scared too. They got to think we knows what the hell we doing."

"Okay baby," April said. "You got too much damn sense for a young'un. Sometime I think you ain't really my Chile," she joked.

April shook Mary. "Wake up pumpkin," she said softly. "Be quiet. I don't want to wake nobody baby. That's right, shake your sister. We got to get gone," her nerves were still jittery.

A rat scampered past Mary's foot. She screeched, and Jo Ann grabbed her and put her hand over Mary's mouth. Mary and Jane were both awake now. Jane hadn't learned to be afraid of rats yet. She would just point and giggle when she saw one. This was an adventure to Mary and Jane.

Slowly they crawled out of the slave quarters, using the door to the Outhouse. Once outside on the thorny, rock covered path that led to the outhouse, they were safer. Sweat and fear make a deadly combination in the woods. Insects kept biting. Thorns and briars were reaching out and scratching. A stray wild dog caught their scent, "Garr, Woof, Woof," she barked loudly.

"Get down," warned April. They waited, hearts thumping. After 2 minutes, April said, "Let's go."

"Oh lord please let us be going the right way," said April.

"I got this mama," replied Jo Ann. "Zack taught me everything about the North Star. We fine. Keep pushing."

Still the gloom, the darkness and the fear of the unknown, had April and Jo Ann jumpy and on edge. Fear was the 800 pound elephant on their back, what will we do when we get to freedom? Where are we going? How will we survive? Those were some thoughts running thru April and Jo Ann's mind, along with the big one. What if we get caught?

The little General, Harriet Tubman gathered her troops at the edge of the woods. The crickets were chirping. The stars lit up the sky. The darkness was all around. An occasional dog barking not far away could be heard. Snakes roamed during the night too. You had to be careful in this thick grass.

"Ms. Tubman, I's in your care now. I'ma see freedom or die trying. We ready, lead us to glory," said April. You could see the fear in her face.

At barely 5 ft. tall, dark face, slight build and wisdom lines etched in her face, Harriet didn't inspire a lot of confidence. When she spoke, it was a different story.

"I going to say this one time," replied Harriet. "I knows what I'm doing. I the boss. Don't take no suggestions, don't need none. Do exactly like I say, you see freedom, give me trouble, or try to run back, you get dead," she promised. At the same time she pulled out her .44 caliber colt. She looks up points to the North Star and says firmly,

"When I takes this first step north, ain't no turning back. If you change your mind say so now. Come hell or high water you going to be free. Let's go!"

You know now Harriet won't fail. Harriet is taking you home. It was no longer 90 to 100 miles to freedom. Now you had to get all the way to Upstate New York or Canada to feel safe. The Fugitive slave act of 1851 made it legal for bounty hunters to bring you back, dead or alive. There were people that made their living doing just that?

Ms. Harriet was a source of pride and a hero to many blacks and whites. One night when they were traveling, April stumbled over a log that was hidden in some tall grass. She disturbed a cotton mount rattler. The surprised snake struck out by reflex.

"Oh lord, Noo! Get it. It hurts Jo. Hurry!" Yelled April.

"Ms. Harriet, I can't pull it off. A snake got my mama, Ms. Harriet," cried Jo Ann. Ms. Tubman caught the tail and yanked hard. The damage was done. A few minutes later the wound started hurting badly.

"Oh my, its burning. My leg is on fire." April screamed. Her leg was staring to swell. The bloodied bite marks were ugly, dark pierces. The inside of April's leg felt like a furnace, burning hot coal. Her toes were starting to get numb. Sweat began dripping down her brow.

"Help me up Jo Ann", her mama pleaded. "Shoot, I can't feel my foot. Oh god, I hurt. Jesus help me!" April cried.

Ms. Tubman tried to help, it was for nothing. She had no medicine. Blacks hardly ever had access to medical supplies. After cutting open the wound and squeezing the ugly yellow puss out of it, it still festered. After an hour or so, it became obvious that April would not see freedoms doors.

"Her leg is so swollen. She's not going to make it, is she, Ms. Tubman?," Asked Jo Ann. "She is woozy. She can't see. Please God, Don't take my mama," pled Jo Ann. Mary and Jane were crying loudly. "Mama," Mary kept calling. "Please don't die mama." Scared and helpless, they watched April toss and turn. She moaned loudly. Finally, she signaled Ms. Tubman so she could whisper something in her ear.

"Ms. Truman, the life is squeezing out my body," April whispered. "Get my babies to freedom." Spittle dribbled down the side of April's mouth. Sweat balls were running down her face. "Please make sure someone takes care of my children. Jo Ann she strong and smart, she can take care of the others." April coughed hard. Her chest was rattling. "Jo tough as nails," April said. "I seen a good life. I'ma see heaven's gate. I ain't scared. Please Ms. Harriet, please get my man and my sons? They needs freedom too. Please get my men," she asked.

She smiled, her eyes rolled up in her head. Her chest exhaled one last time. April was gone. Mary wailed first, "No mama, don't go! No mama." Jane cried, "Mama, mama," not knowing why. Only Jo Ann cried with silence. Tears streamed down both cheeks, with not so much as a moan. Jo Ann just shook, and thought about how she was going to take care of her sisters. "My God," she thought. "I'm so young," her heart beating fast. Her mind was racing. She fell to her knees and yelled, "Lord, please help me. Give me strength."

"Chile god hears you," advised Harriet. "His will be done. You got to be strong for your sisters. You got to keep on pushing," she said gently.

"From those that much is given much is expected. You got the gift girl. It's from God, and you are blessed.

You can handle this. Stand tall, be strong," she said. "It's you and God now Jo Ann, rise straight up from the ashes."

CHAPTER THIRTEEN

By late 1860 the country was on fire with talk of state rights. But some people wanted government for one and all. The Republicans and Democrats were slugging it out. Republican Abraham Lincoln had won the White House, and was determined to keep the Union together at all cost. He was determined that slavery would not spread to any other state.

His debates with the little giant, Stephen Douglass, and the way he pulled himself up from country lawyer, to president, said volumes about his determination, character, and leadership ability. Abraham was a great leader. Many historians proclaim he is the best president in our nation's history.

Many states were speaking openly about succeeding from the Union. They talked about creating their own country, with a separate constitution. All were southern slave states that have their own culture and way of life to protect. They did not want to be dragged into the modernized industrial machine of the northern states, unless it was kicking and screaming. To keep up the culture of the south, they needed cheap labor. Slaves, men in bondage, were the answer.

"How in the hell do you sleep at night," Grady asked.

"Niggas ain't men," Grady replied. "They don't have hearts and souls like us Grady," Coldly, ice water running thru his veins, Darby says, "Hell, they count 3/5 of a man. Shit, they can't read, write or think for themselves. I'd just as soon shoot one dead as I would put down a dog with rabies," Darby snarled.

"God is going to show you Darby," Grady, who's his cousin, said. "You are going to burn in Hell. The hate in your heart will eat you up." Darby said, "I'll die and go to Hell before I say a niggar is equal to a white man." IQ 75, common sense 0, spirituality, none, that is the recipe for a bigot and a fool. Darby had them all. A good Ole South Carolina Redneck.

Grady, proved to be an example of the level handedness that was spread throughout the country. But the economics of the times meant slavery was what drove the culture. Despite the economics of the region, many Southerners owned no slaves. Therefore, brother was often pitted against brother.

With the country literally being torn asunder, Jo Ann and her sisters arrived in Philadelphia, PA.

"Thank you Rev. Alcott for taking us in. You are so kind. God bless you," said Jo Ann.

"Child, don't thank me, thank God," said Rev. Alcott. "This is his will, baby. We are just vessels." Rev Alcott was a fire and brimstone preacher. He often preached about the wrath of God, especially concerning Negro equality.

"Why Jo Ann, once I was a sinner, and a backslider. I drank, I fornicated, I abused everybody, black and white," explained Rev. Alcott. "I was on the way to medical school, like my father. Then I killed a man with my bare hands, drunk from corn whiskey. I promised God I'd give my life to him, if he saved mine," recalled Rev. "He saved me. I gave my life to the Lord, and the rest is history. My father was puzzled. I was not going to be a Doctor. My mother was happy, but flabbergasted. Now I love the Lord and do his work."

Harriet Tubman the ironed willed, tough talking, action charged Moses of her people, came with the sisters at a perfect time. When she landed on his doorstep with the sisters, it was a godsend.

Rev. Alcott was 48 years old, craggy faced, 5'7" tall and 135 pounds. His small stature pushed him to be a book worm coming up. He tried roughhouse with his 2 brothers, but always got the worst of it. But his voice was dynamic. It was booming, it would resonate, and he was mesmerizing. He dedicated his life to the Lord. He stood up for all people that he knew were brutalized, or downtrodden. No one could ever remember seeing him without his black suit and white clergy collar. His blond hair would be soaking wet after sermons on Sunday.

Mrs. Alcott was a stunning, cream complexioned woman. A hair over 5 feet tall, 110 pounds with a Greek nose. (Pointed) She had very sharp thin lips, and very small hands and feet. She had a very pretty voice that led her to take in Jo Ann, Mary and Jane.

CHAPTER FOURTEEN

LATER IN SCHOOL...

"Here is my assignment Ms. Johnson," said Jo Ann. She was doing wonderful in school. The lessons Lizzy had taught her and Willow, were showing. Jo Ann was the smartest student in her class.

"Jo Ann I don't know what I'm going to do with you," her teacher replied. "I'm proud of you." Secretly she was jealous, and mad at Jo Ann for being so smart. "Little Bitch," she thought that no negro girl should be more intelligent than her white students. It ran up her blood pressure to hear Jo Ann rattle off answers to questions even she had to look up.

"My mama never got to tell me about my monthly's, Ms. Johnson. What am I to do? I don't know if this bleeding will ever stop. My stomach cramps something awful," cried Jo Ann.

"My goodness child, is that what that awful smell is? You can't sit in class dripping blood, and smelling like a pig in slop," Ms. Johnson replied. "Go home, right now! Tell Ms. Alcott that I said you are to stay home until Monday. It will be over by then, and you won't smell like a dog in heat," Ms. Johnson said loudly.

"You don't have to yell at me. I'm not dirty or diseased," shot back Jo Ann.

"You little sambo. Take your little black tail out of this classroom, now, right, now," Ms. Johnson yelled again.

Jo Ann, tears swelling up and beginning to fall, ran out of the front door. She ran until she was tired and cried out. Past the hard red clay, and muddy road, through the thick bushes and tall weeds that led to the Alcott's small, but neat home. Jo Ann turned right at the fork, and walked the last quarter mile. The rusty fence and gravel path marked the final 25 yards.

"I'm so tired Ms. Alcott," she said in greeting.

"You look exhausted. Why in the world are you breathing so hard? What is it child?" Asked Ms. Alcott.

"Ms. Alcott do I stink?" Asked Jo Ann. "Ms. Johnson called me, a little sambo," Jo Ann said. "It hurt me she thinks I stink. Can I help? I'm having my monthlies?" She questioned. "Tell me Ms. Alcott. Tell me how to take care of woman's business. She got my heart hurting, and my head banging," Jo Ann said. "I could kill her," she thought to herself. "Snap her neck for making fun of me."

At that moment Jo Ann learned two things she would never forget.

1. Never let a person's words, no matter how cruel, hurt you. Actions are everything. What someone says to you, or about you means nothing. What his actions show you, is all that counts.

2. All things considered, nothing is ever what it seems, even dreams. Search for the hidden meaning. Look past the person's first impression he makes on you. Search for a person's motives. It is that truth that you believe.

Jo Ann was wise beyond her years. Her sister Mary was a blank canvas. She was just beginning to develop. A year younger than Jo Ann, she was chocolate skinned, her lips were full, kinky dark hair. Jo Ann favored denim jeans and Brogan boots. Mary the burlap dresses her mama made her. Her hips, like her grandmother Hattie in the big house kitchen. Sometimes she felt out of place among the white children.

Not Jane. She would soon be 3, and explored everything around her, trying to see what she could get into next. She would not be a raving beauty, but her personality just bubbles. At two she sees neither black or white. She sees just a person. She loves all people. Jane is truly the woman of the future.

LATER IN THE WEEK...

Jo Ann and Mary both had been pacing and running to look out of the window at passerby's, butterflies were flipping in both of their stomachs for two days now. Through the Underground Railroad, word was passed that Moses was running a mission. (Code for Ms. Tubman} She had sneaked back into slave holding country and was coming back with some cargo (slaves). It was a week now since she started the engine, loaded up with wood for the journey, took off, huffing and puffing into truly dangerous territory. By now she was famous, this firebrand of a woman with a heart big as a mountain. All over people would hold their breath, worry, toss and pace the floor at night, until God saw her safe and sound in freedom county.

"Ms. Harriet say this time she gonna tote Homer, Willie and Richard if she can.," Mary said.

I'm so nervous, I been to the outhouse ten times tonight," answered Jo Ann "I could jump out of my skin!!"

CHAPTER FIFTEEN

Five days later, Ms. Tubman limped into town. The expression on her face when she came through the door was grim. Five black men and two women, drooped over, exhausted, dirty and fear stricken stared at Jo Ann and Mary. Jo Ann and Mary leaped up and looked over their shoulders.

"Where's my brothers?" She asked frantically, "Where's Richard?"

Jo Ann cried. Mary, paralyzed with fear, heart racing, whispered, "Please Ms. Harriet!? Where are my kinfolk?" She was weak in the knees.

"They knowed I was coming," Harriet said. "They knowed right off. There's a Judas with our people now," she stared in the fireplace.

"What happened Harriet," asked Rev. Alcott. "Rest child, get off your feet. Jo Ann, get Harriet some hot tea. Bring some for everyone."

Harriet stated her case, "We got away only because of your father and God's will. Your father fought those slave catchers tooth and nail. He held them back so we could run far and fast, but they tracked us after they killed Richard. They wouldn't give up. They trapped us. About two hour's ago in the big field by the river. Homer, your brother, held them off so we could run. We ran across the river crossing, but Homer didn't make it. Now they probably gonna take him back for the bounty or hang him. Either way they get paid. So your pa died while we got away, and your brother was caught later. That's a damn heavy price for one family to pay. I'll never forget. I mean never," said Harriet. "Oh yeah, your pa told me to tell you Willie, your brother, was sold south to Charleston, South Carolina," said Harriet. "He sold to be a breeder to some plantation name of Kings Mansion, right outside of the big bridge, biggest plantation in the area. Ain't anybody heard from him since last year? I'm too old and too tired to go after Homer, so I guess in a day or so dead or alive he be in Grand Harvest."

Jo Ann couldn't think straight. She was 16, had started a new life, people trusted her, treated her with respect. She even met a couple of boys who were inclined toward her. She had never been on an outing with a boy before, but she could tell in a few days, weeks, months, she would get a chance. “What to do? What to do?” Thought Jo Ann, out loud.

The door flew open, Rev. Alcott and 4 other men were checking their firearms and mounts.

“We got to get that boy,” Rev. Alcott spoke first!

“Let’s ride before they get too far,” one of the men bellowed.

“Come on, I need to get me one of them bounty hunters,” the other man, chimed in.

“My God, they don’t even know Homer,” Jo Ann thought. A tear dribbled down her check. She tore off into the house, she grabbed the carbine rifle from over the fireplace, threw on jeans and a flannel work shirt, and was back in the barn saddling up in less than 10 minutes.

”I’m going too,” she said.

“I’m going to see someone in Hell before they hang my Homer.”

“Let’s go,” said Alcott.

“Let’s ride men,” said Jo Ann.

“May the Lord have mercy on our souls,” wished Rev. Alcott.

CHAPTER SIXTEEN

It took three hours of hard riding to make up the difference, after two hours of resting up, and making a plan. An hour before dawn Rev. Alcott, Jo Ann and the others were looking down from the ledge on an out cropping. The bounty hunters camp was directly below. The smell of coffee drifted up from the campfire. You could see the embers and flames dancing, and hear them crackling from their position. You could also see something unexpected. They were asleep, out like a light from rock gut whiskey. Tossing, turning, moaning in their sleep, the bounty hunters were dead to the world. Even the lookout was learning against a boulder, snoring with spit dribbling down the side of his bearded, pock marked face. Homer was tied to the trunk of a massive tree. Although, sitting down, the rough bark of the oak tree and the rope tied so tight, cut off circulation and kept him from resting. The chase from yesterday, and the alcohol had done them in.

When Jo Ann outlined a plan to free Homer, the men were stunned. She would take the lead, sneak into the camp and free Homer, and shoot anything moving. Then Rev. and company would follow up with a full bore attack. “Can you actually pull this off?” Rev. questioned. “Anybody got a better plan?” Asked Jo Ann. “Ok let’s get to work.” And work they did. Jo Ann silently belly crawled onto the edge of the camp. She swiftly cut Homer’s binding and was getting ready to free his feet, when a damn horse whined and rose up in panic. The hunter’s reaction was slow, and predictable. Half scared, and very excited, Rev. Alcott and his men charged the camp, yelling and screaming. There was more noise than gunfire.

“I’m hit, oh God, I’m hit,” screamed Homer. Sure enough he was shot. Whose bullet had gotten him was anybody’s guess. They emptied revolvers and rifles until the smoked emptied.

“Damnation!” A surprised Rev. Alcott looked around in wonder.”

“All of them laid out like wood soldiers,” he said in surprise.

“We ain’t got a darn scratch,” one of the men bragged.

"Girl, where in the world did you learn to handle a rifle like that? I ain't seen shooting like that since my pappy," he roared.

"Oh no, look over there," Rev. Alcott pointed at Homer. Blood leaked dark red from a hole in his gut. Homer, half – conscious and in pain cried, "how, how did you get here Jo?" Coughing, hands trying to hold back his intestines, Homer now croaked, and whispered, "So, here, come closer baby girl." Tears starting to stream down her face, heart racing, she bent her head to Homer's lips. Homer whimpered, "Tell them I died free Jo. Let them know I died free. I love you girl. I love you." With that he was gone. Jo Ann raised up and fainted right on the spot.

CHAPTER SEVENTEEN

In 1861, seven states had succeeded from the union and having created the Confederate States of America, started a civil war. Brother fought against brother, father against son, best friend against best friend. A man by the name of Jefferson Davis was appointed president, and Joe Johnson, a West Point graduate, accepted the leadership of the Confederate Army.

Jo Ann, still in a state of shock, and grieving over her brother Homer, and the death of her mom April, and step dad Richard, had undergone a major transformation. She was often moody now. She would go into a state of deep depression for weeks, often not speaking to anyone. Then she would be sharp tongued, and mean spirited for no reason to Mary, and even little Jane. She took little or no interest in the attention from the boys. Her Bible study went lacking. She said her prayers only once or twice a week. It was like a light switch had been turned off in her body. The warmth that she had generated in the past became cold and distant. It was winter time in her soul 24/ 7. What people did not know, was that an idea for revenge had been percolating in her head like a pot of fresh boiling coffee?

She was in the final stages of her plan this fine September day. The purchase, of this beautiful stallion, from Mr. Jones Livery stable, was the first step in her plan, and it had just been completed. She needed a strong steady horse that would hold up on her ride to Harrisburg City. It would be a hard ride, and this piece of horse flesh would have to carry her. She had made an excellent choice. She had been accumulating supplies and other materials over the last five weeks. While she locked herself in the basement of Reverend Alcott's church, she turned to study herself in the mirror once again. Once the war started, she found her a way that would lead to getting her revenge for all that had been snatched away from her. War! Cruel, dirty, merciless, hard – core. There were women among her circle of friends that cared deeply about the union and wanted to see slavery abolished totally. They talked about what they could do to help the war effort. Some had fathers, brothers, even husbands that had joined the union army. They wanted to help in any way they could. They mostly volunteered as nurses. Some sewed uniforms, made flags, and worked in the factories taking their husbands places.

Jo Ann did none of that. Her taste for blood and revenge was going to be up close and personal! First she had to get as far away from Philadelphia as she could. Then she had to undergo an amazing transformation. She would take the scissors and cut her hair as close to bald as it could get. She took two straps of canvas from an old sail boat she found down by the river and bound her breasts tightly to her body. She practiced muddying her complexion with creek dirt and made her eyebrows bushy. Jacket 2 sizes too large a pair of mule riding britches, some hard tack riding boots and a Bowie knife strapped to her side and the look was almost complete.

"Damn, now all I need is this Fedora Hat". Jo Ann happily commented. "Now I'm a new man", she said. She was Jonathan Douglass from New York City.

One of the least talked about facts of the civil war is that over two hundred and fifty women fought for both the northern and southern cause enlisted as men. Jo Ann was the only known black to do so and also pass for a white man. Her one goal was kill! As many and as often as possible.

"I'll fight until I die", she said. "My family will be avenged, I'm not afraid to die", she said. This is how Jo Ann got to be a member of the 78th. PA. Volunteers. This unit would show again and again during the course of the war that it was an outstanding unit. Headquartered in Harrisburg, PA., they were a hard group to reckon with on the battlefield.

Jonathan entered as a private and mostly kept to himself. Not too many friends or associates for fear of being discovered. Always reluctant to talk about himself, take part in practical jokes or even take part in services on the Sabbath. The soldiers that participated in this war were the most devout in the history of the country. Mostly all thought they were fighting for Gods mandate on humanity and Sunday religious attendance was always heavily populated on both sides.

Jonathan seldom drank, never gambled and the only thing he seemed truly to enjoy was rifle drills and target practice. There he was a master. At 50 yards with the Sharps he could shoot a hat out of your hand!! He had a peculiar habit of walking into the woods to do his business. 80* and his uniform jacket would still be buttoned to the top.

"Damn did you smell that", the soldier said. "I know Jonathan smells like old blood. Damn he must be on his period or having monthly or something," the Cpl. said.

"Man shut up before he hears you", the private replied. "Jonathan can shoot your eyes out of your skull fool" he said.

He was polite, would lend you money, and help you do your chores and do your guard shift if he had to. Although they had not had a major battle, he had shown his courage in the minor skirmishes they had run into.

"The boy ran headlong, into that snipers nest. Did you see that shit?" Sgt. Kelly exclaimed. "Damn, he got some balls, that's for sure."

"Sometimes the boy goes into a trance and don't even remember killing a man or two. That shit is scary", Sgt. Kelly exclaimed.

Sometimes his own men were scared of him. Sometimes men in the 78th would just disappear. Three, in a years' time. One day they were marching. The next day they were gone. They all had the same characteristics. Redneck, White trash, bullies. All were disrespectful foul mouthed cowards. One even killed a man by kicking him in the face and ribs one day when he came into the camp hungry.

"Darby, why the hell did you kick that man? He couldn't even defend himself", the soldier said.

The other had called Jonathan a fag. "You never even take your shirt off, you fag", said Pvt. Lester. "Can you piss standing up?" He asked. Lanner Bodine was just nasty. He disappeared too. Jonathan met Edward Kelly around this time.

"What's up Irishman? Jonathan greeted Kelly.

"Top of the morning to you soldier" replied Kelly.

"Knew you were Irish. Your accent gave you away" Jonathan said. If Kelly knew Jonathan was Black and a woman he would have cardiac arrest.

Edward was about 5' 10" 175 lbs, ruddy complexion and unlike most Irish men, kept mostly to himself and was quiet and soft spoken. He also did not want to fight every five minutes because of his

Irish temper. Blessed with a beautiful Irish tenor his voice could bring a tear to your eye and chill bumps to your arms.

"Damn, the boy can fight like a mountain lion," Pvt. Dunbar commented.

"Yeah, him and Jonathan could have a competition for most dangerous in combat," said Johnson. Between him and Jonathan they were like two killing machines.

Edward had somehow persuaded Jonathan to start attending Sunday services regular. His family, 2nd generation catholic had been run out of Ireland by religious zealots and settled in Harrisburg, PA., Father, mother, and 8 children (5 boys, 3 girls).

The 78th was readying for their first major campaign. It was September 16, 1862 against the army of Northern Virginia. That had been gathering for weeks in the fields of Sharpsburg, MD, near Hagerstown on some farmland that would come to be known as the battle of Antietam. This would be forever known as the bloodiest single day of the civil war. At the end of the evening of the 16th and the following day about 5:30 pm, 23, 00 men became casualties. Some fields were literally "Drenched in

Blood". The most vicious fighting was in Millers cornfield.

"Damn man I can't see a thing". Jonathan screamed. "I can't see 5 feet in front me. Where in the hell is Edward," he asked.

A cannon ball hit at that moment and the land collapsed. Jonathan fell down the hill, felt something sharp pierce his leg and yelled. He tried to stand up but couldn't.

"Shit", Jonathan yelled. "I can't feel my leg. I can't stand up. Oh no, that's somebody's hand I got. No, somebody lost their whole arm." This can't be real," he hollered. "Where is my leg? Where is my damn leg?" He asked.

Edward couldn't hear a thing. The cannon ball had ruptured his eardrum. "I'm bleeding like a pig," he said. "I'm lost and I'm dizzy. I got to find Jonathan. He was right here a minute ago," he said. He rolled down into the crater; he bumped into Jonathan by accident. He threw him up on his shoulder, slipped twice in the blood and regained his footing.

"I should have left you down here, painted a sign on your chest and ran", he smiled. "Your ass is too heavy to be hauling".

"Just shut up and get me out of here", Jonathan screamed. "Promise me you won't let that Doc cut my leg off, Edward," he asked. Edward thought he was crazy. He kept feeling breasts rubbing his shoulders. He must be tripping he thought. "Damn I'm going crazy", he said.

Finally, he got Jonathan to the med wagon. Then he passed out. He had tasted war. It was bitter, nasty and ugly. Now he was battle tested and he thanked God he was still living. Between Jonathan and Edward they had shot, hacked, stabbed, bit, kicked and mutilated over twenty men.

"Damn Jonathan," Edward complained. "I never heard so much screaming, felt so much pain, been blinded or had so much smoke caught up in my throat, ever," said Edward.

"My hair is burnt to the roots " Jonathan bellowed. "I got burns on my face and my hands. I might lose my leg. Hell, I slipped three times on blood from my own men. I ain't never seen nothing like this. Edward promise me you won't let them cut my leg off, man. Promise."

"I got you pardner. I promise." Said Edward. "I'll shoot the doctor"

With that he looked at a deep gash on his arm, squeezed the arm to stop the bleeding, and fainted.

CHAPTER EIGHTEEN

During the rest of the fall and winter there were long periods of idleness. The cold set in round the second week in November, 1862 and the men were plagued with constant sickness and disease. Infections were common too.

Edward talked a lot about his family. He talked a lot about his overburdened father. Two of his brothers were union soldiers. As far as he knew they were still alive. Jonathan did not talk much about his family. He did not want to slip and make a mistake. Trying to act like a man all the time was hard. The men teased him about his voice.

If you listened real close there were whispers about a homosexual relationship between him and Edward. It was during this time he found the wounded mutt whose hind leg had been shot. Jonathan had no idea what he was going to do with him. Edward came up with the idea to name him Buster and make him company mascot.

"I'll keep him thru the war, take him back to the farm and teach him to hunt quail", Edward told Jonathan. "The first time he bites a bird and messes him up I'm going to blow his brains out", he said playfully.

"And you'll go to hell right behind Buster, Irishman", said Jonathan. By now they were hopelessly attached to Buster. It was a love affairs sure nuff. Buster loved Jonathan and Edward right back.

Being gay in the 1860's was not unheard of, just not talked about. Most thought of it as a curse from God for something your family did. Truth be told Edward was starting to become confused himself, because he had no idea Jonathan was really Jo Ann, he could not understand the physical attraction he felt toward Jonathan. He had started to fell shamed and guilty whenever he looked in Jonathan's eyes and felt a spark. When they studied scripture or accidently touched hands, sometimes his manhood would rise. Edward would abruptly cut off his conversation, and scamper off in embarrassment. He prayed about it, but still started to wonder if he was gay. All the time he was just experiencing normal feelings for a first love. (smile) The suspense was maddening.

For his part Jonathan was both shocked, worried, and amused. He/she had been aware that she was attracted to Edward as a woman would be to a man. What shocked her was that now she was becoming sure that Edward was aware of it too.

"There is nothing feminine about the way I act", said Jo Ann to herself out loud. Is this man attracted to me naturally? Or does he have feelings for me just because we have lots of things in common, and it makes no difference to him if I am a man or woman?" He asked himself. "There are butterflies bouncing around in my stomach; sometime it feels like a hammer banging on the inside of my head," Jo Ann said.

As the months went by it got harder to be around Edward for Jo Ann. She started wondering if someone would notice. The suspense was maddening. Already Jonathan did some things, that were not normal for men; like going away from camp to wash up or to do his business. He made sure no one got too close when it was that time of the month. Sometimes he left bloody rags behind when the unit broke camp. Two or three men talked about her/his body odor when she was having her monthly. One man she had to make disappear for good. One day he was marching, the next day he was gone.

Lastly, she was amazed, because her 'brilliant' plan to exact revenge for all she had suffered and lost had not made room for 'falling in love'. What a monkey wrench in her plans. Now she was floating, riding in the clouds. She would break out smiling just at the thought of Edward. Her stomach would tingle when she looked up and caught a glimpse of him with his mouth set, concentrating on cleaning his rifle with those hazel eyes. She would think about him for hours at the time, making time almost stand still for her. That is until Buster would nip at her ankle wanting to play.

Most amazing was how wet she would get between her legs at night. She would play with herself until she had an orgasm that would knock her boots off, send her right to sleep thinking of Edward with a smile on her face. Oh boy, this is going to be rough.

CHAPTER NINETEEN

It all came to a head just before Christmas 1862. Lincoln had relented, an authorized the use of colored soldiers to help the Union war effort. Not all of the Union soldiers were happy about this. One of these units was the Second Michigan Infantry. They were not happy at all.

"Damn, soldier, they don't let you do nothing but sort and pass out the mail? Asked Jonathan.

"Yeah, that's about all," said Private Thompson. "That's been my job since I joined up. I can shoot, fight and ride with the best of them," said Thompson. "Ole Colonel Poe is an asshole sometime."

"Well, good to meet you Thompson", said Jonathan," "Tomorrow we might see us some action. Heard we got some colored boys coming to help out too." Jonathan held out his hand to bid Pvt. Thompson goodbye. As he shook Private Thompson's hand, it felt rather soft to the touch. Jonathan was shocked! Never had he felt a man's skin so soft. It was almost effeminate.

"Damn, wait until I tell Edward about this," thought Jonathan. Never to cross paths again in life, Jonathan had just met Private Frank Thompson. In reality Sarah Emma Edmonds, who would serve out the entire war, and according to her memoirs became a very successful Union spy, assuming the identity of an Irish woman hauling goods behind confederate lines, and another Black woman who conducted operations behind confederate lines. A woman enlisted as a man!

One soldier, Pvt. James Donovan, kept looking at Jonathan every time he got close to him. He was trying to see Negro blood in Jonathan. Jonathan had somewhat let his guard down, becoming distracted trying to puzzle out a solution with this maddening situation concerning Edward. 'What to do? What to do? He / She pondered.

CHAPTER TWENTY

DOWN BY THE RIVER BANK...

"Come on Buster", Jo Ann directed Buster. "Hurry up and take care of your business. We can't be down here too long. There's snakes in this part of the country, that's all I need. A snake biting my ass and me falling out dead. Found with my pants around my ankles, and my coochie where my balls are supposed to be", she laughed.

"Woof, woof," replied Buster. Just like he understood everything Jo Ann just thought. Bending over the almost frozen creek water, Jonathan/Jo Ann pulled down His / Her pants, squatted and started to urinate. Donovan, an enlisted man, had followed Jo Ann and Buster down to the creek.

"Oh, shit", he cried out. "Damn if Douglass ain't got a coochie. I got to have me some of that!" His eyes wide as saucers. He jumped up and tripped over a fallen log. Buster, hearing the noise first, barked loudly.

"Woof, woof, woof", he barked. He broke into dead run right at Donovan.

With surprise in his voice, Jonathan said, "What the hell are you running after Buster? Where do you think you are going, you crazy mutt?" When he caught up to Buster, his jaws were wrapped around Donovan's right arm. Jonathan had snatched up his riffle and broke out in a dead run. He found Buster was being swung wildly in circles, with Donavan trying to free himself frantically!

"Booty, real live Booty", he screamed. "I'm going to get me some of that cookie," he snarled. "Bet my life on it", he yelled again. The thought of rape had him so excited; he damn near pissed his britches. The panicked and startled Jo Ann / Jonathan ran up on the two, (Buster and Donavon) locked in a death dance.

"Let go! Buster." Jo Ann shouted. "Now Buster, let go!" Buster loosened his jaws. At the same instant Jo Ann fired two rounds from the Sharps rifle.

"Ah, ah shit I'm hit, damn, I'm hit", hissed Donavon, blood leaking freely from the two king sized wounds. Donavon tripped over into the creek bed. Edward, investigating what was taking Jonathan so long, ran headlong into the shooting.

"Back up Jonathan, now right now", Edward yelled. He fired his revolver one time.

"Oh God, ah fuck, my head, my head..." Donavon words cut off suddenly. He fell in the ice cold, half frozen, clear creek. An off red mixture of blood, water and dirt combined to make a color not quite known. Donovan' whimpering fell on angry, deaf ears. Edward finished the work with a strike from his Bowie knife. Together they half carried, half dragged Donovan to a mound of bushes and leaves. They laid him there to rest, hoping by morning the vultures, and wild dogs would enjoy one hell of a meal. Buster was prancing and dancing as if the execution was his. Nervous and jumpy, he did his business again.

"I'm sorry I got you mixed up in this mess", Jo Ann said to Edward. She could not take this stress, nor the pressure, one minute more.

"Come to me Edward", she reached for his hand. Edward had no idea what Jonathan meant. She grabbed Edward hand, stuck it under her jacket, and Edward gasped in shock and surprise.

"I'm a woman you see", whispered Jo Ann. "It's alright; I'm yours if you want me". Relief, joy, excitement, disbelief spread thru Edward's body. He pulled Jo Ann close, put his mouth on Jo's lips and kissed her tenderly.

"I love you Edward," Jo Ann declared. "I love you." Edward was so happy; he forgot to ask his true love her real name.

CHAPTER
TWENTY ONE

They had buried Donovan's body under those bushes and fallen logs by the creek. They hatched a plan that would keep them from being discovered, if it wasn't investigated closely. They let Donovan's horse loose, and pilfered his supplies and bed roll from camp. They told two or three people that they saw Donovan ride out of camp right after supper. Hopefully, it would be assumed he deserted. Desertions were high in the cold weather. Many soldiers got lonely for a hot meal, a warm bed, a woman, and a roof over his head. They were hoping like hell that people would think Donovan just got tired and ran off. Just hold your breath and pray.

Throughout the X –mas season, and past New Year's 1863, Things did not look very good for the union troops or Jonathan in particular. President Lincoln, along with most of the union thought the war would be short, brutal and come to a quick conclusion. The southern states were proving to be a formidable opponent. They were fighting like mad men, and although badly outnumbered, their leaders were proving to be more than a match for the Union generals.

Men like Robert E. Lee, Jubal Early, Stonewall Jackson, and Jeb Stuart, were excellent leaders. The union enlistment period which was 90 days, began to grow monthly. When the president decided that he needed a draft to bring in new recruits, lots of citizens got angry and refused to be inducted.

The draft riots in New York City were ugly and violent. They were fueled mostly by Irish citizens that did not feel the need to go to war with slavery as one of the issues being fought over. Also, it was well known that rich people could buy their way out of serving. This created a lot of ill will between those that had means, and those that did not. Back in Dorchester County, as in a lot of areas in the state of Maryland, a lot of citizens went off to join the ranks of the confederate army. Brothers sometimes fought against brothers. Father fought against son in this conflict. Master Johns' sympathies were with the confederates, so that he could continue living the only lifestyle he had ever known.

His son Zack, having wanted to be a sailor for years, joined the union navy so that he could be a part of the U.S. Naval fleet. He got his start at Annapolis which was a major Port, and where naval warfare instruction was just starting to become a major part of the war strategy. The blockading of the water lanes was seen as major way to cut off southern supply lines, and choke off the cotton shipments headed for Europe. The southern states needed this money and the supplies that would be brought back, to survive. Also armored ships were becoming involved in the war effort. This was a new type of fighting. It was dangerous and took many skills to be able to maneuver these types of ships. Captains that could prosper in this type of environment were extremely valued. Zack got his respect and his promotions quickly, and was a considerable source of pride to Elizabeth, even though he wore the uniform of the union.

This war tore some Mothers hearts apart. It made you pull your feelings all different ways, and never, ever have a peaceful minute of rest wondering about your children. There was talk in the naval circle that Zack was an officer that could eventually reach the status of the legendary Edward Preble, one of the navies most decorated officers ever.

CHAPTER TWENTY TWO

Life at Grand Harvest and other Dorchester County plantations continued pretty much like before the war.

"You know John if I didn't know better I would say that incident in the barn between you and Jo Ann really changed you", said Lizzy. "You give me my respect. You get up on Sunday and worship our Lord. By God, I look over at you and you are listening and nodding your head. Are you thinking about your immortal soul?" She asked. "I'm finding myself falling in love with you again", she said. She kissed him on the forehead and smiled.

"Well June is gone and I'm bored and old, so I decided to fall in love with you again," he said. "Meat Ball could have killed me in that barn, whatever made her jerk that shot I'm grateful", he smiled. "Willow is 19 now, it looks like Zack loves the Navy better than Grand Harvest, so I'm going to turn it all over to Willow, teach her what I know and get the hell out of her way. She's got balls and more gumption than I had at her age," he admitted. "So let's just see what the hell the good Lord has in store."

"I hope who ever she settles down with don't mind getting their hands dirty. It looks like this war ain't gonna touch our land. Thank God for that. One day these slaves gonna be free Lizzy," he proclaimed. "I seen beat, raped, hung, branded, tongues cut out, and balls cut off. I seen it all," he whispered. "I never treated my niggas that way," he said.

"Daddy did, Grand pop too. I hope they remember how I treated them, and don't up and killed all of us." He said. "If they did, you couldn't much blame e'm," nodding his head as he spoke. "Willow gonna have to get ready for that, we will see soon enough how it goes. Just hold your breath and pray."

"You think the Union gonna win?" Asked Lizzy.

"Yeah, old Abe gonna set every black face free in Dorchester County. Free as a bird. And you know what Lizzy? I think that's the way God meant it to be," John predicted. "If you say I said it, I'll call you a lie, but I think a man got a right to live free Lizzy," admitted John.

June was in Baltimore, and would stay there. Willow knew from a very early age that June was gay. She knew June had been in love with the slave girl for as long as she could remember. She saw the way June faked like she enjoyed courting by men and flirting. Sometimes it tore at her heart strings. She did not know how it felt to be in love with someone of your own sex, but she felt the pain that she saw in her sisters eyes whenever Sally May was around. At least momma had kept her word, and let Sally May move to Baltimore with June. Maybe June would have some kind of happiness in her life. Maybe she would announce 'It' one day?

Meanwhile Willow tried to keep up with word from up north about Jo Ann. Willow truly thought that she and Jo Ann were sisters. Most white girls would have been horrified. Willow was ecstatic! She could not have been happier if she found out Santa Claus was real. She promised herself that no matter what, she would always try to keep up with Jo Ann and help her if she could.

After Jo Ann ran away with her family, Willow was scared to death she would be caught, whipped or maybe even hung. When word filtered back that the bounty hunters would be coming back in boxes, Willow was overjoyed. She made arrangements thru the Pinkerton Detective Agency to have all information about Jo Ann relayed back to her. The last she heard, Jo Ann was in Philadelphia with a preacher and his wife. She was doing fine.

CHAPTER
TWENTY THREE

MEANWHILE DOWN IN WASHINGTON CITY....

"Listen to me", growled President Lincoln. "I'm sick to my stomach with these bumbling idiots. When is one of these no accounts going to end this nightmare of a war?"

Secretary Stanton, himself on the hot seat frowned, took a deep breath and dove in, "The whole country is sick and tired Mr. Lincoln. Look I have listened to every strategy that God and his children have dreamed up", said Stanton. "The truth is we have not had a general with guts enough or smart enough to trump Lee. Damnit, I'm at my wits end. Sir, we've got to do it sir, we have to" Stanton begged.

"Get him, right now, send for him," urged President Lincoln! "I don't give a damn if he wakes up drunk every morning. Two days from now, he better be knocking on my office door, or some heads will roll," threatened Lincoln.

"He's a butcher sir", warned Stanton. "He loses more men in a day, than most generals do in an entire campaign. What will the press say? The damn newspapers will scream like banshees," said Stanton.

"Let 'em scream", replied Lincoln. "They can scream till they are blue in the face. I want this damn war ended. Now, not a year from now. Grant can end this war. I want him to chase Lee to hell and back if he has to. That fool Jefferson Davis has plucked my nerves for the last time," barked Lincoln. "I want Lee gone. I want Davis arrested, and Richmond in flames, and I want it done soon! Do you understand me Stanton," The voice echoed off the office walls. Rarely had anyone witnessed a tirade by the president. Today he was in rare form. His blood was boiling!

"Get Grant here!" He raged again. "Get Sherman to tear up the entire confederate army, if he can. Burn and loot and run them rebels into the ocean if need be," said Abe. "God will forgive me later," he rationalized. "I'll hold my breath and pray." "We will talk on judgment day. Right now I want Richmond!" General Ulysses S. Grant took command of the effort to end the war, by any means necessary.

The 78th PA, volunteers were part of the push that swept thru parts of Mississippi, Tennessee, and then turned upward, joining Sherman in his famous Atlanta campaign. Jo Ann and Jonathan basically merged into one person. Feeling more comfortable because she knew her feelings for Edward had evolved into true love, she was a little looser around the men in the company. She enjoyed the fanciful banter and stomach turning laughter that came now, she learned to play the dozens, (your mother is so poor, she can't even pay attention) and could give a sleeping comrade the hot foot with the best of them.

Over the last 4 months Jonathan had also dragged one of his men to safety after taking a rebel slug in the right shoulder. He saved another by a daring, all out charge right into a startled, surprised and totally shocked prison camp that he led.

"Man, that Douglass is a hell of a soldier", one corporal remarked.

"I'd follow him anywhere," another proclaimed.

"If it was a choice between him and God, I'd have to flip a coin to choose," still another said.

"Damn, the praise don't get no better than that," declared the corporal.

"Hell, if I had known all you had to do was get shot, I'd did it year ago," said Jonathan. He was talking about his promotion to Squad leader. Edward had gotten a promotion also. Each of them now led their own platoon. They most times fought side by side. Jonathan now walked with a slight limp, but he never lost the leg he so worried about, and his secrets were still safe.

"I should have let the doc cut that leg off", joked Edward. "Then I wouldn't have to worry about charging hell bent into a snipers nest, you crazy fool" he said. "Seriously, you really must think you can't die in this crazy war? Your blood really is red, Jonathan."

"When my time comes I'm ready. Right now God got an angel on my shoulder. I talk to her every day," Jonathan replied. "You just jealous, pretty boy," laughed Jonathan. "Sorry about your brother." Jonathan said. Edwards's oldest brother had been killed at Gettysburg.

"Thanks Jo," said Edward. "I got a bitter taste in my mouth, and a hankering for revenge now. But hell you helped me thru the hurt & the pain. Thanks again, I really owe you," sighed Edward.

OVER A CAMPFIRE...

Old Buster was the love of both of their lives. The dog was the heart and soul of the platoon. Everyone loved Buster! I do believe some of the men would have killed who ever mistreated Buster if they were ever caught doing so. The only thing Jonathan never talked to anyone about was protecting their relationship. (Jo Ann & Edward) If someone got too close, or if Jo Ann suspected someone in the company was getting too close to the truth, they would be marching one day, and missing the next. So far between 1863, and 1864, there had been three more "Desertions". Soldiers that for whatever reason did not reach the next night campfire. This had to be Jonathans doing. He had become an expert at making people disappear. His secrets were still safe, he hoped.

CHAPTER
TWENTY FOUR

After meeting up with General William Sherman to take part in the Atlanta Campaign, there was a lifting of spirits and moral in the ranks of the 78th. The tide was turning for the union. The north could smell blood and victory if they could just press on the advantage they had gained. Sherman and Phil Sheridan, along with General Grant were determined to end this conflict.

Jonathan, caught up in the excitement of the company had started making his own plans. Since the Atlanta Campaigns objective was to crush and destroy anything in its path, Jonathan decided he would mutilate, dismember, gut, and decapitate anything that he had a chance to, in the name of the family members he had lost. He wanted to become a one man wrecking crew. A force of destruction so viscous, that he would be talked about for years to come.

His first chance came in May, 1864, in what would be known as the battle of Pickets Mill. Union troops, perhaps over – confident, committed what historians say was Sherman's biggest blunder of the push to Atlanta. The fighting was hard hand to hand combat, with Sherman letting his force not only get ambushed, but out flanked. What he thought would be a walk in the park turned out to be an all-out, give it everything you got, fight for your life.

Jonathan, whose squad of snipers and sharp shooters, were supposed to pluck off rebels like shooting fish in a barrel, got cut off from his men in the confusion of a rebel attack. Once, then twice, they came screaming, that blood curdling rebel yell that could scare the pants off a man.

"Damn it" Jonathan yelled. "These Rebs think they can just scream and make us lay down?" He jumped up, charged right at the Rebel attack, and cut down two with his Bowie knife, three more Rebels fell to his .44 revolver and the other 3 turned and ran.

"Would you look at him," the soldier from Jonathan's unit was still in awe.

"Walking around like he was still in Sunday school," said another soldier.

"I have never seen anyone fight like that in my life," still another weighed in.

"Shit, he could have taken on the whole reb army and still won," the first soldier said, shaking his head in amazement.

"Of all my days on earth, I will always remember this one. They will be talking about this madman from the 78th for the next 100 years," crowed the bugler that sounded the charge. "Look at Jonathans' uniform. You can't ever tell what color it is in some places. Damn, is that brains on the top part? Look, the man's got brains on his uniform" The boy ain't human. The man was tongue tied and awe stricken.

"I thought that extra uniform was for church. He keeps that because he knows the one he got on will be too smelly and bloody to keep wearing," Sgt. Crow exclaimed.

"Look at his face. Look at his eyes. He seeing some stuff we ain't even seeing, He talking with the devil. They must have made one hell of a deal," Cpl. Warren said, as he bent over laughing.

Edward had accounted himself brilliantly also. His squad suffered no casualties. Although it was not a victory, his men saw him step up to the plate. They were proud of him.

A couple of days later, after Sunday church service, Jo Ann and Edward had a private moment together.

"We can't stay gone too long," said Jo Ann. She was nervous and jittery.

"I know. I just wanted to be alone with you for a while. This war has me wondering what I'm turning into," replied Edward. He was laying on his back with Jo Ann in the crock of his arm. He surveyed the hilly terrain where they had fought like tigers a couple of days earlier. He said, "I know this is crazy, and I know one of us may not walk away, but if we are both still breathing, I'm asking you to marry me". He grinned, and looked Jo Ann right in the eyes.

Jo Ann's heart skipped a beat. She had been hoping and praying for this moment. Now she was stuck. Tongue – tied, she stammered, "You, you, s – s –sure?"

"Damn right I'm sure", cried Edward.

"Well since you never cuss, then I guess that does it," smiled Jo Ann. "I better say yes since your mouth is a prayer book."

By the time the kiss was over, the fears started running in her head. "How in the world will we explain this to your parents?" She asked. "Where did we meet? How did we court? How did we fall in love? Where is my family? Who are they kin to? How much land do they have? When can we meet them?

"Hold on, wait a minute", Edward yelled. Let's take them one at the time", he said.

Then she thought about the big one. "I'm black as a berry," what about that? All she knew was that she was head over heels in love. This was her knight in shining armor. Every time she would break out in a cold sweat. Her stomach would get knots in it. Her head would start swimming. This was the kind of fear that could cripple you!!

CHAPTER TWENTY FIVE

Jo Ann had two sisters to look after when this fighting was over. Mary could probably take care of herself, but Jane, never. She felt guilty just thinking about abandoning her baby sister. She loved Jane like a lioness loves her cubs. But Jane was so black. Her hair was so kinky. Her teeth were white as saucers of fine china. How could she explain Mary and Jane to Edward? Even worse, to Edward's family. She grew up watching Willow's sister June living a lie, thinking no one knew the real her. But it was etched in her face like a painting. Jo Ann had felt her pain. She would never go thru such sorrow. Never!!

It was during dinnertime around the camp fire, when one of Jonathan's fellow comrades. (Big Ed Hawkins), began telling jokes aimed to lighten up the mood after the fighting. He was from the Harrisburg, PA. Area and had grown up on a farm not fifteen miles away from Edwards family. He and Edward had known each other as children, and went to the same school. They each learned to read and write around the same time.

Edward was a good sport. He even joined in when Big Ed started teasing him.

“You’re right Ed. I was a stupid little red topped Irish boy,” admitted Edward.

“Yeah, your front teeth were so crooked, I remember we called you beaver mouth”, joked Ed. “How about that time I stole your coat and you had to walk home with no coat & hat. It had to be negative ten degrees outside”, teased Ed. “You were shaking like a leaf on a tree.” Ed laughed so hard he almost got cramps.

“I think I was sick for a week or two”, remembered Edward.

“Some of that stuff was really cruel Big Ed.”

“I know, little Ed. I know,” said Big Ed.

“Man I couldn’t help myself,” he confessed.

They fell off one by one until the cracking embers from the fire burned down to charred burned out wood. Everyone had had a jolly good time.

When it was bugle call the next morning, and time to set out marching, everyone felt better. Everyone except Big Ed. When he didn’t answer bugle call, the Sgt. sent someone to roust Ed and let him know he had breakfast clean – up duty for being late. When the Pvt. that went to shake Ed awake backed out of Ed's tent, eyes wide as skillets, he could not even speak. Inside lay Ed, penis chopped off, and stuffed in his mouth, eyes wide open in terror, as if he saw the devil himself, and blood everywhere. So much blood you could not tell where the death blows were located. What was frightening was that no one heard anything last night out of the ordinary. No man could kill like that without a sound. It just was not humanly possible.

After clean – up and a very short interrogation, the 78th volunteers from P.A. were back on the road to Atlanta. Much of the talk that day, were whispers about what happened to Ed? Who was responsible? Which one among us could possibly kill like that? Was Edward avenging old wrongs?

CHAPTER TWENTY SIX

Jonathan and Buster marched their platoon toward Allatoona Mountains. They rested, Sherman planned. They fought 2 small skirmishes and a battle on pine mountain June 14, 1864, where one of the worst generals in the confederate army, Leonidas Polk was killed. Of course this was just hearsay concerning his military acumen, for the Episcopal bishop turned warrior was very popular with his men. His death led to wide spread mourning in the South. This battle let the people of Atlanta know what they were in for. It also let Jonathan, Edward and the rest of the men know that this was unlike any of the others they had followed. Edward and the other combined troops tried again, and again to uproot the confederate troops led by Joe Johnson. They fought like cats & dogs. Around 4,000 union soldiers lost their lives on that mountain. For the first time the people of Atlanta, some twenty miles away, could feel the sounds of war! Sherman could see his target. Jonathan could feed his thirst for vengeance, not just on enemy soldiers, but civilians like his two brothers and his step dad. From Kennesaw Mountain, he found the strength to go on. He found the will to take another step toward revenge. By mid July, Jonathans 78th was ravaging the city of Atlanta.

For Jonathan a life changing situation occurred. “Damn Douglass”, the old soldier cried. “You blew that old man’s head off his shoulders for nothing. The man didn’t even have a weapon. I ain’t never seen you do that before.” He continued. “You must have got up on the wrong side of the grass this morning. You saw green instead of brown and went to killing everything walking. I ain’t never seen you execute a man before. What the hell is your problem?” He asked.

“Mind your business soldier,” Jonathan replied. “If I need a sermon, I’ll find the preacher?”

“What in the world is wrong with you?” quizzed Edward.

“I can’t eat. I can’t sleep, something is gnawing at my insides like acid eating on it,” complained Jonathan. “Man, it seems like nothing is going right for me. I wake up in the morning, I’m tired. I feel like I ran 100 miles at night. I get headaches every day. I'm depressed even when I'm around you, and you light up my life." He said. "Every time I close my eyes I see that man's face. He just asks me "Why did you kill me?" Hell, he was only hungry," Jonathan added, "You shot me because I asked for food?" He keeps saying, "I forgive you," with a smile on his face. "I got me a Bible, and I been reading it," Jonathan said. "Been on my knees, asking for forgiveness."

In the weeks that followed, finally Edward said "Jo you can't just not fight. You gonna get us killed." The thought of Edward lying dead because of her bought her around. He would continue to fight and kill but, he had found his revenge. It had left a sour, bitter taste in his mouth. It had left a hole in his soul. It was over!! It was done No more killing for revenge.

CHAPTER TWENTY SEVEN

Further fueling his change of attitude and to seek redemption were the horrors and atrocities that Sherman and his troops were hearing about, that came from the confederate prison camp at Andersonville. Just two hours south of Atlanta, word had traveled up to the union troops that human evil that could not even be imagined was occurring every day at Andersonville. There was talk of people eating rats and roaches to survive. People were dying of malnutrition at record rates. Infection and disease were so common that no attempt at all was made to clean the sewer and trenches where human waste overflowed the campgrounds. Smallpox, dysentery, diarrhea, and every other type of sickness common to the time raged out of control at Andersonville. At times they did not bury the bodies. They just let them swell, burst and out came a smelly liquid that spilled across the camp grounds. All together over 33,000 union prisoners occupied the small prison from its opening, until the end of the war. Sherman could not take the time, and did not have orders to take the prison or liberate the inmates, so Jonathan could do nothing to aid and assist those still confined. But the stories moved him deeply. The suffering of his fellow comrades in arms hurt him, and a lot of the other union troops. They would not forget.

As Atlanta burned, families large, and small, old people mostly, loaded their wagons and left town. The cruelty inflicted upon the city was legendary. Never had Jonathan seen or imagined anything this barbaric. Edward was stunned. He had never thought humans capable of inflicting this type of punishment and brutality on each other. He thought only "colored people" were capable of such things. As time passed, things got uglier. All you could see for miles around were flames and black soot.

By November, Sherman had burned, looted, stole, killed, or run out of town every living being that moved in Atlanta; or so it seemed. He turned his attention to his famous march for the sea. With 60,000 soldiers he was ready to crush anything in the path to Richmond, Va.

Jonathan and the rest of the 78th were ready to move. They wanted this rampage to go down in history as the one that ended this bloody war. Jonathan and Edward were anxious for different reasons. Edward had started writing letters back home to his family.

"I'm in love with this wonderful woman," he told them. "There is lightness in my heart and spirit," he said. "She is a gift from God this is a truly special union," he said. It never occurred to Edward his parents would be perplexed and confused. They wondered for hours at the time.

"How could this happen?" They asked each other. "In the middle of a bloody war. How could you have time to fall in love? How could you meet someone and court them? Have you lost your mind?" They wondered. "We should ride to Washington D.C. and ask the war department to relieve him. After all we have sacrificed two sons already," they said.

For Jonathan it dawned on him, he had a lot to worry about. The question of race was just too much and too big to overcome in one family meeting.

"Why the hell are you passing as a white man?'" Jo Ann knew would be the first question asked of him, he thought. I could not possibly answer that question and make it sound sensible. That is a time bomb ready to explode! That is a murder charge waiting to happen, all the killing Jo Ann has done during this war.

"Damnit, Edwards family would disown our kids if we had any," Jo Ann said out loud. "Nowhere to go, and nothing to live off of," she muttered. She felt like a boiler about to burst open. Her head felt like a lumber jack was driving a spike to split a log. Jo Ann...Jonathan...Jonathan...Jo Ann.

At first It was easy to separate the two, Jo Ann and Jonathan. The transformation was slow, then it took on a life of its own. Blending revenge, hatred, fear and an intense desire for justice, Jonathan kept growing inside of Jo Ann' body, until at one point in his creation, he had taken over. You could not find any indication that a loving, caring, compassionate female resided anywhere in Jo Ann's body.

CHAPTER TWENTY EIGHT

Jo Ann' natural humanitarian nature almost disappeared completely. Buster, who needed the feminine loving, compassionate, caring Jo Ann, brought her back from the brink of insanity. Buster was the only thing that let her hang on by a thread. It was why she loved him so dearly, and appreciated the canine so much. Without the dog, Jo Ann would have been lost to decent humanity. She probably couldn't tell you that, but it was a self-evident truth. Buster was her savior.

The epiphany that saved her sanity for sure was the murder of the defenseless man in Atlanta. It was then she realized she hated Jonathan, and all he had become. It was like being outside her own body and looking at a monster. She also discovered something that chilled her to the bone, made her recoil in horror, and scared her to her very soul. She vomited. She shook her head back and forth trying to clear it. She tried to bring her eyes and her mind into focus.

"I AM A MURDERER," she had to admit to herself.

"Jonathan, come on," Edward called. Buster was barking so he could go play.

"I'm coming out. Just hold your horses," cried Jonathan.

"Can't take time to do anything around here without you having a prissy fit." After wiping the stench from the vomit, opening the tent door and smelling the fresh air, Jonathan focused his attention on Buster.

He was jumping up and down ready to go. Jonathan untied Buster's rope and Buster shot out of the campground. Laughing and running behind him Jonathan yelled. "Don't run off somewhere I can't find you, you little fur ball. Don't think I don't know about that little slut you been running around with at night. I been tieing you up to keep you from getting shot, cause you keep screwing the farmers dog," she said.

They scampered after each other playing and rollicking, bouncing off each other until suddenly Jonathan ran right into the barrel of a colt .44 revolver. Behind the barrel of this gigantic gun was a confederate soldier, wounded and bleeding lightly. It looked like light bleeding because he had bled heavily, and did not have much blood left. He was shaking and scared. He looked right at deaths door step. He was determined to have company when he went thru that door. The old Jonathan would have disarmed this tired, ragged, wounded soldier and put him out of his misery by snapping his neck. Instead Jonathan held up his hands, asked the confederate please not to shoot and told him he was surrendering to him. After considering Jonathan's offer for all of one minute, the wounded confederate burst out laughing, coughed up some blood, and pointed to his gut.

"How in the hell am I going to take you prisoner blue coat? Are you deaf, or are you blind," he cried in a weak southern drawl. "I don't even know where my unit is. I was hoping you had a canteen filled with some damn water, and a biscuit or two. I ain't ate since last night." Jonathan for the first time in mouths felt real compassion overcome him. A lump settled in his throat, and he was neither mad at the wounded white boy with the gray uniform on, nor did he have any desire to do anything to him but help if he could.

He sent Buster scampering back to camp to get Edward and bring help. He took off the rebel's jacket, rolled it up and laid his head on it. He walked down to the creek, filled his cap with cool creek water and walked back to the dying soldier. He cradled his head. Jonathan let him slowly sip on the water, after moving him to a shady spot, and exchanged biographies while they waited for help to come.

Amazingly, perhaps because he knew the man would die, perhaps because he was at the breaking point and had to confess, he felt this was a sign of some kind from God. He told the young soldier the truth. First he said he was not a man, but a woman. At that the dying man just smiled and said, "Yeah, I have met angels before when I thought I was dying." Jonathan did something bizarre. He took the man hand, slid it under his union blue jacket, unloosened the tie down, and let the man feel a breast. At this the soldier almost jumped out of his skin.

"Lordly I done died and gone to heaven. It didn't even hurt, and I don't even have my wings yet."

At this Jonathan replied, “Well we must all be going to the same heaven, because I’m black. As African as any slave your family ever owed.” The boy searched his face for the lie and could find none. This was beyond his reasoning. His mind would not wrap around this. First, a woman, now a black woman. Fighting a war as a soldier. Nooo!!!

At this point, Jonathan heard Buster bark coming up the hill. Behind him were Edward and a small squad of men. They thought an ambush had happened. They had no medical supplies, because they did not think of a medical emergency when he bolted up the hill to where Jo Ann was comforting the soldier. By the time he got there the young gun, had passed on. All Jonathan would say on the way back, over and over was. “What have we done? We are killing off our own people. God help us. What have we done?” It is a question that would be asked many times over by many grieving families, both northern and southern.

‘What in the hell have we done as a country?”

CHAPTER TWENTY NINE

By December 20, Sherman and his troops, of which Jonathan's 78th PA. Volunteers were a part of, had torn a path thru Georgia that would stretch 600 miles long and twenty five to fifty miles wide. They traveled 600 miles in 40 days, and did over 100 million dollars in property damage. December 20, 1864, also saw the city of Savannah, Georgia abandoned. This had been a walk in the park. Over 150,000 guns had been confiscated. Over 25,000 bales of cotton had been seized. Now it was time for Jonathan to turn into Jo Ann and work her plan.

The other plan was Jo Ann's strategy to execute and attack. She couldn't try her plan out, or share it with anyone for fear it would lead to betrayal. So here she is hiking through the woods near the platoon's campsite with her most beloved allie.

"Well Buster, it's like this," she began. "Edward and I love each other and I trust him more than anyone in this world. He makes me feel protected. He listens to my plans for the future. He wants to be part of them. He wants a house full of kids, just like me. He is kind, and he pays attention when I talk. He is never too busy to listen," she said.

"But damn Buster, what you think gonna happen when I say I'm colored? I can't change that, and even if I could I wouldn't" she said. "I love my people, we struggling right now, but in a little while I'ma show these white folks I'm just as smart, and just as good looking as any of them."

Jo Ann was forgetting that she too was a white woman, partly, and there was good in them too. Buster turned around, stopped dead still and looked at her. He thought to himself, "child are you crazy, them white folks are gonna hang you and shoot me." Okay I'm with you sink or swim. "Woof, woof, woof", barked Buster. So began the seduction of Edward Kelly.

CHAPTER THIRTY

Sherman's objective was to establish a base at Goldsboro, N.C. and join up with Grants army, then lift the siege and end the war by destroying Lee's army. Back in Jonathan mode his platoon was licking their chops. This is what they had been waiting for.

"I can't wait to get my hands on them traitors," yelled Junie Broomstead. He was one of the young guns, at 19 years old. Jonathan was anxious too, but he knew to preach caution and he knew to practice discipline.

"Just follow my lead men", he cautioned. "No dead heroes," he said. "We are going to tear those Rebs a new asshole. Everyone stay in formation. Don't break ranks, no chasing after Rebs on your own. We gonna create havoc and raise hell."

They knew that the confederate army was suffering desertions at an alarming rate. A lot of soldiers were just taking their rifles and going home.

The confederate morale was very low. Most felt the war effort was lost. They tried hard to recruit, but there were very few men left. The soldiers kept getting younger and younger.

Jonathan's platoon landed on South Carolina like flies on molasses. The rivers and swaps gave them more trouble than the Confederate Army. On February 17th, the mayor of Columbia rode out to surrender the city to General Sherman. This was the capital of the state. The platoon entered the city almost immediately and found a cache of liquor that was hidden. After consuming as much as they could, they proceeded to vandalize, set fire to, steal and pilfer everything not nailed down! The city of Columbia was ripped apart. The confederates did not put up much resistance. They wanted Jonathan and his men out of the state as fast as possible.

In Charleston, the leader of the procession that entered the city was a black union soldier on a mule. He was carrying a banner that read "Liberty." The black soldiers of the famous 54th Massachusetts followed behind him singing "John Browns body." Black citizens of the city stomped, waved and cheered until they were exhausted and could not yell anymore. Jonathan felt great and he was proud. For himself as a black soldier and for having a hand in freeing black people everywhere they went. They were walking advertisements for freedom. The contradiction for him was no one knew he was black!!

One significant incident came out of the pillaging of South Carolina. It became the place where Jonathan/ Jo Ann lost his only living brother. This made Jonathan sad and heartbroken whenever someone mentioned the state. Around 3 days before the arrival of the majority of the platoon, Sherman sent a scouting party ahead to gather intelligence and come back with reports on troop strength and movement by the enemy. Arriving late in the evening, and taking the plantation belonging to the Howell family by surprise, the scouting party found liquor in the cellars and silver buried in the basement of the main house. Thinking there could easily be a fortune buried here, the union advanced troops and rounded up the Howell family, 12 members in all, and 14 or so slaves that still remained in the service of the family. The troops were drunk and feeling superior because they were armed.

The slaves mistook their intentions. (They thought they were going to be escorted to freedom).

They started questioning the slaves about what they thought were hidden treasure. One of the slaves was Willie. Jo Ann brother. He had been sold to the owner of the King Mansion, Jesse Howell II, and had been the main buck for breeding. He was married, raising a family and been blessed with 3 health precocious child. May and June: two daughters a year apart. The oldest was 3 years old, and Donald the only boy 1 year old, and just starting to bounce around and explore his surroundings. Willie was a natural leader, and the other slaves looked to him as their spokesman. So it was him by coincidence, or just plain bad luck that was being interrogated.

Sgt. Dirk Owens, mean tempered, sloppy build, stocky, and thick shouldered, the Irishman struck fear in a lot of men with his brutish ways. But Willie was not intimidated by him. Besides, he really thought the purpose for the Yankees lining them up and asking questions was some kind of test before they took them in and liberated them. He soon realized otherwise and he and Sgt. Owens became engaged in a mental tug of war that led to a physical confrontation.

When Willie started to get the best of the overweight, out of breathe Sgt., two soldiers cracked him with their rifle butts and black jacks and tied Willie up, trussed up like a chicken. With his wife Bertha and his 3 little ones watching, he forgot himself for a moment, and tried to display his dignity and bravery in front of his family. It would prove to be a fatal mistake, tragedy typical of the day and times. Ignorance won over, and they beat Willie down. They dragged him to the back of the woods. They put him on a horse with a rope around his neck; and in the name of the U.S Army and military justice, hung poor Willie within view of his stunned, startled, and scared out of her mind wife. They left the body for the Howells to bury, and moved on to the next plantation, leaving 4 soldiers behind.

CHAPTER
THIRTY ONE

The 78th roared into Kings Mansion tired from the trip and hungry as a Grizzly bear.

"Sure is quiet around here," Corporal Rawlins said.

"Look here Sgt. Douglass, furniture threw every which away in them shacks over yonder", Private Reynolds stretched his neck and spoke.

"You hear that Large? Sounds like somebody screaming. That's kids, I hear! What the hell is going on?" The squad drew their rifles and scrambled over to the cabin with the broken down fence. Brown grass burned by the sun, paper across the windows, and dirt for the floor was there. Out back, four Army horses were tied down waiting.

"Kick it down Pvt., right now," ordered Jonathan. With a powerful thrust, the door flew straight back from the hinges. On the hay filled mattress laid across the floor, a slave girl, mouth bloody from a backhanded slap, was crying. Two soldiers held her arms and legs down. Six Negro men and 3 small children were waiting and crying.

"Please stop," begged the woman.

"Oh God, please don't hit me again. My chilluns can't see they momma like this."

"Don't hurt my momma, mister," the smallest one begged.

Jonathan saw red. Before you could say stop he had taken his Bowie knife and cut half of one attacker's ear off. Blood splattered all over the smoke burned walls. He slashed grisle and cut arteries. With his gun barrel he cleaved to the white meat, the back of one man head.

"No, not that please, my God man, have a heart, screamed the soldier, just before the pot of boiling water from the fire place burned, blistered and steamed his white skin; curling it up and stinking like crazy.

"No he didn't? Asked one man, awed.

"Shit, his face is burned off," marveled another.

"Fuck," said the horrified Captain, he had just entered the room.

"Clean up this trash. Get these bastards out of here," Said Captain Willie.

"Garbage needs throwing away," said Jonathan, "before it starts stinking"

Jonathan was half out of his mind and still angry. He had gone too far. How safe are his secrets now? His head was pounding and he was barely aware of what state he was in. He had lost it. He could tell by the looks on the other men's faces. This one had been a bad one. Later when he calmed down, Edward told him he had never heard of such brutal behavior. He asked Jonathan point blank if he had ever acted like this before. Jo Ann/ Jonathan fell apart. He/ She was so afraid of losing Edward, he fell on his knees and begged. The pleading was so loud and the wailing so deep, Edward was afraid someone might hear, so he relented and took back the chastising.

The next morning, Jonathan went back to the cabin to make sure the slave girl was okay, and got the shock of his life. The woman that answered the cabin door was wearing a necklace that Jo Ann had made for Willie when she was in 2nd grade. She had made Willie, "cross his heart and hope to die," That he would never take it off, and true to his word, he didn't. She looked at the necklace, a chill coursed thru her body, and she grabbed the slave girl and questioned her. She found out it had come off her husband's body after she buried the body yesterday. She offered to show him where. As they walked to the site, Jonathan began to tell the whole story. It was the slave girl bertha's time to be incredulous.

"For the fifth time Bertha," pleaded Jonathan, "listen to what I'm telling you. Willie was my brother. Your husband and me were brother and sister, didn't he tell you his mother's name was April? Didn't he tell you about Homer, Mary and Jane? How would I know that?" He questioned. "I'm, I'm, he could not bring himself to tell her. Bertha, clearly scared to death, kept saying, "Willie say his brother name Homer. You ain't Homer. You ain't even a nigga. Why is you scaring me like this? Don't hurt me. I'll lay down for you. Just don't kill me and my young guns." she muttered.

Jonathan was clearly frustrated. He was frightened that Bertha would expose him, and finally gave up. "Listen Bertha", he promised. "I swears on my brothers body, I'm gonna take you and the kids away from this. I'm going to take you away, I swear. I'ma finish this war, and these children gonna be proud colored folks," Jonathan said. "Just don't forget. Don't forget I'm coming for you", Jonathan said. "I'll be singing Moses come to carry me home, and you'll know it's me," "Jonathan said.

"Why? Why you gonna do that for me white boy? Asked Bertha. I'm just a poor nigga woman. Your men done killed my man, put their thing in me, scared my kids, scarred my back and legs, took my pride, and made me take them in my mouth. I can't hurt no deeper. Why you gonna help Bertha?" She asked. "I'm glad you saved us, but I still don't know why."

"Just know I'm coming back", Jonathan promised. "I got to go now, but I'll see you again. Keep telling yourself, it won't be long now."He smiled, and a tear rolled down his cheek. He knew he would be back. He just knew, he just didn't know when. One more secret.

CHAPTER THIRTY TWO

Sherman pushed north. He took Wilmington, N.C., and closed the south's last major port. Jeff Davis was worried. He appointed Joseph Johnson to command the confederate army forces. That was supposed to stop or at least try to slow down Sherman jugganaut.

By March, 1865, it was obvious to everyone the Confederate Army couldn't protect your dog in the backyard! They were weak and demoralized. No money, no food, the only strategy left was to try to sue for peace. During this walk in the park which Union troops would not even call victories; there was plenty of time for Edward to think about what he would do after this war was over. He had already written about 10 letters home. He told everyone of his new found love. He told of his romantic relationship, and his plan to marry and start a family. He was trying to decide if this would really be a good decision. The fact that was undeniable, was this; Jo Ann had "issues," Edward wasn't ready to go as far as to say the girl was nutty as a fruit cake. But he was ready to concede that if you marry her, you are going to spend a lot of sleepless nights wondering if your kids rising sun went all the way to the top. A lot of sleepless nights wondering if all the marbles were in the bag?

Hell, you might wake up after an argument one night, and half your head be on the other side of the room. This lovely lady had a temper like a raging bull. How could someone so beautiful be so loony? For Edward had made himself look past the mud cake Make – up, the man looking short hair cut, the strap downed breasts, and the clothes that were two sizes too big. He had made himself talk to Jo Ann about wants, needs, and wishing for the future. They were a lot alike. They made a good pairing, in Edward mind. He really felt the only person in the world he would sacrifice himself for was Jo Ann. But her volatile nature frightened him. She might explode and he would have to kill the Jonathan in her. That was the way he made himself think of it. "The Jonathan in her". He did have sense enough too. That scared him. What to do? What to do? It kept him up at night.

For her part, Jo Ann thought a lot about the future too, during the times that the fighting was slack, and the battles were almost nonexistent. There were times when you could forgot you were at war. Each time they made camp, the black population that just up and left the plantations and followed, got bigger and bigger. Some of the black men tried to enlist right on the sport. A few that had special skills like blacksmiths or cooks were even allowed to enlist.

"What can you do woman," asked the soldier.

"Sir I can clean your clothes," the negro woman answered. "Look here sir; I got other things. "I just need to get away to freedom. Please sir, take Jenny Mae with you", she pleaded. He said. "Maybe a few of my friends will need a try out too. You start tonight girl," he said with a smirk on his arrogant face. "Thank you, sir, she agreed.

Many such deals were made like this. Just black girls trying to get to freedoms door. Jo Ann was not sure if Edward was confused or not. He had never spent time alone with her. Never made love under the stars with the breeze bellowing softly.

"You're a damn killing machine J," he had said. "Cold blooded as any man living." That bothered Jo Ann. She couldn't be responsible for who would end up laying in the dirt with his throat slit from ear to ear. Although she would never hurt Edward, she wasn't sure if Edward felt secure, protected and comfortable around her. In fact, if truth be told, she wasn't sure if she trusted herself when the black rage came. The color issue had to be faced too. How in the hell could that happen.

"Excuse me honey, but I'm African. "Pardon me love, but this baby you put in my stomach may come out a little dark. My dear I've been meaning to tell you, but that slave girl I saved from being raped was my brothers' wife. Listen, I know I am a little on the light side, but I'm really Octaroon. You know I am black and white, but I'm really African. The babies will be fine. Just don't let your daddy shoot them." Jo Ann spoke of all of these, both nervous and scared.

If I can get Edward to agree to give me and my family a trial period, say 60 days or so, I know he will like Mary & Jane. I can't let him feel like I tricked him', she thought. We can't hide from the rest of the platoon after the war is over, either. General Sherman would personally hang me if he finds out I'm a woman. He might shoot me when he finds out I am a niggra woman. Then hang me again for good measure. I have got to start taking better care of myself. I have put on a few pounds since we are eating regular.

"My goodness, Jo Ann's eyes grew wide as saucers. My tits are getting too big to hide. These straps won't do any good in a minute," she said. "The straps are so tight one tit jumped out the other day, scared me silly. Buster."

"Woof, woof, "Buster answered. Translation: This war better be over quick or both of us will be hung.

"Edward thinks I'm losing my mind" she said. "He just might be right. At least I threw that kill book away. Last count was 68. I know, I know Buster. It was sick to keep it in the first place. My God I must have over 150 by now. That still won't bring April, Homer, Jasper or Richard back. At least father Abe did away with bondage. At least my people ain't got to suffer like that. Nothing will ever be as bad as feeling that whip, or looking at them scars on a man's back, or watching your chile sold down south. What in the world was you thinking about Lord," Jo Ann pondered. "Now slavery finished maybe Edward and me can go west to Texas, or up in the mountains out west", she thought out loud. "Wherever he goes, I'll go. I love him so much. Does he feel what I feel? What you think Buster?" She asked. "Woof, woof, woof", answered Buster. Translation: of course he loves you. A man would have to be a fool to be with your crazy butt if he didn't. You are an A – 1 lunatic!

A bead of sweat rolled down Jo Ann's forehead. Normal, except for it was 10* outside. It was colder than a whore's heart. Perhaps a symbol of things to come, it was never this cold in North Carolina.

CHAPTER THIRTY THREE

The cold front broke quickly. Spring with all its beauty, threw itself on the landscape with a burst of warm weather and beautiful colors. Jo Ann's plan was in full bloom by the time General Grant arrived on April 9, 1865, at the Appomattox Court House.

By coincidence or fate, which ever you choose to believe, Jonathan's squad and Edward's squad was picked to ride escort duty for a wagon train full of bounty captured during the plundering by Sherman's troops. The Atlanta campaign allowed the Union army to confiscate almost 500,000 dollars worth of gold, silver, art, antiques, and relics from southern households. These were being sent back to Washington as bounty of war. They were protected by the two most ruthless squads, Jonathan's and Edward's. Men that would kill at the drop of a hat.

They started out on March 12, from the North Carolina border and by the time the wagon train would reach the safety of Washington City on April

11, 1865, the war for all practical purposes would be over.

During the long trip, Jonathan / Jo Ann tried to engage Edward every chance she / he got. They took long walks 'to stretch their legs'. One evening they walked up a ridge, disappeared around a corner of rocks and trees, and taking a very dangerous chance, made love for the very first time! Jo Ann losing her virginity, and surprisingly Edward losing his too. He might put a baby in his love ones stomach. Jo Ann hoped so. By the time they arrived, tired hungry and appalled by the foul smelling City of Washington on April 11, two things were foremost on their minds.

"Hot damn, Lee gave up," the man hollered. "The war is over, the war is over. Thank God almighty!" He rejoiced.

Jonathan & Edward needed two things, a hot bath and some sleep in a real bed with a roof over top of it.

"A few weeks and we will be out of this man's army Jo," said Edward. He immediately started thinking about home. All Jo Ann was thinking about as she looked around was this miserable, muddy, stinking city, "Oh noo." They turned over their contraband and rode down PA. Ave. Thru the part of the city known as the Navy Yard. Nearby was their post, Ft. McNair. The post was there mainly to protect Fed. installations from attack.

“Look at all those run down shacks”, Edward was startled. They are called Shanty. They looked like a strong wind would blow them down.

“Wow they are everywhere,” Jo Ann was shocked. “Look, chickens, pigs and rats. We fought four years to save this,” she asked. Garbage filled the sides of the mud racked streets. Poultry, and in some cases, pigs strolled down the street. The nation’s capital was not much to look at, even worse to smell and one wondered if the heavy cost in bodies & blood had been worth the sacrifice on either side. One thing for sure though, four years of fighting accomplished what politics could not. The United States of America was again one nation. Whether or not it was under God was open to debate.

After retiring to their quarters, Jonathan and Edward agreed to meet and go for a stroll later on that evening. They gave themselves about six hours to sleep and rejuvenate their bodies from the long ride. They would walk somewhere off of the post and enjoy a good civilian meal, cooked at one of the eateries they had passed on the ride in. Army food was the last thing either of them wanted.

Edward stripped off his clothes, and sprinted to the first hot cauldron of hot steaming bath water he could jump in. The hot bath cost 5 cents, even in the army bath – house. In this day and age, hot water was still a luxury, and bathing was still not a regular pursuit of men. He also paid the extra penny to have his uniform washed, and hung out to dry.

For Jo Ann this was much more difficult. She had to mount her horse, and ride off of the post, to find a bath house. "I need a room with a tub, please sir," Jo Ann inquired. The clerk at the desk turned his nose up at the smell coming off Jo Ann's uniform and almost turned her down. Instead he charged two dollars extra. He put that right in his pocket. This was just a fair warning of what was to come.

"Damn, this is a nightmare," Jo Ann complained. "I can't do anything in this town in private. These are the nosiest people in America. You look up and someone is staring you in the face. After two weeks, two more citizens of the nations' capital suddenly disappeared. Had they seen too much of

Jo Ann or was it just coincidence in play? Was another crisis about to unfold?

As April 11th came to a close, Jo Ann and Edward found themselves eating "Home Made" beef stew, with sourdough bread, sipping hot tea, and recalling all they had been thru. Buster waited patiently outside the eatery, sucking and gnawing on A steak bone.

CHAPTER THIRTY FOUR

Celebrations, 500 gun salutes, parties, Impromptu dances in the streets; Washington was a buzz about the news of Lees surrender. People both white and black were overjoyed and relieved. As "Dixie" played, Lincoln claimed it jokingly as a, "Lawful prize of war.

Jo Ann and Edward took the time off for celebrating, by riding over to the rooming house that Jo Ann had rented as Jonathan Douglass. Edward climbed up the back steps. He entered through the back hallway, and they spent the entire afternoon of the 12th making love in a soft feather bed. Jo Ann gave Edward lessons in the art of slow, patient foreplay, and lovemaking, and was hopeful after 3 hours that a baby had been firmly implanted in her womb. She need not have worried, because had she bothered to pay attention, she would have noticed she skipped her period after that first hurried, clumsy attempt at love making. By the time of the rooming house adventure, she was nice and pleasantly pregnant.

By x – mas day her dilemma would be how can a soldier that has just been announced as a medal of valor winner, hero of Pickets Mill, and participant in the Atlanta campaign be expecting a baby? Worried, because she had not been feeling too well, and after yesterday just realizing that she has not had a period, she confesses to Edward that she is scared she is pregnant. Edward is overjoyed. He jumps up and down, swings Jo Ann round and round, and then realizes they are in a mostly public place.

"Excuse me sir", asked Edward. He had stopped two soldiers that were walking down the street.

"I have a bad case of the ladies disease. You know I picked it up from Hattie whorehouse in town. I need to see a doctor. Can you point me in the right direction? I need one that will be discreet," he said.

"That would be Thomas E. Stonestreet," the soldier replied. "Good man won't say a word. Been to him myself, lad. Here is his name and address. It was rather out of the way in Bethesda, Md., but that was even better for Jo Ann and Edward.

On the day they traveled, Jo Ann switched from army dress to burlap dress and a brown wig. At doctor Stonestreets, they found two women talking about Mr. Henry Brown.

"You know the gentleman that mailed himself to freedom in a wood crate," she said.

"Oh him," the other said."

"Yeah from the south to New England with water and biscuits, He is now making speeches about the evils of slavery," she explained."

"Hello doc," Jo Ann held her hand out in greeting.

"I need to see you about an urgent matter. I have not had my monthly in a couple of months and I need to know if I'm with child." Jo Ann explained. "I can pay", she said. "This is not welfare."

After an hour the doctor saw Jo Ann and the exam was completed. They were both deliriously happy. It was 90% certain she was with child. It would come around X – Mas.

They were on cloud nine. Halfway back Jo Ann asked Edward to please stop and get off of his horse for a moment. Edward, thinking something was wrong bolted off his steed, and grabbed Jo Ann off of her horse. Buster, who had been puzzled by what to him were two separate Jonathans', started to bark in confusion.

After grabbing Edward by the hands, looking him right in the eyes, she tenderly said, "I love you no matter what you say or do." Jo Ann laid the simple statement at Edward's feet.

"I am colored. Black as a berry, and the child of a slave woman." You could hear a rat piss on cotton. Silence, except for the hammering in Edward head and the thumping in Jo Ann's heart, there was absolute silence. For about a minute no one spoke a word. No eye flinched. No body part moved a muscle. Finally after what seemed like two days, Edward said softly, "I knew." Jo Ann strained to hear, she asked, "What, what did you say?" Edward grabbed her. He pulled her to him and said in a whisper, "I knew. I guessed, but I don't care. All that matters is I love you more than life. We will deal with the rest when it comes." The flood gates broke. Tears flowed freely from both woman and man. Smiles told them they were tears of joy.

Buster was perplexed. "What was this lump? in his throat? Are dogs supposed to get these? Why am I so happy? I have no idea what just happened."

So he did his usual. "Woof, woof" and wagged his tail uncontrollably. Something good had just happened. He just missed it, he thought.

The ride back home was mostly talk about the tickets the doctor had given the happy couple as a gift for learning they were to be parents. There was a play at Ford's theater in Washington, titled, "Our American cousin. It was for Friday, April 14, and that was Good Friday. A special treat was in Store. President Lincoln would be attending. Jo Ann and Edward fussed briefly because Jo Ann did not want to go dressed in his/her Army uniform. Edward said they could not do otherwise. Suppose someone saw them? The seats were good ones, almost up to the first row. The doctor had good connections. Both of them would have to make sure their uniforms were pressed and boots were shined.

CHAPTER THIRTY FIVE

They would find someone to watch Buster and go have a nice time at the play. It was supposed to be funny. Both of them needed some time together to get used to this new revelation in their lives. In these days an times, inter – racial couples were almost never seen in the United States, unless it was a white man and an Indian woman. That occurred mostly in the river states, or in the mountains out west. White men, even in northern cities were almost never seen in public with women of color. The rate of men and women that were white & black, and married was probably too small to even consider counting. Now Jo Ann and Edward had to consider seeing racism raise its ugly head, and finding out how it would feel to be an outcast among your own people. This could get messy, ugly, and dangerous. On top of all that, there would be a child to consider. An innocent brought into the world who thru no fault of its own, would be treated very differently by everyone.

As Friday approached, Jonathan & Edward looked around for suitable garb and a new pair of boots. They were caught up in the celebration of the city but also wondering what the future would bring for each of them. Jonathan especially was having a hard time. His feminine traits were beginning to show more and more and the work it took to keep them hid was beginning to be almost too much. He was always on guard and exhausted.

Finally, Friday was here and the word had been passed thru the squad that Jonathan and Edward had tickets to tonight's play. Both had new army outfits and boots. Both had brushed their horses and wiped down their saddles. Both were excited about getting their first look ever at president Lincoln. Both had forgotten that neither had asked permission to be excused from tonight's base curfew! At the last moment it occurred to them they needed the captain's permission to miss lights out. Candlelight's and Kerosene that is. Hurriedly and nervously they both bolted to the entrance of the captains' office praying that he had not left town for a Good Friday holiday.

Captain William Ruth was a West Point

Graduate, that because of a war wound in the Mexican conflict had been given desk duty in Washington, D.C. Known as a by the book officer, he did not have a big fan base among the enlisted men. One thing saved Jonathan and Edward, He loved the theater and he loved plays.

"Promise me a handbill and full accounting of tonight's play," the commander demanded.

"Done, Captain," Jo Ann promised. "I will make you think you were sitting right beside me. You will be transported to another world," said Edward. They practically ran out of his office before he changed his mind.

A SHORT WHILE LATER...

"This place is wonderful," Jo Ann whispered. "How did you find it? The food is really good. You have not been cheating on me, have you?" Asked Jo Ann. Before Edward could answer, they heard a conversation from the next table.

"Good evening Mr. Booth, beautiful evening sir. My wife would love your autograph sir. Would you do me the honor?" the patron asked. The smallish man with the dark hair and good looks was rather dashing. In the back of her mind Jo Ann had heard of the famous Booth family of actors. A father and two brothers. They were famous for their Shakespearian acting.

"Why certainly sir. How should I address it? The pleasure is mine since this may be the last time we see each other for a while. After tonight, I shall be taking my talents elsewhere." he said. A part in larger drama awaited him.

At 8:30 P.M President Lincoln departed for Fords Theater. General Grant and his wife had been invited, but the general declined. The rumor around town was that Mrs. Lincoln and Mrs. Grant did not see eye to eye. As the play was in progress, Mrs. Lincoln arrived and was cheered by both cast and the audience. Mr. Lincoln was seated in his special rocking chair and the play continued.

Jonathan and Edward were thrilled to see President Lincoln, Finally after all the years of struggle and fighting they got to see the man that was their Commander and Chief. They clapped, yelled bravo, and were happy as small kids at the chance to express their emotions.

Shortly after 10 P.M a shot rang out from the president's box. A man jumped from the box. Jonathan swore it was the actor Booth that they had seen earlier, and staggered across the stage. He shouted, “Sic Semper Tyrant’s,” (Thus always to tyrants) at the same moment, someone shouted, “The president has been shot.” “Catch him, hang him!!” Jonathan almost knocked Edward down as he sprang from his seat. Before Edward realized it, Jonathan was out of the aisle, up on the stage, and chasing the actor who was limping badly, having caught his spur in the American flag, and broken his ankle landing awkwardly. Jonathan hit the exit door flying, catching a glimpse of Booth as he hobbled down Baptist Alley toward a man holding a horse. As he hopped up on the horse and grabbed the reigns from the man, Jonathan dove at the horse and tried to grab Booth’s leg from the saddle. The man that was holding the horse panicked and misunderstood the move. He immediately jumped on Jonathan’s back and held on shouting,” Sir what the hell are you doing? This here Is Mr. Booth. Let Go! Stop! I say let go.” Booth for his part, took the knife and slashed down twice, screaming because of the pain coming from his ankle. His knife hit the mark twice, puncturing Jonathan’s jacket on the left shoulder and causing him to yell and scream out too.

As booth righted the horse and began to dart

down Baptist Alley to the street, Jonathan pulled his revolver, drew a bead on the galloping horse, and pulled the trigger! It was a rat hair too late! The man that was holding the horse bumped Jonathan's gun hand just enough to make the shot go wide left. Lincoln's assassin would get away for the moment, and he would flee into the night. Jonathan's rage would show no mercy, nor cool off until he let off the steam. The man in the alley would know no relief. For the next minute or two, a beating the likes of which has not been seen before or since took place in that alley.

Jonathan's gun was broke into a thousand pieces by the skull of that man. It is doubtful if he ever fully recovered from that beating. God only knows how he survived to tell his side of the story some 90 days later.

Jonathan and Edward could not wait for the police. In the excitement they disappeared. No one would ever know how close Jonathan came to catching Booth that night. No one ever knew how the 12 day man – hunt that followed, almost never happened. No one but two soldiers that quietly eased back to the fort, and silently crept into bed.

CHAPTER
THIRTY SIX

Jonathan and Edward were both making plans to muster out of the army in May, 1865. Jo Ann/ Jonathan wanted out as soon as possible. Two months pregnant and on some mornings feeling out of sorts, Jo Ann/Jonathan knew that soon her belly would start to swell. The morning sickness and cravings would be an everyday occurrence. In two weeks there would be a medal ceremony honoring Jonathan's squad, Jonathan would be receiving two medals of valor. Edward would get one, for their actions during the Atlanta campaign. After that both would be free to leave the Army and go back to civilian life. Edward's dilemma was drawing closer by the minute. What in the world could he possible tell his family that would make them understand why he was not coming home? No explanation short of "He died" would be enough. He looked at this from every angle he could think of. He talked it over with Jo Ann until they were blue in the face.

Nothing sounded remotely plausible. Finally he came up with a solution.

"I love the army", he said. "I will confess that I love it so much I am never leaving. I have decided to make it my career. I'm in for life," he said. "Since I'm not mustering out, they will give me a 30 day leave to go home and visit my love ones. I'll have some reunion time and get married," Edward planned. "You will meet everyone, then we will venture out West to deal with the Indian problem. It might work. It just might work," he speculated.

Jo Ann was stunned, could they get away with this? One minute a decorated soldier, the next minute, pregnant and an officers' wife having morning sickness and cravings. It would be possible for any of Jonathan/ Jo Ann's men to recognize her. It would be impossible to realize the killing machine and the enlisted man's wife were the same person," argued Jo Ann.

"Where Jonathan? Where could we possibly go and not be found out. How could Douglass fall off of the face of the earth?" Her face squinted up like tasting a sour lemon. "Add that to the fact that both of my sisters are dark as blue berries.

They would be like two Concord Grapes in a field full of white grapes. They would stand out like a sore thumb," warned Jo Ann, in the highest of voices. "This is a train wreck waiting to happen," she howled.

"Okay, so I'm desperate," replied Edward. "We have to try something," his voice showing his worry. "No one will survive this train wreck," Edward said.

"Our dignity and reputations will be shot," Jo Ann said. She was picturing in her mind Edward standing on top of Navy Yard Bridge, minutes before plunging in the Potomac River. Out of shame and desperation was born an idea so absurd it just might work. Jo Ann had lured one soul that roamed the streets at night into a dark, out of the way alley. Once there she proceeded to chop, mutilate, stab, beat, kick, and choke the man, until he was literally unrecognizable as human.

"Damn, I feel a whole lot better," Jo Ann said after the murder. "I really understand now, I am a sick puppy. Really seriously deranged," she said out loud. "It would be better if I just hung myself from a big oak tree, and let God do whatever he wished with the body."

Jonathan has got to disappear, it will have to be untraceable and no one should successfully be able to inquire about his where abouts. Jo Ann could only think of one way that could happen. “Sgt. Douglass must die. Nice, quick, immediately. No autopsy, no remains.” Jo Ann said.

Edward looked horror stricken. “Now what?” he thought. The idea Jonathan could just disappears from the face of the earth after receiving the medal was pretty hard for Edward to swallow. But, with choices and time very limited, swallow he did. He had no choice but to join the execution of the plan.

CHAPTER THIRTY SEVEN

"Soldier you are one of the most fiercest warriors I have ever met," General Grant said as he pinned the medal on Jonathan's chest.

"Thank you sir. It is an honor I will never forget," said Jonathan.

General Grant was confused. As he was pinning the medal on, he could swear that he felt a nipple on the end of a swell of a breast. "I'm getting too old for this," the general thought. Men passing for women, heroes with tit's, he scratched his head. "I'm going crazy!" he whined.

Around 9:00 P.M Corporal Kelly and Sgt. Douglass mounted their horses for the ride back to the post. As they were swinging their mounts out of the stable of the White House grounds, Sgt. Douglass horse raised up and threw him to the stable floor. What happened next according to Kelly was tragic.

"My damn horse panicked."

“My head. Ah shit, he kicked me” Douglass yelled.”

“A moment later Douglass blacked out,” according to Kelly.”

“A kerosene lamp in the stable flipped over and burst into flames,” he said. “The damn hay caught on fire and flames spread like mice running!!

“My horse ran out on the gallop,” Cpl. Kelly said. “I couldn’t get him under control. He damn near crushed my leg.”

“The stable lit up like a Christmas tree,” said Edward.

“Flames and smoke shot skyward,” he remembered. By the time some help arrived you couldn’t get within 20 yards of the barn fire. They needed to make sure the fire did not spread over the White House grounds, and on to the main dwelling. By the time they found Edward and realized Jonathan was still in the barn, the fire was out of control.

An hour later it had burned itself out. A badly decomposed body with two medals pinned on the uniform, was discovered in the rubbish and debris. The body was unrecognizable. It is presumed to be Sgt. Douglass. He was the decorated war hero from Pickets Mill. His body was caught in the stable fire, and burned beyond recognition. Edward was taken to the army hospital at Walter Reed to recuperate. It was estimated it would take about a month.

After Edward had been in the hospital about a week, his parents came down to visit him, to get him better so they would have him home again, finally. It was then that he dropped the bomb. “I love the army life dearly, I am not mustering out.” He began. “I am going to make a career out of the army,” he said. His mom & pop were shocked! They had never considered that Edward would want to stay in the service. They were so taken back; his father could not talk for more than five minutes. His mom & sisters just cried. You would have thought it was from the shock of the accident, he and his wife decided not to say anymore, and just let the shock wear off.

“He will come around. He doesn’t know what he is saying right now. Let him be and he will come around. Smile, laugh, and pretend everything is fine. Edward will come to his senses.” Mr. Kelly counseled his wife. They just knew in time, everything would be okay, and Edward would be too.

CHAPTER THIRTY EIGHT

Phase II was more difficult. About a week and a half after the accident, on a bright May morning, a young lady in a plain blue coat, bright blue head scarf, yellow dress and plain shoes appeared at the front desk of the hospital. She signed her name Jo Ann Thomas of Washington, D.C. She asked to visit Corporal Edward Kelly. The desk clerk looked at the woman, about 5'5" tall, 155 lbs. She had pretty doe like eyes, and full lips. he wondered aloud how lucky Corporal Kelly was to be receiving such a pretty visitor. Under her arm was a newspaper. Wrapped around her wrist was the handle of a picnic basket. Upon Inspection of the basket, the clerk observed 4 pieces of cold fried chicken, some biscuits, two apples and a banana. Quite a feast for an injured patient, Corporal Kelly was indeed a lucky man. For five days in row this cute, pretty young lady appeared each morning, and stayed until evening. She read the paper to Corporal Kelly. She walked on the grounds with him; she sat thru supper each day, and fed him day and evening. The nurse at the desk spread word that a love affair was afoot on the ward, and that Corporal Kelly was a lucky lad.

Out of the hospital, Corporal Kelly settled in for assignment not to fight Indians, but as administrative asst. to the Post commander at Ft. McNair in Washington, D.C. This was to be Sgt. Kelly's promotion and permanent posting. A plum posting for most, a miserable assignment for Edward, He hated the diseased, rat infested, foul smelling city. Even if it was the nation's capital, he just looked at it as one big muddy city. Who ever thought they were doing Edward a favor by posting him to Washington City was sadly mistaken. He couldn't have been more unhappy.

Jo Ann was even more unhappy. This put a monkey wrench in Phase II of the plan. Phase II was to get assigned to some border state outpost. He would send for Jo Ann later to join him. After that he would pretend to hire Mary (Jo Ann's sister) as a maid, and have baby Jane (Jo Ann's baby sister) act the part of Mary's daughter.

"What are we going to do now?" Asked a clearly worried Edward. "Someone is surly going to recognize you on the post or in the street. All of the sniper crew ain't even gone from this miserable city. Some of our men are reenlisting and staying here."

"Just let me think Edward. Don't panic on me now," replied Jo Ann. I'm going for a walk. Stay cool, give me a minute, I'll keep us safe," Jo Ann said cooly.

While walking home one day from visiting Edward at their favorite eatery for dinner, Jo Ann accidently bumped into a short, stocky, plain faced black lady. She carried herself with a great deal of formal bearing and dignity.

"I'm sorry miss; I should have been paying attention. Here let me help you with those packages," said Jo Ann.

Taken back, and totally surprised, that a white woman had just apologized to her and offered to help her pick up her packages, the black lady just stared and shook her head. Jo Ann noticed that there were bolts of nicely stitched cloth, two or three sewing kits, and knitting needles.

"Why that's very kind of you," said the lady. I'm Clara Down, extending her hand and giving Jo Ann a firm hand shake. She looked her right in the eyes as an equal. Although she was black, she did not seem intimidated or overwhelmed by the white woman who had knocked her packages askance. With a bright smile on her dimpled face she remarked, “My goodness that is a really pretty dress you have on. Did you make it yourself?”

“No, I’m clumsy with needle and thread, replied Jo Ann. “I would probably sew my fingers together if I took up dress making,” she joked.

“I bet you could learn in a hurry if the right person taught you,” Ms. Down’s remarked. “Your taste seems to work for you. At least with the dress you are wearing.”

Ms. Down’s went on to say, “your shoes are nice also, and that silk scarf seems handmade.” Together the outfit was very pretty. The color matched her complexion perfectly.

“Are you a professional designer by any chance? Asked Ms. Downs.

“No, of course not,” Jo Ann laughed. In what seemed like five minutes, an hour and a half passed. The white woman and Negro lady chatted and got acquainted. A friendship was born.

"I hope you don't mind me saying so, but you look like you are quite well to do," Jo Ann inquired. "

"Believe me I'm not," said Ms. Downs. "I'm just a humble Servant of the Lord," Ms. Down's replied.

"You're just so ..... I don't know how to say it," said Jo Ann.

"Neat for a niggra" said Ms. Downs, smiling. "Yes, I've heard that before. Thank you, I guess," she said.

"No, I wasn't trying to insult you man," Jo Ann said. "Please forgive my manners," Jo Ann spoke.

Ms. Downs was surprised. Jo Ann did not look down her nose at Ms. Downs. They exchanged addresses. They made plans for a dinner date this upcoming weekend. Ms. Downs could not believe her eyes or ears. "

"Would a white woman really be seen in public with me at a nice eatery?" She asked herself. She was a black woman with a formal bearing, but she knew people would be whispering behind her back.

"Could it be I have made a friend?" She asked. Is this woman one of these abolitionist I have heard about? I just never met one before."

Jo Ann was just happy to have a female friend. "I have never had a woman for a friend before in my life except Willow. I wonder what women talk about" she asked. I'm starved for girl talk and lonely for a female companion. I don't even know how to act like a woman," she said. "Damn, I feel great. Thank you Lord for sending Ms. Downs to me." It never even crossed her mind that people would talk because there was a difference in their skin color. After all, this was Washington, D.C the nation's capital.

She got a further shock at dinner later that week. As they waited for their Roast Beef and Potatoes, the 53 year old Ms. Downs told her a very unusual exciting story.

"I lived in the White House, with President Lincolns family. I still look after Mrs. Lincoln when I can. I sew all of her clothes and she is a very good friend of mine. Mary Todd Lincoln is very troubled. Her brother, three half brothers and three bother – in - laws all fought in the confederate army. She was a true Kentucky Belle. Some considered her a smart aleck meddler that sticks her nose in Abrahams, business. Now that he is gone she doesn't know what to do with herself She spends money like there is no tomorrow," said Ms. Downs.

"Abrahams, election was like giving Mary the key to the candy store." And on it went for a couple of hours. It was obvious Ms. Downs was a trusted member of the Lincoln inner circle. Now she was a friend of Jo Ann's. Her gut told her Ms. Downs was trust worthy and kept secrets in a time of war. Her gut told her she was contemplating, the right thing.

"For some reason I feel like I have known you forever, Ms. Downs. My gut tells me I can trust you, and I am so filled up with secrets I'm about to burst open. So here goes," she paused, took a deep breath and let it out. "I am a niggra woman just like you. My name is Jo Ann Douglass. I am a runaway from a big plantation on the eastern shore. I escaped with my family, went to Philadelphia to start over," she said. "My mom and my brothers are dead now, that hurts." Tears started flowing. "There are times I can't sleep at night it hurt so bad. I have seen my share of fighting and killing. I'll trust you to keep that to yourself," she asked.

Ms. Downs was mesmerized. She just listened, then she smiled. She nodded and reached across the table. As tears flowed from both women, an 800 pound gorilla was lifted from the room.

"Thank you Ms. Downs, for listening." Ms. Downs had no idea she didn't know half the secrets still buried, and would probably fall flat on her face if she did. Ms. Downs said, "you come from a good family. God will forgive you, and look out for your troubles. I am holding your hand so we can pray together. The good Lord will bless you child." The white patrons looked on in amazement. If they only knew.

CHAPTER THIRTY NINE

After bearing her soul, to her new friend the final phase of her plan fell right in focus. In Ms. Downs mind there was only one way that you could possibly keep such a gigantic secret in a city like Washington. "You have to open up your closet. Take the laundry out and air out your dirty laundry in front of everyone. That way it is no longer dirty and nothing can hurt you," said Ms. Downs.

"First things first. You have a family to protect. That means you have to hurry and say I do. That is the start of our family. After that announce you are with child. Now the tricky part. You are proud of your family and your heritage. You loved your mother fiercely. Your mom was a slave from the famous Grand Harvest. Your poor father was murdered, killer unknown. The master was sympathetic. He insisted that you take his last name. Your mom got sick, passed away. You moved to PA. to freedom, after he freed you. The family that took you in, is still taking care of your sisters. Now that you are married, it won't be long before you send for them. Your husband knew everything. You told him from the start. God has been merciful, you have been blessed," she spoke proudly and strongly, thinking that this just might work.

"The rest is up to the Kelly's' and God. But remember, the best laid plans of mice and men often go astray. Man plans, God laughs," she said.

CHAPTER FORTY

Three weeks later they were married by the Army Chaplain in Ft. McNair. It couldn't have come a minute too soon. For soon after that, morning sickness became an everyday visitor to Jo Ann. "These cramps are killing me. I hate being pregnant. This morning sickness and vomiting is too damn much," Jo Ann complained.

"Hell, you are eating everything in sight," Edward told her. "Your tits are growing, your butt is getting round as a wagon wheel. Even your hair is growing," said Edward. "You are really starting to look good woman," said Edward. "Even Buster don't know who you are sometimes," he laughed. "You smell like Jonathan, you just don't look like him," he said. "Dogs get confused too. This Jonathan was 100% nicer."

Since Edward had to move in the married quarters, the other soldiers did not see much of Jo Ann. "I'm just so scared someone might recognize me," said Jo Ann. "It's like an itch I can't scratch."

Jo Ann kept looking for a good place to buy a small house off of the base. That way contact with army personal would be kept to a minimum.

Already, Edward had turned down 2 invitations to dinner with the post commanders family. He pleaded sickness as an excuse. Captain Brady would start getting suspicious, if Jo Ann didn't start socializing with the other soldiers wives. She wanted to wait until the right time to make her big announcement. She knew the news that not only was she pregnant, but that she was black, would be the talk of the post. It may even spread through the city. For a white man to marry a black woman in 1865 was practically unheard of.

What really worried Jo Ann, was not the reaction of the army, but the reaction of Edwards family. She knew how he felt about his mom and dad. She knew what was in his heart when it came to his siblings. She was thinking that he was missing the hostility that would come from them when it came to her. For some reason, Edward thought their attitude would be like his towards her, and the racial issue. She did not think so. She had lived in the north, and understood that most white folks felt just like southerners when it came to race. They thought that blacks were inferior beings, and had no equal place in the world beside whites. They would be hostile to the notion of a son, a brother, a family member, seeing a Negro Person as an equal, much less marrying one, and making her part of the family.

"I don't believe your family would just accept me with open arms, do you?" Asked Jo Ann. "I would fall on my face laughing if I wasn't so scared. I know that they will hate me as soon as you say the word married," Jo Ann argued. "Do you really think in these times after four long years of struggle that anything has really changed?" She asked. "Look around you. I don't see one mixed race couple anywhere. The only thing a woman with my skin color can do is be a prostitute, may be a mistress. People like us don't get married. We don't start families," Jo Ann said seriously.

Edward replied, "I don't care about everybody else. I love you. We are going to spend the rest of our life together. Bet on it," he yelled. "Whoever don't like it, that's their problem. Till death do us part, that's what the deal is. Ma and Pa will love you," he said. Jo Ann shook her head. She almost laughed. "You are so naive Edward," she said.

CHAPTER FORTY ONE

It was a warm evening, muggy and humid. The heat of the July summer was suffocating. Edward and Jo Ann left the post and headed toward the park on foot, Jo Ann was trying to find the words to tell Edward of her plan, and her decision about the course that she thought best for them to take.

"Stop being so stubborn, and listen Edward," Jo Ann said. "Don't fight me on this. I really ain't in the mood for one of your goody two shoes lectures about how understanding your momma and poppa are."

"You got your nerve Jo Ann," Edward shouted. "You don't even know them and already you have them labeled as bigots. That's not fair. Give them a chance, they will get to love you just like I do," he predicted.

"You don't believe that Edward," Jo Ann said. "This being accepted into your family," she stomped her foot. "Damn it this ain't looking across the field and accepting the nigger girl in your daughter's school class," Jo Ann said. "If you really believe that why don't they even know we are married? Jo Ann asked. "They are white and I am Niggra and they ain't going to want no Niggra woman for their precious Edward. You know it, and I know it."

"This will be the straw that broke the camel's back," Jo Ann insisted. "We got to go up to the farm, tell them everything, and if they pitch a fit, you going to have to choose Edward. Me or them! If you choose them I'll just get on the train and ride. I'll go to Rev. Alcott's and get my sisters and make my life like I can, the best I can."

"If you leave me Jo Ann, I'll jump off a bridge. It will not be because of me," Edward replied. Once in Philadelphia she would become a single mother with two siblings to look out for. There, she would try to put the pieces of her life together. She would have to try to mend a shattered, broken heart. This more than anything, scared her the most. For she truly worshipped the ground Edward walked on. She loved his last year's drawers!

Thinking so deeply and concentrating so hard on what she would say, Jo Ann completely missed the four men that had been following her and Edward at a discreet distance. Now they had fanned out. One was up ahead, one on each side of them, and one still following behind. The foursome did not make a particularly dangerous looking gang. One, 6'0" 190lbs, good sized biceps and legs. The other three rather average, between 5'8" and 5'10" 160lbs. to 180lbs. Closer looks would have revealed various bruises and scars from recent brawls. Some were from strong armed robbery attempts. Obviously, they were thugs down on their luck. A man and woman taking an evening stroll was an inviting target, too good to pass up.

So the lead man known in the underworld as the "stick" man, suddenly stumbles, loses his balance, and takes a nasty headfirst fall. Edward, observing the fall, rushes up to the stricken man, who appears to be semi – conscious and in pain. At that point, the two men fanned out on each side, "the wing men," converge. They close in from the side, weapons (in this case two 8 inch knives) at the ready. The "trailer", the last man, walks up from behind. He forced Jo Ann to join the gathering by sticking his knife in her back, and pushing her forward. At this point the man on the

ground spins and shows Edward his weapon. Nice, orderly, pulled off in perfect unison. One exception this time. Wrong victims, Jo Ann pivots, grabs the young thug's wrist, twist's his arm, and flips him forward in one motion. Surprise and his own momentum carries him over on to the ground, as his weapon is wrenched from his grip, the blade is plunged in his chest. The other three converge on Edward. He kicks the one that was on the ground hard to the face. Then he steps on his wrist to get the knife out of his grip. The thug on his left has stabbed Edward in the neck. That is a scared reaction to the counter – attack by Edward. The thug on Edward's right plunges his blade in Edward's right hand. Edward shields his face from the stabbing motion. The rest is a blur. In less than two minutes the attack is over. The attackers are hobbling away. Hurt and embarrassed, they do not realize they are lucky to still be alive. Edward is injured. At first glance it does not appear serious.
A closer look by Jo Ann reveals otherwise. The blade has cut an artery. The blood is pumping out in spurts. Jo Ann is panicked as Edward is choking on his own blood. Now he is in a sitting

position. She cannot stop the flow of blood. "My God this can't be happening!" She thinks.

"Help! I need help!" she screams. She cannot leave Edward. She must get some help. She starts to panic. "Help me!! Please help me," she yells. Over and over until her voice has exhausted, she yells. Five minutes pass by, 10 minutes pass by. Finally a passerby hears the desperate cries. He races over to Jo Ann, who by now, is cradling Edwards blood drenched uniform, and blood soaked handkerchief by his head, in her lap. She thinks she is still screaming, but no sound is coming from her shocked and exhausted body. She is shaking, and tears are flowing freely.

Her Edward is gone. The love of her life is no more. After four years of war and carnage. After missions so dangerous, and battles so fierce you could not see your enemy 5 feet in front of you, he's gone. After a marriage so brief that only a few people even knew of their union, dear Edward is gone. "What now? What in God's name do I do now?" She asks, still shaking.

CHAPTER
FORTY TWO

December 25, 1865, was a very cold, very snowy day. The temperature was around 30.* It was a crisp winter afternoon. The snow made the day feel like you were standing in the middle of a postcard. The snowflakes dancing around, wet and tingly, making you taste the wetness of their droppings with your tongue. Mittens wet on your hands from the snowballs you've thrown, knowing later on a sneeze or two will be the result. Far from the horse drawn sleighs being pulled up and down the avenue, Jo Ann was giving her final push.

"Oh Lord, don't bust my coochie wide open," begged Jo Ann.

"The head is right there Ms. Douglass," the doctor said. "C'mon now push hard! Act like you want to see it right .... Damn ..... Now," yelled doctor Lacy.

"Oh, ah my Lord, what the hell was up there," cried Jo Ann.

"Perfect, he's perfect, Jo Ann," Doctor Lacy acknowledged. Kicking, screaming, and big headed, "Big Blue" Douglass barreled his 7 pound 10 ounce, form into the world.

"My Christmas gift from God," said Jo Ann proudly. "This makes all I been thru worth it," she sighed and laid back. "Me and you against the world Big Blue," she fell quietly to sleep, a smile on her face.

Lost in her dreams, Jo Ann flashed back to the time some five months ago, when Edwards family had rejected her so soundly, ripping into her dignity and tearing her heart out.

"I'm so sorry Mr. Kelly, Mrs. Kelly," the post commander said.

"Edward and his wife are such wonderful people. Jo Ann did not deserve such a cruel blow so soon after their union."

Mrs. Kelly and her daughters almost fainted all together. Mr. Kelly's eyes popped open wide as onions. He sputtered, "What in the devil are you talking about man? Wife? Union? You deaf? You have made a terrible mistake. You notified the wrong family, fool," he yelled. Mrs. Kelly could not speak. She just kept blubbering and repeating, "Oh God, oh Lord", over and over again.

"My brother wasn't married idiot," both sisters chimed in.

"Mama don't cry," one daughter begged. "This dunce is a lunatic."

"Lt. Whitestone go get Mrs. Kelly right now!" The commander exclaimed. I will not stand here and be humiliated by some back wood hicks. I said, get her now! Move!"

"Captain what in the blazes is so important?" Questioned Jo Ann. "Is my house on fire? I don't see the smoke," she joked.

"Mrs. Kelly meet Mrs. Kelly," said the commander.

"And no, your house ain't on fire. But your future may well be on the way to hell," commented Lt. White stone.

The two Mrs. Kelly's met eye to eye. The stare down looked like Wyatt Earp and Jonny Ringo, at high noon in Tombstone.

"Who in the name of Jesus are you," barked Edward's mother. Not giving an inch, Jo Ann replied, "Your sons wife and the mother to be of your grandbaby."

“Grandbaby,” Edwards’s mother screamed. She grabbed for her husband. She missed, and fell on the floor, her head spinning like a top.

“What Grand baby? Where in the Sam Houston did you come from? Who are you? How did you marry my Edward without us knowing?” Mr. Kelly sputtered.

“If you shut up and listen,” Jo Ann said. I’ll tell you everything. Close your mouth girls,” she said to Edward sisters. “A fly will land in your mouths, they are open so wide.” She said to the group, “I know this news is a terrible shock to you. First to find out Edward is gone, then to find out he had married so hastily. I just want to tell you it was my idea, not his. He wanted to take me home to you and tell the world that he had intentions to wed. That he was in love and spoken for. We were in love and proud of it. We were mates in our own little world.”

Mrs. Kelly, tears streaming down her face, could stand it no more, she blurted out, “Then why? Why would you rob his family of the joy of seeing him united with the love of his life, if what you’re saying is true,” she said. “I don’t understand.” She looked Jo Ann right in the eye seeking an answer.

After a silence of about 30 seconds, Jo Ann sighed, took a deep breath and said "My blood isn't white. Edward said you would not understand," she lied.

Edwards youngest sister Ava was first to respond. "You mean my brother married a Niggra?" "I don't believe it, you are a liar," screamed the older sister. "One day my brother is fighting, a war, the next day he is romancing a niggra? I don't believe you," said Sarah, the youngest sister.

"You tricked Edward. You put some kind of roots on him," Darlene, the other sister said.

"He probably couldn't see your skin clearly. You pulled your dress up, and Edward was dazzled," snickered Sarah.

"Where are you from?" her mother – In – law asked. "Who is your family," Mrs. Kelly inquired.

"Where are your roots?" Mr. Kelly wanted to know.

"Did Edward ever see your black, dirty sisters and brothers?" Mr. Kelly asked.

"Were your family slaves? "Mrs. Kelly asked.

"Who do you belong to?"Asked Darlene.

"We might have to buy her," they all said together. Then they laughed.

Jo Ann did her best to explain to the flabbergasted family. Trembling, nervous, mouth dry as a desert, she extended her hand to Mr. Kelly. He looked at her like she had small pox.

Jo Ann said to the group, "I don't need you. I'll make it on my own. Keep your money and your farm. You will come crawling one day," she predicted. "One day you will need your grandson and come begging to me."

"My brother would not dirty our family name like that. You tricked him. You didn't tell him."

Edward's father said something that would forever live in Jo Ann's head rent free.

"You colored trash," he yelled. "You had my boy killed so he would never know the truth. You are a liar and a murderer. I'll see you burn in hell for this."

Horrified, Jo Ann bolted from the office like a frightened deer. She thought it might get ugly. She had never imagined she would be accused of murder. That hurt more than anything had hurt her in her whole life. It was almost too much to carry.

That was six months ago. Edward's family took his body back to Harrisburg, where he was buried on family land. Jo Ann never heard a word from them for years. They never even inquired about their grandson. They did not respond to Jo Ann letters asking for a meeting to clear the air. She was not kicked out of her home on the base. She was legally a window due all Army benefits. Her life became a living, breathing hell.

CHAPTER
FORTY THREE

8 MONTHS LATER....

It had been a rugged eighteen months since Edwards's tragic death at the hands of four street thugs that were never brought to justice. A good man, a war hero, and a wonderful humanitarian who was accidentally and unluckily killed by some down on their luck nobodies. It did not seem fair. Surely God knew that. Surely he knew that for Asa to have a chance in this cruel, ruthless world he tumbled into, he would need a father to guide him and not only about his heritage.

"It's just crazy Clara," complained Jo Ann. "How could the Kelly's be that ugly? They wouldn't even acknowledge their own grandson. They insist Asa is no kin to them. How much does a son have to look like his father?" She wailed. "Damn it, he is the spitting image of Edward. I get chill bumps when I look at him," she said. "He looks like a small version of his poppa."

"That okay baby," Ms. Downs replied. "Mark my words. One day they going to need that child," she predicted. "They gonna come to him, hat in hand. I feel it in my bones. It gonna come full like a circle. God don't like ugly. They gonna pay the piper," she said, with fire in her eyes!

Word got around that Jo Ann was not white. "People might as well mark me with a scarlet cross," said Jo Ann. "The women on this post avoid me like the plague. I have done nothing but treat these people with respect. Now they give me their butts to kiss," Jo Ann said sadly.

"The other day I was at the general store," replied Ms. Booker. She was half Indian and the only friend Jo Ann had on the post. "I heard ole lady Church and Ms. Brown talking about you. They said you set Edward up to get his pension," she chuckled. "I butted in and reminded them that the money isn't even $50.00 a mouth. You can starve living off of a pension check."

Jo Ann said, "I even went to Freedman's hospital to have Blue. I don't trust these army doctors. They might try to kill my baby," she said. "I'm so worn out I really need a doctor for my head."

She gathered her things to go meet her best friend, Ms. Downs. She also had a check up to go to with the nice doctor at the clinic. She had started to trust Dr. Davis even though he was a white doctor. A compassionate man that at most times didn't get paid near what his services were worth, he accepted eggs, chickens and even fresh killed rabbit as payment for treatment.

Later, in the company of Ms. Downs she was a little tired so she unburdened herself with a little conversation.

"Clara, I feel like I'm losing my sanity sometimes," said Jo Ann. "It feels like I'm coming and going at the same time."

"You are feeling guilty because you lived and Edward died," replied Clara. "That is a natural feeling for people, especially if someone you love has died. Edward would want you to live. Edward would want you to be strong and go on with your life and happiness, again. You are young and beautiful. Time heals all wounds," she said. "Not to mention you'll have a baby to raise," she said in a gentle voice.

She brought Jo Ann, back from the brink. She talked, she fed Jo Ann, she walked miles with her thru muddy, sloppy, trash strewn streets. Mostly she listened with a silent and compassionate ear. What she did not do was coddle Jo Ann. When the time came... "Alright child, enough is enough," she said. "Enough of the dead, time for the living. Take those black clothes and throw them out. You have nice things. Tomorrow I want you to start showing Washington City your wardrobe. This weekend we are going to the theater. Mary (Ms. Lincoln) will look after everything. I'ma get you ready to raise this child. He can't raise himself," she commanded. "You are beautiful, but that opens the door. Your mind is what will keep it open, and let you take advantage of your opportunity." Clara spoke. "I'm Niggra and I was poor. You got toughness about you. A ruthless streak that I can feel, so use it. The pity party is over, me and Buster won't have another minute of it." Jo Ann resolved to raise her child the best she could.

"I' ma do the best I can Clara," Jo Ann promised. "I'm going to get my sisters, and one day I'm going to bring Homers children up here to live. Bertha's going to bring them children up here to get a good education and be somebody." Jo Ann was determined to save them from a life of poverty.

CHAPTER FORTY FOUR

Jo Ann started to put her plan together. She had a place to stay because of the army, but she knew the time was limited. She knew she had two years left on her widows' lease. A monthly stipend, and food allowance was also included. Most times the other wives would give you a hand, but not in Jo Ann's case. She was an outcast. Nobody offered her as much as a piece of bread.

Sometimes she would walk with Ms. Downs, Buster and little Asa over to Ms. Lincolns' bungalow. It was time for the big charity event of the year. All the newspaper people would be there. "Mary, are you coming to the Ball Saturday night?" Mrs. Della Rose asked Mrs. Lincoln. "We always have the biggest turn out of the year," she said proudly. "Everyone will be there." They were trying to get Ms. Lincoln out of her deep depression from Abraham's assassination.

Mrs. Rose was in a quandary. Her cousin, Frederick D. Thomas was in town. He was one of the wealthiest men on the east coast, but socially he always presented a problem. Everyone knew he was mixed heritage. He had an Indian mother and a white father. They needed a dinner companion for him at the table that wouldn't mind being with a mixed blood man. When she mentioned the problem discreetly to Ms. Downs, she replied, "I have the perfect partner for him," and she smiled. "Ms. Douglass here will make an excellent companion. Why ask Ms. Lincoln. She is young, pretty and single."

"Excellent," said Mrs. Rose. "Down right perfect." She discreetly pulled Jo Ann to the side and extended the invitation to her. Jo Ann was stunned. Jo Ann had never been to a formal dinner in her life. She would not know which fork or knife to use if there were only two in front of her. She would not know what to talk about. She did not know a thing about politics and paid little attention to current affairs. Most damaging of all she did not own a formal dress, or a piece of jewelry. She knew nothing about lip color, or rouge, and had never had her hair done by anyone other than her mamma.

"My Lord, this will never work," Jo Ann said. "They will think I'm a backwoods hick, a country bumpkin. This is a disaster waiting to happen," she fretted.

"We accept," Ms. Downs said cheerfully.

"We", Jo Ann almost shouted. "We what?" She almost fainted. Stuck on stupid, she had no idea what to do.

"Ms. Douglas will be delighted. Have Mr. Thomas pick us up at 5:30 P.M. that should give them plenty of time to be seated by 6:30 P.M. A red rose should be sufficient for a corsage; Jo Ann just sat in silence. She had no idea what a corsage was. After Mrs. Rose left, Jo Ann jumped up out her chair. "Are you crazy woman?" She ranted. "I don't even own a dress. What will I wear? A Cpl. Uniform and brogan boots", she said. "I will make a fool of myself. They will know I'm a slave girl. I can't, I can't do it," she said. "They will laugh me out of Washington City."

Ms. Lincoln, who had said nothing during the entire incident, spoke up. Her eyes were full of sparkle, and there was a spark in her voice.

"Child you are beautiful, you are bright, and you stand out. Clara and I will watch little Asa. By the time Clara finishes with you, no woman in Washington will be your equal. By Monday morning you will be the talk of the town," she said.

Ms. Lincoln's prediction was astonishingly true. With a dress from one of her client's wardrobe, some jewelry from Mrs. Lincoln's collection, a pair of Ms. Downs slippers, a hair do designed by Ms. Downs and make up done by Ms. Lincoln personally, Jo Ann was the talk of the dinner. She was stunning, and people were, talking about her like they had grown up with her, and known her and her entire family for years.

The other half of the conversation was not so good. People were, talking about her being the widow that had her husband killed for his army pension.

"That's her," they were whispering. "Yeah the one that had poor Cpl. Kelly done away with. Yeah you know, the war hero," They said. "The word is, she is niggra. Can you see it?" They muttered.

For his part Fred Thomas was flabbergasted. He was knocked off his feet at first sight. He was speechless. A feather would have knocked him unconscious. Love at first sight was too light of a description.

"Please take all my wealth and put it in your account madam. If that's not enough for you I will rob 6 trains, 3 banks, and kidnap a Vander built, and hold him for ransom," Mr. Thomas begged Jo Ann.

The buzz was loud and strong. Fred was smitten, as the months passed, the society pages were full of pictures and articles about the widow Kelly, and the wealthy Fred Thomas, at one gala or another. A chance encounter had brought Jo Ann back to life, put some sparkle in her life again, and turned Fred into a hopeless romantic. He found more and more reason to spend time in Washington City. Jo Ann enjoyed his attention, and surprisingly so did the little fellow Asa, first crawling, then toddling, he followed Fred around like a puppy, and before long was calling him "pop – pop."

CHAPTER FORTY FIVE

The society pages were not the only news that was circulating in the country. 1866 saw the country beginning an economic boom unheard of, and unlike any in the history of the world. The U.S.A. was certainly the place to be on the business front. Chicago, Pittsburgh, New York City, Baltimore, Washington and St. Louis were just a few of the places that with hard work, creativity and some investment capital, fortunes were being built. The Carnegies, Vanderbuilts, Mellons, Rockefellers, and Thomas's were starting to amass fortunes in their chosen industries. National celebrities, like Mark Twain, were being established. They were no longer just confined to a region. They were famous all over the country because you could now travel the entire country in days by railroad, in record times. Gold and silver were making people explore the western territories. The telegraph and the Pony Express advanced communication and exploration so that people started to push the Indians onto reservations.

While all this was happening at a dizzying pace, something horrifying was happening under the surface in the bustling city of Washington, D.C. Between Sept. and Dec. 18, 1866, three men were found brutally murdered in the city. The police department was not remotely prepared to deal with the situation. The Washington D.C. Police Dept. was a poorly organized, slip shod group that was cobbled together to protect the Senators and Representatives in Congress from being mugged and molested, while doing the nation's business.

After the civil war ended thousands of out of work soldiers and newly freed slaves roamed the city daily. There were many muggings, robberies and homicides that were getting out of control. The police force was doubled in size in the year 1866 and each dept. was given a Chief Officer. In charge of homicides was a young Irishman by the name of Michael O'Connell. He was an ex Pinkerton detective, who was brought onto the force as a favor to the memory of his dad. At onetime his dad was a friend of President Johnson, before he was killed while serving on the force.

Michael was a shade over 6'0" tall and close to 200 pounds. Quietly confident, 35 years old and carrot topped, he wore his hair rather long, and had a mustaches the same color as his hair on his head. Dimples on his cheeks and a trademarked gap toothed smile complemented a beautiful Irish tenor that let you know he sung in the church choir on Sundays. His complexion let you know he spent a lot of time outdoors, hunting and fishing.

"Johnson, where is that report I ordered? "O Connell asked." "You should have been finished yesterday," he bellowed. Not a patient man, his Irish accent always came out when he was anxious. Like now. Slackers were not tolerated in his world.

"Damn O'Connell give me a break," his Cpl. begged. "You just ordered it yesterday."

"I've got to interview these witnesses today," O'Connell said. "The man just lives a half a mile away. You should have tracked him yesterday. The chief is on my butt. Get on it man. I'm going to make an arrest on this even if it's you!" He promised.

Odd that O'Connell chose police work. He was an A student and finished high school early. He was in his second year at Harvard when he dropped out to join the Pickerton Detective Agency. His mom thought he had lost his mind. But he loved brawling, and solving a good puzzle was his hobby. The Law Enforcement bug bit him and it was a wrap.

"Damn it, I've had my share of black eyes and busted lips. My brothers kicked my ass for breakfast most mornings, but I learned to give as good as I got," he said. "If you don't get me some suspects I'm going to put my foot where the sun don't shine Cpl," he threatened.

The older cops laughed. O'Connell was one of them even if he was a little on the young side. He could knock down an Irish whiskey with the best of them. He was familiar with the relatively new surveillance techniques also. He used informants and paid them.

CHAPTER
FORTY SIX

He was the first to realize these three killings were connected and signaled Washington that it had its first known serial killer. The first victim was a bully, loud and obnoxious. Harry Ward was his name. He had an especially bad habit of embarrassing the colored help that cleaned the offices. He took pleasure in feeling up the woman of color that passed thru the hallways of Congress on their appointed cleaning assignments. On more than one occasion he was seen backhanding one of the stable boys that were tending to the carriages of congressmen.

One evening Ward was found about 10:00 P.M in the stable, throat slashed from ear to ear. Blood was everywhere.

"My God, his penis is cut clean off," said one detective. "Looks like a razor cut", said another. "Someone jammed it down his throat. Look, his eyes are gouged out too. Someone was really mad at ole Ward. He pissed somebody off, didn't he?" The detective asked

Four weeks later, October 15, 1866, another murder took place in an alley in the back of Union Station. A busy railroad depot, a large house of prostitution that did big business on a daily basis, had one of its frequent customers, Jefferson "White Horse" Riley of Yazoo, MS.... the famous slave holding, cotton selling family, found in the same position. Ear and throat slashed. More blood than law allowed, and intestines and guts all over the place. The Riley Plantation was famous for its cruelty to its slaves, and ole White Horse could flick a fly off of a slaves back at 20 yards. His horse whip was nicknamed Sir Whip – A – Lot. Since Mississippi had just rejoined the Union he did not have any real business yet. So he spent most of his days talking stupidly about President Johnson, and getting drunk in Ma Belles House of Prostitution. He was mad because President Johnson was the lone congressman that did not agree with succession with the rest of the congressman from the south.

"I smacked that ole Nigger silly", old White Horse joked. He was talking about President

Johnson's butler, a man of color. Despite having a train to catch that evening, someone delayed his departure permanently. The back of his skull was crushed, white meat and bone mixed together, blood and gore everywhere, and guess what? A penis jammed straight down his throat. It was detached from the rest of his body by a razor. He appeared to be eating a hot dog. Half a head attached to his neck, he was eyeless and his bowels had broken. The stench smelled up the entire alley.

"My God," said O'Connell. "This one is worst that the last one, I think someone is sending us a message. I hear you loud and clear."

When they found the third one O'Connell actually laughed at the boldness of this killer. Robert Chester III had actually expressed joy at the assassination of President Lincoln. He owned one of the most right wing, conservative newspapers in Washington City. He had begged General Lee to resign from the U.S Army to lead the confederate troops. Owner of over 100 slaves, he was the leader of the Klu Klux Klan in Virginia.

"You little black bitch, I should put my foot in your ass," he said to the new colored prostitute at Ms. Minnie's whore house. The pretty new girl hurled an insult right back at him. More than a little intoxicated, he called her, “a black cow,” and hit her with a right hand punch. She went down and he kicked her, breaking a rib.

“I should have killed the bitch,” he shouted. “Come on girl, get your ass up those steps,” he shouted loudly. He was red faced and drunk.

Six hours later he departed. Ms. Downs happened to witness the incident and told Jo Ann. “If I was a man I would have punched him back,” Ms. Downs commented. Jo Ann had much more in mind. A punch in the face was the least of the retaliation Chester faced.

One hour later Jo Ann, dressed as Jonathan, confronted Chester in the back of the brothel, the alley smelly and dirty.

“Fancy meeting you here, Chester,” said Jo Ann.

“Do I know you sir?” Said Chester, still half drunk.

“You will in a few minutes,” replied Jo Ann. She proceeded to punish Chester until he was practically unrecognizable. Jo Ann grabbed Chester around and twisted his arm around his back. With the razor against his throat, Chester walked carefully into the alley.

"Far enough Chester," Jo Ann said. Chester halted. Jo Ann slit his throat immediately. "Bleed you sadistic bastard," shouted Jo Ann. At that she pushed him to the ground. She stomped, "take this," his face the recipient of thick brogan boots. "Next time you hit a woman, it will be the devils wife," roared Jo Ann. "Go straight to hell. I'll see you there one day."

"My God, please stop," croacked Chester. Blood spurted thru his hands. They were wrapped around his throat. "Please, Please," he whimpered. Finally he moved no more. He twitched once more in reflex, but he was dead.

"This Cracker is a dead Cracker." cried Jo Ann. "You got what you asked for." She turned, and walked slowly out of the alley.

CHAPTER FORTY SEVEN

Washington, D.C had its first serial killer. When O'Connell viewed the corpse after responding to a message, he could not tell a face belonged to the body.

"Jesus, Mary, and Joseph," O'Connell announced. "There is no face to the body. If I announce this there will be total panic, if I don't the press will crucify me. This is going to be a dance with the devil," O'Connell said. "X – Mas, New Years and St. Patrick's Day all in one. Ok, you want to dance; I'm the one to hook up with. I'm the prince of darkness, Mr. Killer. You think you can scare me, I'll be right on your ass," O'Connell promised. "I'll find you; I'll track you down and put my gun in your mouth. When we dance Mr. Devil, I'm going to blow your brains out for sport. Okay, here I come," He bellowed. "Here I come with my gun in my hand. The Civil War was a tea party compared to what I'm going to bring to your chase. You can take that to your grave. Not a threat, that's a promise," said O'Connell. The gloomy darkness and putrid, disgusting smell filled the alley, and the broken bottles, and shards of glass made a proper mattress for the corpse.

O'Connell's investigative technique was based on the dark side of his personality. He put himself in the mindset of the man he was looking for and took it from there. That made him the victim of lots of depression, mood swings and temper tantrums. He would sometimes go days without eating and would lock himself in his office for hours at a time, transforming evidence that he found at a homicide scene into human thought, ideas and actions.

"Damn man brings my hair up on my arms," said Det. Donald.

"Sometimes he stinks, smells like a whorehouse. Breath almost knocked me down. Damn cigars and rot gut," complained Donald.

Bloodshot eyes, slow ambling stride, the Devil himself broke in the room. As he tilted his head round slowly, he stared Donald right in the eye.

"Got something you want to say to me, shithead?" He asked.

CHAPTER FORTY EIGHT

Jo Ann and Ms. Downs were talking about the type of design house, like the kind the French have overseas. Jo Ann laid her plan out. "I want the kind of place where well off women can do their shopping. Plenty of room, places where they can see their clothes. I feel it Clara. I'm chilled to the bone, swellin proud, fallin out happy. Butterflies are flippin in my stomach. I want to be known as the best in Washington City. Feel it Clara! Squeeze me, hug me. I'm really, really feelin my shop."

Ms. Downs said, "I will help you run the shop. We can turn a profit off of people I know alone, we'll be special." Their faces and hearts lit up. They were beating a hundred miles an hour. They hugged.

ONE NIGHT AFTER MAKING LOVE...

"Fred, I want to take on a business venture," Jo Ann blurted out. The smell of love making and perfume gave off an exotic Aroma.

"What do you think about that?" For the next two hours she bared her dream. Fred was amazed. He had no idea Jo Ann had such business sense. He was so impressed he offered to put up 100% of the start – up capital, along with another request.

"Marry me?" He asked excitedly. He told her in no uncertain terms, "if you turn down my marriage bid, I still want to back your business. It will be a gold mine," he predicted. "I don't pass up a chance to make some money."

In the comfy, feather bed surrounded by the candle light, the spacious pale green bedroom smelled like roses. This plan felt like dollars signs waiting to happen. Two deals were closed at once Jo Ann said. "Of course I'll marry you, big head. I love you, you scoundrel," smiling like a lit X- Mas tree. They established Douglass & Thomas Clothing House in 1867, the city's finest. They were married in Calvary Episcopal, church on H Street in Washington in March of the same year.

ONE WEEK LATER...

"I love our home," Jo Ann exclaimed. The 3 bedroom Victoria style house was rust colored brick, a walk-up with a short front porch, and a steep slate roof, two bay window and a cozy study and smoking parlor that almost reached out and hugged you. The place said "Welcome", and made you feel comfortable and "Home." It was everything Jo Ann had never had when she was growing up at Grand Harvest.

The building that was to be Jo Ann's first store was within walking distance. It was hard to find a good location at first, especially since she was a woman.

"Damn, my feet are so sore and swollen, I can hardly feel them," complained Jo Ann. "I can't afford these outrages prices they are asking. No one wants to rent me any space. You would think I want to buy some ones first child," Jo Ann said. She was clearly frustrated.

"Don't fret it honey bunch," Fred replied. Secretly Fred had made up his mind to step in. He would use his name and influence to make sure Jo Ann got what she wanted. He would buy the entire building and save Jo Ann's rent money for her each month.

"I will give you an extra 500.00 a month to finish on time," Fred told the contractor. For Fred it was a done deal. He would make sure everything was on time and the goods were imported and stocked. Fred one upped everyone by becoming the first clothing store outside of New York City to have purchases delivered from Paris, France to Washington D.C direct.

"How in the world did you manage to have these delivered from Paris Fred?" Jo Ann quizzed Frederick. She was truly flabbergasted. "Who would afford us such a privilege?" Jo Ann asked. "We are nobodies. How are we so important in the fashion world?" Jo Ann truly did not understand how important or influential Fred's name was. His reputation was impeccable. He was truly respected internationally. Politically, wealth wise and in business circles he was a heavy weight. Jo Ann just did not understand how heavy.

"It is amazing" Jo Ann said, "The editors for Harpers, New York Times, Washington post all write me and ask my opinion. I'm just a country girl. What do I know" she asked. By 1869 Jo Ann's bank account was six figures. "I can't believe this Frederick. Where did this money come from? How are these orders possible, Clara? Is God this good?"

She asked. In 1869, the promise that had nagged at Jo Ann every day finally came to pass.

"Thank you God," Jo Ann whispered.

A volcano was rushing up from the pit of her stomach. She swayed.

"Thank you Lord," she sang a little louder.

"I'm so grateful. I'm so lucky. I'm so happy," Jo Ann shouted.

The chill bumps broke out. The tears were flowing. Her joy was contagious and shining thru.

"To those that much is given, much is expected. Halleluah! Halleluah! Thank you Ms. Harriet. Thank...you.

CHAPTER FORTY NINE

"Go get those children and bring them back to me," Jo Ann said excitedly. "My brothers children are coming home, Fred. My kinfolks are coming home with Moses. Fred, you hear me? I want them right ... now!"

"Okay Jo, Chester will leave today," Fred said. Excitement was in the air. The mood was cheerful. Jo Ann was running around the house grinning from ear to ear. Buster was barking and playing, the children felt like X-Mas was coming. "O Lord, thank you," Jo Ann closed her eyes and cried. "Thank you for all of my blessings."

TWO DAYS LATER...

Bertha had done the best she could in poverty stricken Charleston, SC. Having 3 mouths to feed, washing clothes for a white family, it was all she could do to care for them. Illiterate, but determined, Bertha almost fainted when Chester found her, and told her what he was looking for her for.

"Oh God, thank you. Oh Lord, please don't let me be dreaming. Sir, can we leave now? I don't want to wake up and this be a dream," she said. Two days later Bertha found herself in a hotel getting ready to meet Jo Ann.

"Oh Lordy," Bertha exclaimed. "Please don't let me wake up in Charleston. If this is a nightmare, you are pretty darn cruel God."

"Bertha for the fifth time," replied Jo Ann. "You are not DREAMING!! I looked for you for months. Feel me, I'm flesh and blood. Woman, you are not seeing a ghost. This is no fantasy; God has blessed both of us." Bertha's face almost glowed, she was so happy.

"How can I ever repay you?" Asked Bertha, tears rolling down her sunken cheeks. Etched in her face was the look of someone that has struggled mightily. Although not yet 30, Bertha's face had worry lines, wrinkles and bags under her sad eyes. She was bowed from toting burlap sacks full of laundry. Her feet were calloused, her hands felt like steel wool.

"You must learn to smile again," said Jo Ann. "You must be humble and grateful."

"I know Ms. Douglass," whispered Bertha. "But with people like me, ain't been nothing to be grateful for. Ima need me some practice time," she said.

"You will get the hang of it," Jo Ann assured her. "My Lord is a good teacher. You will meet him bye an bye. One day soon the sun will shine right on you and yours. Believe me," she promised.

BUT WHAT IS IT THEY SAY MAN PLANS ... GOD LAUGHS.

HERE ..... WE .... GO ....

LATER IN THE YEAR...

"I can't believe it Fred," Jo Ann was practically jumping with excitement. The little cramped room with the broken legged chairs, wobbly deck, an stuffy smell, might as well have been a Castle. It was to Jo Ann. Finally after months, the adoptions were complete. The children were in bright new clothes, pigtails for the girls and a haircut for Donald.

"My brothers children are officially ours," beamed Jo Ann to Fred. "I'm so happy I can scream," she said. "I know Willie is looking down on us smiling," she said. "I feel him, I really feel him."

AT THE OFFICE...

"Chester, I hate to admit it, but the woman is ruthless in business matters," said Fred.

"You're right Fred," Chester replied. "That meeting with Dupree yesterday, she ate him alive. I felt sorry for the old guy. He never had a chance," Chester grinned.

"Damn I'm glad she's my wife. I wouldn't have a chance battling that she devil in negotiating. She's got no mercy or compassion in her heart," Fred was clearly impressed.

Fred was talking about how he just lets Jo Ann go and count the money as it comes in. Fred's name kept the vultures away and Jo Ann's tenacity kept the vultures from preying on the woman. She could play dirty with the best of them.

Jo Ann army experience prepared her for battle. Her slave days taught her how to win a war. She won battle after battle every day. The war was won when she became the first black woman to own a business in Maryland.

"I wonder how my sister is doing" she asked Ms. Downs. Sometimes it still felt like her and Willow were joined at the hip. It would be eerie sometimes how she could be thinking of Willow and the next day a letter would come in the mail. Jo Ann's face would frown up, her left palm would itch and her right eye would blink uncontrollably. Jo Ann would go sit on the white washed front porch and sit down in the rickety swing and a letter would come from the Post Man. This was a new experiment In Maryland. There were men who would bring the mail right to your door.

"Willow laughs about Zack being a war hero," she said. She says "Zack would blow Mr. John's head off if he knew how he called Ms. Lizzy bad names and got drunk and mistreated her," remembered Willow in her letter.

"Now that we have no slaves he can't order Roscoe to clean up or Ms. Hattie to cook," she wrote. "It is so funny to see the pain in his face,"

Willow wrote. "I am so sorry Ms. Lizzy passed," wrote Willow. Hell we don't even know if we are blood sisters or if my daddy and yours are the same man."

LATER JO ANN AND ZACK TALKED...

It seems now the white relatives of Jo Ann are in a bind. She is wealthy, they are not. How do you tell your super rich sister, "I don't care how much money you have, you Niggra and I hate you," said Zack.

Master John doesn't know if he is coming or going. He would proclaim, "Hell no, that mulatto ain't my child." The horse was out of the barn. Too late now to lock the door. The rumor of John being Jo Ann's daddy was all over Dorchester county.

"I ain't got no extra children," he would bellow. All the time burning his mind up, wracking his brain, looking for a clue to who in the hell was Jo Ann daddy?

"Damn you Lizzy," he would cry over and over again. "You and that damn Jasper done messed up the best of my life. You cock hold me, then got the nerve to die on me. You left me all by myself, you Jezebel. God is going to take your wings and put you out!" He shouted.

"Oh no", Zack cried. "No the hell you didn't you, old dog. All these years, and now you tell me Jo Ann is really my sister," he roared.

"All I ask of you is just look out for the chile Zack," said John, "I didn't tell you to give up your right arm. Ok, I made a mistake. I made a chile that just happens to be a different color than you. Hell, she is still your blood. Both of you bleed red! She acted more like you than Willow and June put together," John reminded Zack. "You said so yourself, plenty of times."

Zack couldn't deny that. Over the years he often was amazed about the bond he felt with the slave girl with the heart of a lion.

"Okay, you win," he said. "If she ever needs me I'll be there. You got my word and my promise. Lizzy made me promise her the exact same thing," Zack shook his head in amazement. The Douglass family was crazy. All of them, certifiable!

Speaking of family, Willow on her way to Baltimore after a trip to New York, decided at the spur of the moment to visit June and her family. Willow happened to be sitting in the window seat. She was gazing at the sights going by. A tall gentleman, brown eyes, patrician nose, rather thin lips with a dimpled chin, and near perfect white teeth, plopped down in the seat beside her.

"Hi there good looking," he said, white teeth dazzling. "You must be tired because you been running thru my mind all day," he said.

Willow replied, "If, that's the best you can do, I think I'll move my seat."

From there it was on. Soon, John Dodd from Washington, D.C. introduced himself as a property developer fresh from looking at some real estate. Willows instinct took over. She smiled, batted her eyes and licked her lips. She rubbed her leg against Dodd's enough times that by the time the train pulled into Baltimore, each knew the others entire history. In reality John Dodd's was a Washington Post News Reporter who lied regular for a living.

In five days time the headlines in the society section read like a confession. The words screamed, "Society queen Jo Ann Thomas revealed to be a Negro." Jo Ann has never one time denied her racial background. She still was shocked to see it smeared all over the paper. Someone had found Master John at Grand Harvest and talked to him too. He made a statement about Jo Ann's mother that made her sound like a whore.

"No," Jo Ann screamed! Her face flushed. Breath caught in her throat, chest heaving up and down.

"That lying old man. Who in the hell found out about Grand Harvest? Damn Master John makin mamma out to be a whore for every damn man twenty miles around," she said. "I'ma kill him. Strangle the life outa the son of a bitch," she yelled.

No wonder bad luck followed. From Thanksgiving 1869 thru the New Year invitations to galas stopped, orders dried up.

"This Dobbs man has ruined my life. Nobody messes with me or mine. He gonna...pay. He..gonna...pay...soon."

CHAPTER FIFTY

It was 1870 and whites were still fighting the civil war. Some whites were determined blacks would never have equal rights and started passing laws aimed at getting rid of the gains that blacks made in politics. They were determined to wipe out all of the things that Congress had made into law to help blacks.

A WEEK LATER... A SMALL SOUTHERN TOWN

“Mister, what have I ever done to you?” The black man asked. He was scared half to death and urine was running down the front.

“You was born the wrong color boy,” the man replied. He had a white hood on his head and was riding a chestnut colored Mare. “Hang the nigger and burn the house to the ground,” the man said with excitement in his voice. He did his dirt under the cover of the hood and showed his boldness in the darkness of night like most cowards.

"Please mister," pleaded the Negros wife. "My man a good man, he work hard, he a good papa. Please don't do this, sir." Three children watched in terror, crying loudly. As they loosed the horse and the hate in their heart with it, the same type of hate was being released in cities though out the north in business deals every day. Same hate, different type of terrorism.

CHAPTER FIFTY ONE

Jo Ann decided to turn back the clock and summon Jonathan from the closet. Too much of this violence and terror was invading her life lately. John Dodd would hold court at his local drinking hole in the evenings 3 or 4 times a week. He was a bragger and a showoff and was known for his nasty remarks and despicable attitude toward Negros and woman. Tonight he was in rare form.

"Drink up Dicky," Dodd's roared. He was red faced now; the alcohol was slurring his speech. He was experimenting with long hair, and sported a full beard these days. A red vest with his two piece suit, cheaply made did not quite go with his brown Brogans. His run over heels gave rise to his occupation, Journalist do a lot of walking.

"Last rounds," the bartender said while wiping the bar clean. Dobb's stumbled. "Damn floor keeps movin," he said.

"Get your druckin tail outa my bar dobb's," Roscoe told him. "Hey you! Come here and tote this fish outa my tank," Roscoe waved the stranger over.

A homeless man warily approached Mr. Dodd's.

"Spare the price of a meal sir?" Asked the beggar.

"Here man." Dodd's replied. "Take this change and leave me alone," Dodd's voice was still slurring words.

"Move and you are a dead man walking," the bum said harshly. He pulled the .44 caliber gun out of his pants and stuck it in Dodd's bulging belly.

"Leave out in a peed or you'll be headless in a few seconds," warned the beggar. They walked until they were in Shanty Town, a collection of run down clapboard Shanties and rough pine cabins located mostly in alleys.

"Just keep walking slowly," said the beggar.

"Where are you taking me man," fear clearly in his voice.

"You can wear this bullet in your head, or you can walk with me, your choice," replied beggar man.

Five blocks of walking past chickens, stray cats, two sporting ladies, looking for tricks, and two separate groups of blue clad union soldiers and they were in an alley where an abandoned store front was located. It looked like some kind of storage warehouse or stable.

The beggar had lost his slow walking, slumped over persona. He was now spirited, upright and strong voiced. He had transformed into something that tingled Dodd's spine and caused him to sweat even in the cool weather.

"What have I done, why in the world did you pick me?" He asked.

"Shut your face. Just shut up," Jonathan warned him. " My finger keeps itchin, my hand wants to squeeze."

Kind sir, I have nothing. I aint no politician, no general. Hell aint nobody goin to miss me when I'm gone," he said. "Hell, I know you taken me for somebody else. Look mister I aint him. I'm poor as a church mouse," he said.

"Didn't I tell you to shut your damn mouth," yelled Jo Ann.

In return for his efforts to speak and identify himself, he received a backhand blow with the revolver that knocked him down to his knees and left a lump the size of an orange on his forehead.

In addition he was gifted with a split lip and a sharp kick to the ribs. Blood poured out of his mouth and a dull thud beat in his rib cage. The swift kick to the head was icing on the cake. He could see the stars thru his puffy eyes; He could also hear the ringing in his ears.

"I know exactly who you are," his assailant said. "Believe me I have the right man." As a chloroformed soaked cloth was passed over his face, he collapsed onto his back and lay still. Forty five minutes later, he woke up groggily and realized. "Damn I'm tied up like a chicken." He peeped thru the slits in his eyes and saw his tormentor holding a jar of honey in one hand and a jar of red ants in the other.

"Aagh, please no," he screamed. "What have I done to you?" He asked, voice croaking like a frog. 'Why me?"

In answer the assailant did three things. He poured honey on Dodd's from head to toe. He opened up the jar of ants and let them have a go at the honey. He pulled up a chair, opened up an old Washington Post Newspaper, and began to read slowly and precisely, an article about Jo Ann

Douglass Thomas and her Negro heritage, complete with family tree!!

After an hour passed, a new toy was opened. Introduced to the party were five sewer rats' that had not eaten in two days. "I'ma open up my torture bag," Jo Ann said. "Rats almost bit my finger off." Dobb's screamed. "What the hell are..." A small block of cheese was forcibly jammed into the rectum of Jo Ann's favorite reporter. Mr. Dodd's screams could be heard even thru the muffled rag jabbed into his mouth. Of course nothing could cover up the stench of the urine and bowel movement caused over the next three hours by the rodents. Finally at 2:00 A.M, the ultimate "Hello stranger." A Cottonmouth rattle snake pulled from the edge of the Potomac River stopped by to introduce himself, up close and personal. For Mr. Dodd's death was an expected relief. The unabated terror, the heart stopping, ruthless torture, the continuing pain, along with the unknowing guessing game of where is the hurt coming from next, combined to make Mr. Dodd's wish he'd never been born. A human being tortured long and this deadly had never before experienced this kind of humiliation. Death was an experience his swollen, poison filled body smiled at. He had danced with the devil and lost.

The sight was too gruesome to describe when the body was discovered three days later. The foul smelling gases escaping the room could be detected a block away. The penis protruding from the mouth of the victim, a fitting crown for the king of nasty killings. "How far back do these killings go?" O'Connell wondered. Detectives had to start digging to find the origin of these awful killings. O'Connell was truly baffled.

"Damn it Ryan, I don't have the foggiest idea when this maniac started his spree," said O'Connell. O'Connell, one of the department's brightest minds, was always at or near the top of his class academically. At the age of five he could think logically to work out a problem. As he got older he learned Advanced Mathematics and Latin, mixed with academics, he was Middleweight bare knuckle boxing champion. His father taught him to fight and his brothers kept him sharp.

His father drunken bashing of Michael came early and often, along with the beatings passed out to his mom and brothers. As a policeman he was always ready to take a gift or a bribe. The catholic upbringing most likely kept Michaels father from killing him. At 16 enough was enough. He caught his father in a drunken stupor one evening and put a straight razor across his throat.

"Touch anyone of us again and I will make sure you sleep with the fish," he told him. The beatings stopped.

One evening it went too far and Michael emptied six shots into his father's torso, after he had beat his mother bloody. His mother confessed to the crime. His father's chief of police classified the shooting as accidental and Michael got clean away with his first murder.

TWO YEARS LATER....

"I'm taking a job in New York mother. I'm joining the Pinkerton Detective Agency," he suddenly announced one day. "I'm bored with college, I need some action in my life," said Michael. With that his quest for education was over and the law enforcement bug took a full bite out of his soul.

"I'm good at what I do," he often told his mother. He was right, but he was lousy at character judgment. He fell in love with every slut he met.

"I love you Michael", was a declaration that burned him over and over again. His integrity was unquestioned, but his weakness for woman was legendary. Blondes and stray puppies. He couldn't resist either one. "His name is Ike," Michael told detective Robinson.

"Michael, this is the third one this year," said his partner. "The dogs come looking for you, you fool," Robinson smiled. "They can't wait to get you home and poop on your floor, rub your nose in it."

O'Connell with his baggy trousers, bright colored vests, Bowler hats, fancied himself stylish. With his crooked carrot colored mustache and expensive brogans rakish wouldn't be a bad description, vain would be even better. In the manner of bankers and local gentry his obsessions for brogans was legendary. He changed girlfriends almost as often as shoes.

"Mary Dudley is a keeper Robinson," he said. "I think I will marry this one. She is a keeper, you'll see." He often failed to realize he was searching for his mother. He loved all women because they reminded him of her. All in all he was a fairly good man with a very dark side.

Complex was just the beginning. There just was no telling who Michael would be today when he woke up. It led him to a lot of lonely, empty days with sinister thoughts running thru his mind. But, the detective in him would clamp on and hold on until his case was solved, his man under arrest. He was a young Sherlock Holmes. He was very good at his job.

CHAPTER FIFTY TWO

By February 1870, May was 10 years old, June was nine, and Donald was seven. They were hyper kids that found it very hard to sit still and concentrate on learning lessons in a structured classroom. They were not stupid children, but they were slower than almost all of the kids in their class.

May and June had been placed in 3rd grade. They were just starting to learn reading skills and Donald was in the first grade and learning his A B C's. He was starting to get used to socializing with other children.

The girls still had their southern accents and sometimes the other kids would tease them because of their speech. Becoming used to school was not easy for the kids. They would tell Aunt Jo Ann about the hard time the other kids were giving them, but Jo Ann did not want to address the issue with the head mistress. With luck it would resolve itself in time. It didn't, one of

Fred competitors, John Stevens had a son that was the class bully. He was in May and Junes class.

"Hey chocolate drops you so dark you both look purple," teased Billy. "Look at your nappy hair, short, kinky, you look like monkeys," he teased. "How many lips you got? On top of that you stupid. Don't nobody understand what you are trying to say," he laughed. "My dog got more sense than you two," he joked.

"Shut up you ugly boy," June warned. "You got the brains of a brick," shouted May. "Don't make us lump your face up Billy Butthead," May barked.

Billy was 3 inches and 15 pounds heavier than the girls. It made no difference. Today they felt like scrapping. They lit into Billy like white on rice! Wild cats roaring. Two black eyes, a busted lip and a sore face later, teachers pulled the sisters off of Billy. He was terrified. The sisters were so angry they were tongue tied. Billy lied, and the sisters were suspended from school. Jo Ann brought the sisters back to school to the Head Mistress.

"How could my babies hurt that oversized gorilla?" She asked in amazement. "He could probably beat me up," she said. "This is ridiculous."

The Head Mistress hinted that a donation to the building fund would smooth things over. Jo Ann, insulted would have none of it. She told Fred, and he had his Coachman take him right over to Mr. Stevens house. It was huge sandstone and marble, manicured lawns, three large fountains, and wrought iron fences surrounded the entire property. Fred was impressed by none of it. He confronted Mr. Stevens and Mr. Stevens was flabbergasted. When he saw how small the girls were, he called Billy and chastised him right in front of the girls, took his belt off and whipped Billy right there, and made him say "I'm sorry."

Of course, after that he promised Fred he would ruin his businesses if it was "the last thing he did." And so the war was started between the Steven's and the Thomas's. It would last for two generations.

Jo Ann and Fred were expecting their first child. Fred was so exited he could hardly concentrate on business. U.S Grant was now president of the United States, and Reconstruction, economic prosperity and modern technology were in full swing. But black suffrage, freedom and equality for newly freed slaves, plus representation in federal and state legislatures was on shaky ground. Northerners wanted to make sure that the same issues that caused the war did not become a reason to fight the war all over again. In Washington feelings were mixed. There were plenty of anti - abolitionists in the city. People that smiled and said the right thing in the day light but, under cover of darkness worked to destroy everything the Union Army had fought for.

Jo Ann and her family represented everything they hated. Nobody wanted them to be treated on equal grounds with whites. Have the same jobs, go to the same schools serve on the same juries, and certainly not benefit from the same laws. Jo Ann and Fred put on their fighters gloves. "Dear Lord, I know I am coming to you a lot lately," Jo Ann whispered. "But, they have thrown bricks thru my windows. They have poisoned my horse and my birds. I am going to commit murder very soon," she said. "The stress is going to kill our baby. I can't take it much longer. Please God, just carry me a little longer. I want my child to be healthy. Please bless my baby," she pleaded.

CHAPTER
FIFTY THREE

She never made it to the hospital. With Buster prancing up and down, Fred a nervous wreck, Bertha practicing mid – wife duties, Diamond "Baby girl" Thomas was born right in the shop on the sewing table.

"Push harder chile," Bertha directed. The table was piled with towels and some soft straw from the stable next door. There was hot water from the wood stove, and extra candle light to go with the Kerosene lamps. Bertha's face was sweat drenched, and her hair was plastered to her head. Jo Ann face was etched in pain, and her hands squeezed the table for all they could give for the fifth or sixth time.

"Wah" the newborn wailed.

"Damn look at the feet on that chile," Bertha said.

"Gimme my youngun," said Fred.

"That's the prettiest baby ever came a peep hole," He grinned.

"My Valentine day gift from the man upstairs."

"Right on time. Mamas birthday," Jo Ann sighed. She layed back to rest, a smile on her face.

It was February 14, 1871, Valentine's Day, and April, Jo Ann mothers birthday.

Jo Ann and Fred started to improve their relationship with the community, and were invited to more affairs and outings after Diamond was introduced to the neighborhood, and the people living in it.

"Mama, Popa, this is Ms. Jo Ann. This is the tigers mama," little Ricky said excitedly. He was almost out of breath.

"Good to meet you," Said Mrs. Hunter, Ricky's Mama. "Every other word I hear is about your girls. I understand they are a handful."

"Ricky is a good boy," Jo Ann replied. "I think he likes my girls. They like him. It seems we can learn a lot from these children. Purple red or green, color never matters to them," Jo Ann said. "They just see a new friend."

"I'm glad you came up with the idea of clothes readymade for children. I hate sewing and I don't like passing my children clothes from one to the other," Mrs. Hunter said. "It is so easy just to ride into town and pick something out of your shop for the little ones. How did you come up with that idea?" Mrs. Hunter asked. "I heard the idea has caught on everywhere, even in the country and on the farms," Mrs. Hunter smiled. "For a few pennies I can save a lot of time. That's wonderful," she said.

Indeed, pennies sure add up. Jo Ann's clothes for children have made her the first woman millionaire in the United States and the only black one of any gender. She is famous. The sewing machine has allowed her to employ fifteen woman that sew her children dresses, shirts, britches, coats and underwear, which young people are just starting to wear on a daily basis. The railroad has enabled her to ship her clothes all over the country in a short time.

CHAPTER FIFTY FOUR

Jonathan Douglass was now just a memory. The Sgt. Douglass that received the Medal of Valor no longer existed. The ruthless, heartless, cold blooded Jonathan that lived inside of Jo Ann, at times reared his ugly head and came out to play. When that happened someone would die. Someone that violated the sense of justice instilled in Jo Ann would die viciously, and horribly. Someone that had betrayed God's law or worse Jo Ann's law. Do Unto others as you would have them do unto you. You do not violate a man because of his race, creed or gender. You don't step on a man because he is poor or uneducated. Street justice took Jonathan's place.

"Somebody's got to pay," became a mantra Jo Ann lived by. "I will cut your nuts out, slit your throat from ear to ear, pull your intestines out, punch out your eyeballs," she warned. "Do my people dirt, I'm coming," Jo Ann threatened. "Harm my brothers or sisters, you wake up on the brown side of the grass," she promised. Between 1871 and 1873,

O'Connell had eight more broken, mutilated, cut up corpses added to his case files. Each one, minus a penis. Each penis stuffed in the mouth of the victim. Each time the city held its breath and people wondered, "Whose next?" "How bad will the next one be?" "Will William be home for dinner tonight?" Under the surface of the city lived fear. Pulse pounding, cheat bumping, heart stopping, F E A R!!

"Why is he doing this?" Wondered O'Connell. "What is driving this maniac? How does he pick these people? These ain't criminals. They ain't homeless bums. They are not related. This is a sick puppy," O'Connell said. "He is going to make a mistake. He'll slip, this monster will slip. I'm just as brutal as he is. I'll wait, I'll be patient. Torture is the link. I know what it is to live in fear," said Michael. He flashed back: For Michael had a secret, one that culminated with the death of two people. No one was alive to bear witness, which served Michaels reason for entering his pursuit of a career in Law Enforcement just fine.

As he sat at his desk puzzled by the lack of leads in the investigation, his mind wandered back to the time he was a sixteen year old kid that was growing physically much faster than his mind was developing.

"Damn it boy," his father shouted. "Didn't I tell you keep your goddamn opinions to yourself, unless I asked you something. This is between me and your momma. Stay the hell out of it!" Michael tired of his dad yelling and punching on him and his mom and summoned some courage from some unseen power. "I told you, you drunken piece of shit, don't put your hands on mom again. Don't you know you broke a damn rib last time? How many times can she tell the fuckin doctor she fell?" Michael was trying to sound manly; in truth he was scared to death.

Mike Sr. Looking thru whiskey focused eyes, bellowed. "Look at you, shaking like a goddamn leaf on a tree. I should turn you upside down and beat you blue." The liquor smelling like back alley rot gut Whiskey. He Grabbed Michael by his left arm. He caught him and swung him around, landing a vicious right hand to Mikes jaw, stunning him and leaving him almost out on his feet.

At 6'1" 230 lbs. Michael's father was a lot of muscle, but mostly fat from free drinks at the many bars on his beat as a Boston cop. Fear made

Michael grab for the gun in his father's holster. He was a second faster than his dad was. Gun pressed right against the gut, Michael unloosed six shots to the stomach. The .44 Caliber bullets tore up kidney, liver, and spleen, resulting in a bloody mess. Shock still registered on his dads' ashen face. He bled out right there, the only attempt at rescue, a kick in the face from Mrs. O'Connell, after she ran in the kitchen and found Michael, pistol in hand, tears running down his face.

"Mom, I killed him, I did it and I'm not sorry. I hope he burns in hell," Mike said.

"Damn it to hell. I'm glad he's gone. I hope he went right to hell," she sobbed.

"The Irish pig," Mike replied.

"Momma, what are you going to tell the police? Momma, I don't want to go to jail. That scum of a dad wasn't worth two dead flies," remembered Michael.

"He beat me," she muttered. "What?" Questioned Michael. "He beat me," Mrs. O'Connell said, a little louder. "The bastard hit me, knocked my teeth out, busted my lips and while he was choking me by the neck I grabbed the gun and shot him," she said with a little more confidence in the scheme as it came to her.

"You don't look beat up Momma," said Michael. "What are you talking about?"

"Shut up boy and punch me in the mouth. Now!! Not tomorrow right funkin now!"

"I can't Mama," answered Michael. "I won't, you're my Momma." Pleaded Michael. "I'm not gonna hit you."

"You coward. Damn you Michael, time is running, hit me fool," she commanded.

He did four times and hard. Sweat was pouring off his face mixed with the tears streaming down his face. Ten minutes later the police were knocking at the front door of the one story house with the patch wood roof, lopsided chimney and falling down fence. Faded paint completed the derelict look of the dwelling. Mrs. O'Connell opened the door slowly in obvious pain. Black eye, busted lip, and a convincing lie coupled with Sibley Hospital records announcing six separate trips for treatment of trauma, including broken ribs, a sympathetically provided police report, and a police chief that did not want one of his own to be remembered as a wife beater. He made the murder become an accidental shooting with no changes pressed against the perpetrator.

It was this incident that let Michael know that he was capable of inflicting the ultimate punishment. It was the utter lack of remorse and the cold blooded dismissal of any emotional connection that helped Michael understand that he was not like most people. He was a killer a natural born killer. That knowledge has both served to his advantage, and scared him when he has been involved in shootings. He is obsessed with hunting this killer. “Is he a lot like me?” He wondered.

CHAPTER FIFTY FIVE

On one occasion Jo Ann was in the back of the shop going over inventory figures on the children's line. It was five minutes until closing time when to Jo Ann's surprise and the surprise of the single girl still working, Mr. Walter Myers of the Myers Railroad dynasty walked thru the front door of the store. He was alone, no coachman, no bodyguard.

The evening rather gloomy, rain clouds, lingering from early afternoon, an on and off drizzle had been falling all day, and the sun peeked out and ran back to hide behind the clouds most of the afternoon. It all brightened quickly for Jo Ann when the 5'9" 165 Lbs. Myers walked thru her shop entrance. He had salt and pepper hair, a beard trimmed rather short and also mixed with gray, a severe limp where a horse kicked him as a child, and his usual Ill fitted basic brown suit. He, had on unpolished brown brogans, suspenders held up his baggy trousers, and a tight fitting cheap cloth shirt, frayed at the collar, completed his attire. Unless you knew him you would hardly believe this man was heir to a railroad dynasty and very well off.

He had decided to surprise his wife, who was 15 years his junior, with a new gown for her birthday. Jennifer Boone, the housekeeper for the Myers family, told Ms. Downs that in a drunken rage Mr. Myers had raped her, sodomized her, punched her in the face, and knocked out two of her teeth. Face swollen she could not go to the police because she was afraid she would lose her job. Anyway she didn't think the police would do anything.

Ms. Downs told Jo Ann about Ms. Boones plight. Jo Ann was disgusted, and so ready to punish Mr. Myers immediately, that she almost committed an impulsive and foolish act of retribution. Her heart pounding in her chest, her blood boiling, she held her emotions in check and waited. Now today is her day of retribution. Myers just dropped in her lap. Jo Ann's mind hit overdrive, she unbuttoned the top two buttons of her blouse, poured a few drops of French perfume on, ran a brush thru her hair and went out to give her full attention to Mr. Myers.

"Jesus Lordy," Myers said. Spit was running out of his mouth. "You smell so good," he whaled. Spring blooming red roses invaded his senses. "Excuse my lump. This ole chicken just wakes up and rises," he said. "Your outfit is delicious. I could eat it off of you, my dear."

"Come here you naughty man," Jo Ann whispered. "Ima make you forget all about your wife." The Black Widow smiled.

"Relax Walter, just relax," purred Jo Ann. Myers was still not quite sure how he had ended up in the basement of the store with his pants around his pale white ankles.

"Oh God" he babbled. "What in the world is that you are you doing? My goodness, not right there. He wrapped both hands around Jo Ann's butt cheeks. His next move was supposed to be to shove Jo Ann onto the cutting table and mount her. All of a sudden, oops mistake #2. Like a mouse darting to safety, the tables turned.

"Oh shit! Shouted Walter. "How in the hell did you do that? Come on now you are hurting me, why you got your knee in my back? I can't feel my damn legs. Oh hell, you're going to pull my arm out of the socket," he wailed.

"Just shut up before I cut your tongue out, Myers. You think I don't know how, to use this razor? Its 12 inches and I'll cut you every way but loose. Remember Ms. Boone? That's right, your maid. The one you screwed in the ass until she bled. Well I didn't find that funny. Her swollen face or her broken arm were really not very amusing Myers. Now guess what? now it's payday." She flicked the razor within an inch of the neck artery.

It was so sharp it could cut a piece of paper in half at the flick of her wrist. She had demonstrated time and time again that she was capable of deadly results with her use of her razor. Cold sweat and mounting fear had the basement smelling like a wet dog. Myers dared not make a move, much less utter a sound. The only sound to be heard was the urine that ran thru Myers pants as it streamed down his legs. The whimper of his voice was the background singer as he begged for his life, "Please, please no."

Jo Ann finally asked, "Is this how poor Mrs. Bonne felt when you rammed your sorry prick in her backside?"

After touching him lightly with the razor and drawing just a touch of blood from Myers throat, he vomited all over the cutting table. It was like you could reach out and touch the fear coming from him. See It, smell it, feel it. Jo Ann cleanly sliced his left ear straight thru to the bone, leaving it hanging by some gristle.

"Aah, noo, no, my ear, my damn ear is gone," Myers screamed. He bucked and Jo Ann sliced open an eyeball. Blood and gore ran down Myers face. Doing a dance on his spine, Jo Ann whipped the razor across his hamstrings and immediately crippled Myers. It was then that Myers understood he was not leaving this shop alive. At the same time it dawned on him why he was being punished. Puzzled he cried out, "Why? What was she to you? I am your own kind. She is a Sambo. A monkey. Not even a real person. Why do you care about a Niggra?" He asked.

"No", Jo Ann screamed. "She is my own kind, you asshole." That was the last straw. Left, right, right, left. Four flicks of the straight edge. Blood spurting out of Myers neck like a water hose. Jo Ann had lost it. Jonathan had taken over.

Now Jo Ann wanted to know, "How can I fix this? How can I clean this up?" She wondered out loud. She knew, the chill bumps on her arms. She knew, the sweat running down her brow. She knew, her mouth so dry she couldn't swallow. Not today, not tomorrow, but soon. This was the beginning of the end. But right now she must cover up.

CHAPTER
FIFTY SIX

"I got to hurry," whispered Jo Ann. "I've got to find some way to get rid of this body," she said, realizing she was talking to herself. Panic, was seizing her mind. Sweat, combined with nervousness was talking over her body.

Jo Ann dashed upstairs to her office; she yanked the file drawers open one by one, and went quickly thru the contents. She pulled out the most important documents she would need and stuffed them in a saddle bag. She scampered back down to the dark, musty smelling basement and started pouring kerosene from the lamp that she used in her office. She doused the body and the bolts of expensive cloth & silks. She went upstairs got another lamp, and did the same thing with the steps and upstairs office.

By the time she lit the wooden match that started the fire she was exhausted and almost completely out of breath. She tripped going up the steps the last time, and a long painful splinter caught her in her hand.

"Oh shit", she shouted. "I got to get out of here. This damn place is a match box. Look at those flames. This heat is suffocating," Jo Ann yelled. "Damn it, I can't breathe. These flames are a damn inferno. This heat is gonna burn my face off," she said. No one could hear her panicked complaints. Nobody cared that she was destroying her own dream. She had changed into a simple blue calico dress, some flat black shoes, and carried the saddle bag draped over her shoulder.

"Damn lady. I'm sorry, I didn't mean to run you down." the homeless man with the one eye and scarred up face said. It was Willie.

"I'm okay," Jo Ann said. "Then a look of amazed fear came over her.

"I know you. I seen you before," the man said.

"I'm not from around here. You got to be mistaken," Jo Ann slurred the words. Not convinced, the man stared hard at Jo Ann. He was trying to recall.

"It's gonna come to me. I ain't wrong. It's on the tip of my tongue," said the man.

This was the man Jo Ann took a pistol to when she almost caught Booth after the Lincoln assassination. This was the man in the alley holding Booth's horse. Jo Ann had lost it and damn near beat him to death. Now she remembered!

As the flames from the store finally leaped into the alley, the bum turned his attention to the fire.

"Oh shit," he cried. "Look at that fire! I got to get some help. I got to go now."

"Hurry," Jo Ann hollered. "Hurry, before someone gets hurt." And with that she dashed out of the alley. She was praying the man would not recognize her face. After all, that night she was Sgt. Jonathan Douglass!

"Oh Hell, a body." The fireman had tripped and damn near broke his neck. "Call O'Connell man, this here shop belongs to the Thomas woman. I hope it aint somebody works for her," he said. A call to O'Connell sent him hurrying to the Thomas house. Introducing himself to the maid, the woman of interest, Jo Ann had the maid serve O'Connell black coffee. Detective O'Connell waited another ten minutes before Jo Ann appeared.

"My goodness you look so very young to be a detective," said Jo Ann as she opened up the chess game of the minds.

"As do you," parried O'Connell. "Your pictures in the society pages hardly do you justice. I thought the maid had summoned your daughter by mistake," said O'Connell. He flashed his perfect smile.

"Aha, a charmer," laughed Jo Ann. She tried her damndest to present a calm relaxed matron. The way she dug her finger nails into her palm and bumped her knee against the antique desk said otherwise.

"You give me too much credit," said O'Connell. "I'm just doing my duty as I should and you happen to be the target of my mission this morning.

"An official visit. My God who did I murder? Replied Jo Ann. She was only half joking. Suddenly she felt light headed.

"I just stopped by to ask you if any of your employees have been missing? An unidentified body was found in the rubble at your store. From the looks of it the man was there when the fire started," O'Connell informed Jo Ann. The body was charred and burned so bad we can't tell who it is yet. "I thought you might need help," he said.

"Now that you asked, Mr. Brown, Randolph Brown, my cleaning man. After I closed the shop, he could have been there. Tuesday was his time to work, but I thought he came in saw the fire and left. God I hope it wasn't him. He is a good man. Just a little down on his luck," Jo Ann said almost in a whisper. She swooned slightly and grabbed the desk. "He was homeless. Didn't have a real place to stay," her voice was now a bit shaky.

"Well let's hope it's not him," said Michael.

"Sometimes he sleeps in the basement if the weather is bad," said Jo Ann. "I'll send someone to look for him," she said.

"That's kind of you but that's my job," said O'Connell.

They went back and forth for ten minutes. They speculated that the motive was sympathizers for the southern cause, mad at Jo Ann's success, wanting, to teach her a lesson. Maybe even scare her off. Being married to Fred Douglass Thomas did help a little. So far now Jo Ann was in the clear. The heinous murder and the torching of the store, was not yet laid in her lap. But what about the many people that depended on her to eat? All the needy, humble hard working people now would have to scrap and claw just to feed their families. There would be families that would struggle, without their weekly pay. She thought of all the families that would have to go without. What would they do next?

"I'll try to help Ms. Downs, and Mary Rose and Chester Brown as much as I can," Jo Ann answered her own question.

Meanwhile, Jo Ann was now newly pregnant and Fred was fat. With a new contract for his company, he had decided to take some time off. Bone tired and weary from driving himself really hard, he went home to relax for a time.

"You have the most beautiful eyes I have ever known God to put in woman," Fred pronounced. He was stroking Jo Ann's full rounded breasts, while looking straight into those eyes that were like magnets.

"Never, ever leave. You've got to put up with me a long, long time," Jo Ann teased.

"No, baby between you and Diamond I can't decide why God made me such a blessed man," Fred said, a serious look on his face.

This was the most time in a while that Fred had spent with his family. It was a lot dealing with the pressure of the times, the reconstruction efforts and the knowledge that vicious, ruthless people were still fighting the war between the states. They still hated with a passion what they thought of as mixed marriages. Night Riders, the new terrorist group, Klu Klux Klan was wrecking property and taking lives almost on a nightly basis. Fred was acutely aware of many problems.

Jo Ann and Fred, had a chance to enjoy Buster, still the loyal family dog. Asa “blue” was the spitting image of Edward, but Fred loved him too, but his heart was still diamond. The neighbors liked the children, including Jo Ann’s sister, Jane. The family was growing rapidly, so it was close to time to move again.

CHAPTER FIFTY SEVEN

"I'm really excited sir," said David Jones vice president for building projects.

"I can understand why Dave," said Fred. "You have made me proud. This so called reconstruction is almost over," he said. "I told Grant last week that we need to be expanding all over the west since our railroad is now joining the eastern part of the country with the west. There is no limit to where a man can settle and call home." Fred pondered, "Now we can become the greatest country on Earth. There is no limit to what we can do and how we can grow."

David said, "It's amazing. We have a Negro in congress, from Mississippi no less," (Hiram Revels) "Ole Jeff Davis must be having a shit fit with a nigger sitting in his seat. They can vote, and even the Klan is being challenged now," said Jones.

"All because our railroad has united the nation. People can migrate now," said Fred. "Time ain't no issue and mail is cheaper than the Pony

Express, or stage coach. Now we can concentrate on engines," said Fred.

"Grant loves us again," Fred boasted. "The president told me last week he is changing his policy about the Indians," Fred explained. "He realizes now he does not have enough troops to wipe out the whole Indian population. Now he is trying to drive them on to reservations, and keep them, contained there. That's going to mean a whole lot of lies and broken promises to those people. By the time this is finished they will hate every white man on earth," Fred warned. "I wish he would come up with a better plan," Fred sighed. "This one stinks to high heaven. The Republicans were known as the anti-slavery party and right now they are very popular. They also were the party the working class preferred. The 1860's and 70's were good times for them." But graft and corruption brought the party down and a panic in the 70's, turned the country around.

Jo Ann, a ruthless, bi-polar, multiple personality, went thru several changes during this time. She was as complicated as her mental condition-both Angel and Demon. She got pregnant again, this time with twins. Her personality was all over the place. Calm one day, a roaring raging bull the next. Eyes big as saucers and paranoia attacking from all sides at 12:00. By 4:00 she would be taking the kids on an outing to the park. She would jump on of her staff with both feet one day. Have flowers for the same staff member the next day, and give them the day off. Clara Downs watched and prayed she wasn't losing her mind like Mrs. Lincoln. She was really worried about her friend.

"Mind your own business Clara," Jo Ann would tell her. "You are not my doctor. I pay him good to look after me," Jo Ann would say.

Only Ms. Downs knew for sure. "Jo Ann doesn't even have a personal doctor," she would say. "She told me more than once. I don't trust quacks to play with my mind or my health. I talk to my lord. The woman is going batty," she would tell her close friends. "Jo Ann is two people, and both of them are driving me nuts!"

While searching thru the alley in the back of Jo Ann's burned down shop, a small homeless man stumbled up to detective O'Connell and begged for the price of a drink.

“Please get lost man. Don’t you see I’m busy,” O’Connell said.

“If you knew what I know about Ms. High and mighty, you wouldn’t be talking to me like that,” Willie said. “I could solve your case in about five minutes, but no, you want to treat me like a dog. That is why ole Willie never helps the police. You treat me like dirt on your boots.”

One minute from breaking his case wide open, O’Connell let Willie get away. The biggest case in the history of Washington. The most sadistic, ruthless, most heinous killings in the city’s history, and O’Connell let Willie stroll right out of his life. For the price of a bowl of beef stew or some rot gut whiskey, O’Connell could have burst his case open and had a promotion next week.

CHAPTER FIFTY EIGHT

In the spring of 1874, March 13 to be exact, Miles and Noah Thomas came kicking and screaming into the world. Noah came twenty minutes after Miles. Both were healthy, curious kids, right out of the womb. Asa considered himself, one step from a grown up now and all he wondered about day and night was the process that produced his twin brothers.

"Pop, what did you do to get Miles and Noah here?" He kept asking his step-father. "Tell me where they came from? Randolph says a man and a woman lie down together and hug and bingo a baby is born. That doesn't make sense. Mom hugs me all the time and nothing. There's got to more. What is it? I want a son too. Who can I hug?" Asa wouldn't turn loose. Diamond appointed herself junior mom. She was the protector and took her job seriously. Buster watched over everyone. He loved the whole household. The family now lived in Foggy bottom and was counted among

Washington most well to do families. They counted James Wormley as one of their neighbors and he was among the wealthiest Negro's in Washington.

The shop was in its final stages of being rebuilt and the store was bigger and had a better location than the first one. Right up the street from the White House, it was magnificent. It had a place for children's clothes to be displayed, the first of its kind anywhere.

TWO WEEKS LATEER...

The loyal dog Buster died. "I'm going to miss my baby Fred," lamented Jo Ann.

"My head hurts, my heart is heavy. I feel so sad. I cried all day. I miss him already. It's like a dark cloud is hanging over my head. I know he couldn't live forever, but I feel like I lost one of my babies, I hurt so bad my stomach has a hole in it. Buster, I love you so much," Jo Ann sobbed.

"Stop it Jo Ann, please stop," cried Fred. He had his own favorite Buster moments. "How can I feel so hurt about a dog? Man, he was the best damn dog God ever created. The kids are crying like one of us died today," Fred was truly grieving. Buster touched him like nothing he had ever known. People that didn't have a dog to love would never begin to understand the pain the family was feeling.

July 21, 1874 Buster was laid to rest. "Bless you Buster," whispered Jo Ann. Jo Ann tried to handle the emptiness and burning hole that ran right through her soul caused by the loss of Buster, the love of her life. She prayed, she walked 5 miles a day, causing her legs to feel heavy, and the sweat to roll down her brow. She stopped fighting the compulsive craving; the urge that consumed her mind had won. She rose, walked quickly and silently thru the house. She eased down the steps, stepped out of door into the cool, breezy, starless night. Her eyes blazing with her hand wrapped tightly around her razor, she slowly and deliberately walked down the mud coved avenue, into the night. She was searching for the tavern she knew would yield her target for extinction. A victim to feed the thirst, the hunger she knew had to be satisfied. It must be fed for to her to end her grief.

His name was Harry Dunbar. The offense; a man whose sole duty in life was to make sure the Indians that had been shuttled to reservations, the people whose land we swindled, and stole, had food, clothing, blankets and supplies to survive. He chose to steal these funds. He chose to add insult to injury. He fed his greed and uncaring nature with the monies intended for native people. The maggots in the corn meal, the worms in the feed, the stench of the rotten spoiled meat was all due to thievery, he stole from the downtrodden Redman. Now it was time to pay the piper. Jonathan/Jo Ann's wrath was the pay masters payment and would be delivered tonight.

President Grant was indifferent to the corruption. Jo Ann was not. She spied on Mr. Dunbar, she followed him to the outhouse in the back of his local drinking hole. "I got you, bastard," she whispered. "Tonight is your last," she promised. She creped silently to the outhouse, while Jonathan possessed her body. Harry Dunbar could not imagine death coming for him, not for the self Important Harry Dunbar!

Dunbar had just come off of his fishing boat, an over equipped relic that served as a warped, dank smelling, floating bar for Dunbar and his buddies.

"Man let's mosey on over to Hank's," Dunbar said. "Some ole husk buddies (clams), a few slime balls, (oysters) an a belt of corn will do me justice."

"Damn right" Bud Wentworth agreed. He was a crator faced confederate sympathizer that spent the war ducking the fight.

"Damn, that jacket stinks Bud." Dunbar slurred. "Smells like that ole niggra that cleans my outhouse." They both laughed and joked about cruelties an abuses they had inflicted on others. (Black and White)

"Gotta pay my water bill. Be right back," said Dunbar.

Jonathan/Jo Ann is waiting out back for Dunbar to use the outhouse. He is out of sight, hat pulled down low, fishing gear on and black fisherman's booths on feet. Finally Dunbar heads to the outhouse. Jo Ann steps right behind him, rubs a chloroform filled rag across Dunbar's face and catches him before he collapses to the ground. He drags him into the nearby woods onto a sling fitted behind a trail horse. Once far enough away not to be noticed Jonathan stops, ties the body tight on the canvas, muffles Dunbar mouth and continues the ride into the countryside. A cave Jo Ann discovered years ago serves as the perfect place to deposit Dunbar's unconscious form.

"Where in the hell am I, and who in blazes are you?" Dunbar demands to know when he wakes up. "Do you know who the hell I am?" Dunbar said. "Do you know what you have done? I'll have your ass for this boy. You'll hang from the tallest tree I can find." He promised.

It was after an insect stung him on his backside that he realized he was butter ball naked. "What the? Where are my damn clothes?" He asked. "Why is my leg tied to this tree stump? Untie my hands you fool. The games have gone on long enough," Dunbar yelled.

At that Jonathan started to read in a low menacing voice from a paper in his hand. Delivery date, name of a tribe, reservation location and what they were supposed to receive. Every time he would whisper, "Delivery short," Jonathan would administer five lashes with the bull whip. When the lash count rose to fifty Dunbar's skin was flayed, his body was bloodied and he was barely conscious. Of course that is when Jonathan took a break.

After pouring cayenne pepper on the wounds, the screams could be heard for a half mile away. Of course that was before Jonathan decided to pry Dunbar's fingernails and toenails off one by one. Each nail representing the name of a chief. Mr. Dunbar passed out completely.

Forty minutes later he came to again. "Jesus no, oh God please," he croaked. A 12 inch straight razor smiled at Dunbar like new money. His tears came when he felt the urine running down his legs. His bowels broke when Jonathan nicked his penis ever so slightly. He actually begged to be killed. The fear was too much to bear. The man helped exterminate whole Indian nations his suffering had to be special.

"Not my eyes, please not my ... Aah," As one eyeball was plucked out with a pen knife. "Here let me get this for you," Jonathan said, as he sliced the penis clean off with two strokes. Dunbar twitched, humped the ground three or four times and bled out. Of course it was fitting that he wear the penis between the lips. They call it poetic justice, now Jonathan could rest. Busters death was avenged and Jo Ann could grieve easier. Amen.

CHAPTER FIFTY NINE

On August 10, 1874 Jo Ann received a telegraph message from Willow that asked her to come to Grand Harvest as soon as possible. She set right out and her driver, pushing the pair of drays as hard as he could, made it to Grand Harvest the following even. Sore, stiff, dry mouthed and irritable, Jo Ann found the family gathered in the smoking parlor and talking in hushed tones as if a funeral was afoot. Master John had suffered a stroke. His entire left side was crippled, he could barely speak, and his doctor had already requested the priest be summoned to give the last rites.

"Well Zack the years have been good to you", Jo Ann told him. "You must be like a magnet to the women. You have grown up Zack. You have been up and down the whole east coast and you have become famous, I keep hearing your name like you saved the whole navy all by yourself. I'm really, really proud of you Zack," Jo Ann said.

"How sick is he?" Asked Jo Ann. "Will he make it until tomorrow?" Questioned Jo.

"The priest is on the way from town," said Zack. "The ole man ain't scared. He just got religion since you been gone and he want to be blessed, before he closes his eyes for the last time."

Thinking hard and feeling kind of guilty Jo Ann wondered if John 'Getting religion' had anything to do with her almost blowing his head off when she fired and jerked her shot in the air.

"I feel a little spirit filled myself sometimes. I think the older we get the closer we feel to God Zack," said Jo Ann. "You know you have matured into a very handsome old man," she joked. "What are you 6'1" 6'2"? Got to be a solid 200 or so. I really like you better with a beard. My goodness, five medals? Did you win the war by yourself?" She teased. "I'm so proud of you Zack. You still got the deepest dimples in Dorchester County boy," Jo Ann smiled and kissed him.

"Thank you, Jo or now should I say Sis? Yeah, the old man fessed up," Zack admitted. "I damn near had a Heart Attack when he told me," teased Zack. "Always wondered why he was so easy on Ms. April. The crazy fuck was in love with two women," Acknowledged Zack. "Just tell me Jo. Did you know?" Asked Zack "Was I the only blind bat in this family? I'd feel a lot better knowing the truth," he said.

"You weren't the only one Zack," Jo replied. "When I heard it the first time, I damn near made you an orphan," she whispered. "I almost shot master John out back in the barn," she said. "I came this close," she held up two fingers.

"What stopped you sis?" Asked Zack.

"I realized that all these years, he was the only one besides you that treated me with respect," Jo Ann had a tear in her eye. "Sometimes, I even thought I was special to him," remembered Jo Ann. Zack was on the verge of hugging Jo Ann when Willow burst through door, spoiling the mood.

"Jo Ann, my Jo, damn have I missed you," sang Willow.

"Girl, you are a sight for sore eyes," said Willow.

Jo Ann fell into Willows embrace, it was obvious to everyone, Willow loved Jo Ann. She almost squeezed the life out of her. Tears were flowing like Niagara Falls. For her part June was crying too, and really happy to see Jo Ann. Too many years had passed. The girls really had special feelings for each other. They missed talking and keeping secrets, sharing adventures, and stories of forbidden love affairs as kids. Zack just watched, for the very first time he realized what he had missed growing up. He understood that his misguided youth made him miss out on sibling love and he could never get those years back. A lump settled in his throat. He really loved these girls, all of them.

"My God Jo. I heard you are rich. Is it really true?" Asked Willow.

"Unfortunately yes," answered Jo Ann. "It is a rope around my neck that you never want to have, Willow," she replied. "Sometimes I wish I was back here with Ms. Lizzy, April, and master John," Jo Ann said. "Money is overrated," she laughed.

Everyone was proud of Jo Ann. "Meat Ball," said Zack. He used Jo Ann's nickname as a child. "We need to talk. Poppa may not be with us much longer. He wants us all together upstairs. He's got something to get off his chest. Let's go see what it Is," Zack said.

They all trod up the stairs. They circled Johns' bed, and waited for the doctor to finish his ministrations. John smiled when he saw all of them together.

"Lizzy would be so happy," John began. He looked at Jo Ann. "April too," he said "I'm sorry for your daddy," he said to Jo Ann. "God knows I'm sorry. I was scared my Lizzy was in love with Jasper, and I was awful jealous, that's right, me." , said John. "I don't know if I am your poppa or if Jasper was. I will go to my grave not knowing. I know you will hate me. I can't fix what was done. I can't change who I am." Then John made up his mind. Tears were flowing down Jo Ann's face. This girl that John loved in his own special way. "As God is my witness. I swear to you on my children," he lied. "I didn't kill your poppa. I did a lot of things in my life, but I didn't do that. Forgive me all of you. But I loved you all in my own way," John said.

"Thank you poppa," Jo Ann said. "Thank you." As she held his hand he coughed one time. He smiled at her touch. He looked Zack in the eyes. Tears started to flow lightly. "I'm so sorry son," he whispered, his eyes closed, faced relaxed. He passed on to glory. John Douglass was gone. "Now he belongs to the Lord," Willow said.

CHAPTER SIXTY

After visiting and reminiscing for the rest of the day. The family caught up on current events and each other families, and exchanged plans for the future. As Jo Ann strolled around the Grand Harvest grounds, she thought about all she had seen and all she had been thru on this land.

"I remember Brutus McCoy with his branding iron, and the day he burned the letters GH on Uncle Lucas back," she cringed. "Those men that took Jody out back and chopped his foot off for going into town to buy Ms. Lizzy a store bought dress for her birthday." She thought some more. "Master John working us three days without rest to get crop into harvest, because he thought the rains were coming. Julius fell out dead on the second day, and Aunt Mary had a sun stroke and never walked again," she said. "Little Jimmy running out of the barn after that stinkin Brutus raped him and burst his bowels open. All that bleeding. How many young boys did he do that to? Seven? Ten? Who knew? Alfi May watching while they took that long knife and cut Mr. Daniels thing off so that they couldn't have no more young guns," she said. "See you thought cause you had me keep Willow company and let my momma wait on the white folks in the big house that I didn't feel none of this evil, but I felt all of it. I filed it away. I never forgot. You all did okay by April, Hattie and me, but my people, my people you wronged. Master John was better than most, but you all still his children. You my brother and you all my sisters, but I ain't sure I need to lay by you in my afterlife. I just ain't sure. You got a lot to ask the Lord to forgive you for," Jo Ann whispered. "Besides, there are ten other slave girls that could be buried in this here family cemetery. Master John was daddy to all of them."

The memory of bondage ran long and ran deep. It hurt like a knife wound. Willow, June and Zack did not know what to say. They were speechless.

BACK AT THE HOUSE IN WASHINGTON...

Asa was going thru a crisis; the ugly word was he was black balled. He was cast out of the family. "Blue" was a bastard child, with no connection to a father. As far as the Kelly's were concerned, he was mixed race. He had black blood. As for his Blue blood relatives, Jo Ann said fine, "You are all dead to me, I don't need you for anything, ever," This was just one more reason for Jo Ann to work hard.

"I want to go over these investments one more time Mr. Johnson," Jo Ann instructed. She was talking to her banker. Fred had guided her to start putting money into railroad stock and oil companies. It was paying off handsomely. "I'm up when most people are still sleep," she said. "I've got to make sure my babies will be okay." Jo Ann still had her causes. She tried to help the freedman Bureau, and the Indian people. It wasn't too long ago she slept on a hard dirt floor, and shared rags with ten people herself.

The civil war was still fresh in her mind. The cruelty that men did to other men, the horror of Andersonville Prison, the maggots in the food, rats that you caught, and ate. Roaches and insects sleeping with you. Malaria, small pox, food poisoning, drinking water from streams filled with feces. Night Riders, lynching's and killings ordered by white folks who hate you cause you got darker skin than they do. There were people who ran your children over with horses. They raped your daughters and they spit on you, all in the name of God.

The times were still dangerous and the hardships were many. But, Negros were not just taking it lying down. "If you hurt me or mines mister, I'm coming. I know you may kill me one day, but I'm not teaching mine to lie down," Jo Ann promised. Even Fred, not a violent man by nature, drew a line in the dirt at his children. Not a coward, he would kill for his family, his loyalty to his family was paramount!

"I worry about my twins sometime," Jo Ann once told Clara. 'They are little tigers. Get the blood boiling and they are warriors like 'Crazy Horse' or 'Geronimo'. Blue sometimes is scared of them, and he's their brother," Jo Ann bragged proudly.

CHAPTER
SIXTY ONE

THE KELLY'S CAME TO SEE HER...

The Kelly's came to see her. Now that she had kept the Kelly's waiting over an hour she turned her attention to the family that had turned their back on her.

Jo Ann was shocked when she walked in the parlor of the house, Mr. Kelly stooped over, looked to be 125 lbs. at most. Hair mixed gray, overalls with a hole in the knee, and two buttons missing. His flannel shirt did not look washed, and certainly did not smell like it. His scuffed brown boots appeared run over at the heels. A walking cane was made from the branch of an oak tree. His fingernails were chipped, and dirty.

Mrs. Kelly had a burlap sack for a dress; her wrinkled face had dark circles around the eyes, and bags under them. She appeared that a battle with corn liquor had been lost a couple of years ago.

After the shock wore off Jo Ann greeted the couple coldly, and got right to the point.

"What brings you here?" Jo Ann asked. "The last time I saw you, you told me that hell would freeze over before you graced me with your presence. If I quote you correctly," she said.

"What are you doing here? She asked. Obviously ashamed, Mr. Kelly explained. "Our fortunes have changed? Mrs. Douglass," he began. "My holdings have dwindled to 15 acres of land. I won't waste your time explaining how that happened. But that is the long and the short of it," Mr. Kelly said. Mrs. Kelly almost on cue, burst into tears. Her wailing, screechy cry echoed thru the parlor. An embarrassed Mr. Kelly continued, "The bank has foreclosed. My very house is endangered. Have mercy, Mrs. Thomas. I have nowhere else to turn. I need a loan please, dear lady. I will pay it back with interest. Surely you would not see Edward's son's grandparents out on the field? Surely the kinship we share is worth something?" Mrs. Kelly chimed in. "I think of little Astor all the time," she lied. "I am ashamed of what we said in such haste."

If they weren't so pitiful, Jo Ann would have doubled over in laughter. "Asa, his name is Asa," Jo Ann corrected. "This grandson of yours that you wouldn't know if he stood right before you," Jo Ann replied. "Jane go get your nephew," Jo Ann hollered thru the door. "Go get him right this minute," Jo Ann said. Jo Ann was furious. Her blood was boiling. Jonathan was trying to push his way to the surface. Jo Ann fought to keep him away. He was on the verge of a appearance! It would be bloody and ugly if he appeared. Asa saved the day.

"Yes mama? He said as he entered the parlor.

"Asa these are your grandparent's Jo Ann proclaimed, and for the next half hour the story poured out. Asa, both fascinated, and appalled, angry and hurt.

"They need money," Jo Ann explained finally. "And you my son have the final say," Jo Ann said. "Your answer will determine their fate. Do they sleep in the street or not? What say you?" She asked. "They black balled you," she said "In my mind they are dead." While she was talking, Mr. Kelly kept staring at Asa. This boy looked like Edwards twin.

It was impossible to deny this was his grandson. He started thinking about how much he had missed. A tear was falling from his eye. He was heartbroken. Asa, having the heart of his father, understood only that these people would have nowhere to stay, no place to eat or sleep.

"Give them money, mama" he said. 'I never want to see you again," Asa said. "Have a safe trip back home. Go plant your corn and pick your potatoes," Asa yelled. "When you think about me, I hope it makes you sick to the stomach. Stay out of my life forever," Asa demanded.

Within two years time, Mr. Robert James Kelly would be dead, a victim of suicide. He would hang himself one dark dreary night, from the cross beam in the barn of his farm. He left a suicide note addressed to Asa... man plans, God laughs, who when notified, refused to accept it or allow it to be read to him.

CHAPTER
SIXTY TWO

December 25, 1874, was icy cold, windy and the temperature around minus five degrees when midnight rolled around. Christmas lights everywhere, but holiday cheer was not quite awake yet in New York City. Fred Thomas was standing in the short line at Penn Central Railroad Station, and was about to board. He was headed home to Washington, DC from a combination business meeting and investigation. The Klu Klux Klan was expanding in the southern states, especially Mississippi. President Grant was determined to do something about it. He appointed Fred as chairman of the committee investigating the violence that was happening.

Fred had just closed a deal that would add 100 miles of track to the expansion of the railroad going west. It would make him one of the largest stockholders in American Railroads. Soon his wealth would rival Vanderbilt's and Mellon's. He had promised Jo Ann that he would be home for Christmas Day. He would open presents, and eat

Christmas dinner. Last year he had missed it. So here he was catching the midnight express, instead of lying on a feathered bed in a fancy hotel. A promise was a promise. If he had to walk he was going to make it home this year.

"Will we make it to Washington on time James?" Asked Fred.

"Looks like it sir," answered James, the conductor.

"Tracks all clear? No ice or delays?" Fred questioned.

"Far as I know sir," replied James, "all clear, no negative reports sir," James answered.

"Take me home than. Fast as you can, get me there," asked Fred. At the next to last stop on the rails, Joe Hardy, a 10 year vet with the railroad, was ready to go home. Joe worked 2:00 P.M to 12:00 A.m. He made sure all the switching equipment was working. At 11:45 P.M his wife pulled up in the buggy to pick him up. Joe had a couple more Christmas toys to put together, so his babies could enjoy the holiday. It was bitter cold and he had checked the equipment an hour ago.

"Oh hell, I can skip this last one," Joe said. "Ain't nothing changed in an hour. I'm outta here."

Bonnie yelled, "com'n hot cakes, let's go."

"Merry Christmas y'all," Joe hollered. "See everybody tomorrow." Joe rolled out of the switchyard. Robert, his replacement, rolled into the yard, signed in, felt the freezing cold, and parked in the switch yard office. He sat next to the firewood heated stove, and didn't move. A swig of Knotty Head Gin fortified him, and an hour later he was sleep. The switch mechanism was barreling down the tracks. It had an appointment with destiny.

CHAPTER
SIXTY THREE

Four hours later the train came within view of the switch light. The light was green. Everything was a go. Before the engineer realized the switch was stuck open, the locomotive ran clean off the track.

"Oh shit!" "The engineer cried. "This can't be happening!" He yelled. The first seven cars ran off the tracks.

"We're tumbling, damn it! We're flying," a passenger screamed.

"What in the world?" Another questioned, before his car jack knifed. A chorus of yells and cuss words filled the cars. Bodies flying, glass breaking, metal twisting, flames igniting. A crash worthy of a scene from hell. Fred and 85 other passengers were tossed, thrown, crushed and trapped in a burning inferno! Fred's car was up front. They caught the worst of the damage.

"Ah, I'm hurt," Fred yelled. 'Help me, I can't move. I can't move my legs." He had been crushed between 2 seats, and his spine was snapped, leaving his legs numb and leaving Fred helpless. Broken glass lodged in his face, and his broken ribs were close to a collapsed lung.

After a touch & go rescue that took over 2 hours, he felt the bitter cold air on his face. He realized he hadn't hit heavens gates yet. But, he knew he was seriously hurt. Christmas in Washington was not to be. Singed hair, smoking eyebrows, chest burning and lungs filled with smoke, they finally dragged Fred to safety. It was three hours after the wreck when the doctor in the hospital first had a look at Fred's train wrecked body. The conductor and a few others knew exactly who Fred was, and a messenger was dispatched to alert his family.

Dawn was beginning to rise when Jo Ann sleepily answered the door.

"Merry X-Mas sir. To what do I owe this visit?" Jo Ann asked, sleep still in her voice.

"Mrs. Thomas your husband has been in a train wreck. He is in the hospital in prince Georges General. I have no idea about his condition. I was told to bring you to him as soon possible. Can we hurry ma'am? I don't know anything else except they are calling for you." He said.

"Oh God. Give me a few minutes. I'll be right back! Please just a few minutes. Jane, hurry. Get down here now. I've got to hurry," she screamed. "It's Fred. He's hurt I've got to run Jane my God, a train wreck!" She hurried up the steps, threw Wing some clothes on and tossed a heavy winter coat and hat on. She didn't even wash up.

In a short time, she was on her way to the hospital. It was a frantic dash to the bedside that was lost in time to worry and fret. Sweating and panicked, she finally arrived at the hospital. She spoke to the attending doctor who explained, "Your husband will be stitched up to stop the bleeding. He may lose one or two fingers, and he is paralyzed. He has no feeling in his legs now. I have given him Morphine, and tried to keep the infection from setting in. I will do what I can. But, I can promise you nothing." The doctor said. "Let God have his say," he suggested.

Remember, medicine and the practice of it, improved a lot because of the civil war. Surgery, cleanliness, new medicines, all of these thru trial and error, got better. Fred was in good hands. God got the rest. It was 1874 and now medicine had made much progress. So now injuries were not always fatal.

Jo Ann waited and prayed. Fred was hurt badly, but he would not die.

"Fight Fred," pushed Jo Ann. "I love you," she whispered to him. "Fight for your life. Don't die on me man. You better not die. We need you!" She pleaded.

Fight he did. Like the warrior he was. Injured, but fighting, he pulled thru. It was a month long battle. Touch and go, sometimes. Fred won. He did not regain the use of his legs, but death passed him by.

CHAPTER
SIXTY FOUR

Fred woke up to find himself surrounded by love. Jo Ann and the children were there. "My mouth feels like the desert," were his first words. "Damn, what year is it?" He asked. "I decided to come home for Christmas. "Now I'm a little late, huh?" Fred joked.

"You silly fool," Jo Ann replied. "You are a month late." Man plans, God laughs.

It is January, 1875, and the door has been kicked in on America. The centennial year was fast approaching, and America was a mixture of political statements and realities. Blacks, Indians, Asians and women were not a part of the political process. They were pretty much left out. Still, as our country prepared for its 100th birthday, the north and south remained separated and segregated. The north was money driven and technology based. The south was stuck in the old southern ideals and principles. People were migrating.

The white man, most people called Carpet Baggers, was buying land up cheaply, and trying to come up with schemes and ideas to put the land to use, Education and literacy hardly played a part in it. The southern lifestyle of the 1870's didn't have a promising outlook of what the future looked like 20, 40, 60, 80 or 100 years from now. Political corruption and graft was widespread everywhere, and political machines like Boss Tweed and Tammany wall in New York got rich as they got more greedy. State after southern state adopted "Home Rule," meaning white supremacy.

Even though Hiram Revels became the first black man elected to congress. He took Jefferson Davis, the confederate's states first and only president, Mississippi senate seat. After him, black man Blanche Bruce, also of Mississippi. No one could for see that no black men, would serve in the senate for the next 90 years.

Like Jo Ann's use of the sewing machine to help her amass her fortune, new inventions were helping ordinary citizens become wealthy. It was the age of invention and innovation. In the north it was all about the dollar bill.

Jo Ann was now 4 month's pregnant. She now had to prepare for an additional mouth to feed, and learn how to run her husband's Corporation due to his disabilities. She was stepping into the shoes of one of America's richest men. This was unheard of in America, had never been done! No man of consequence was used to taking orders in a large company from a woman.

"Woman is slick as wagon grease," Vanderbuit said. Said she wasn't very good at theses man things. Like to stole my britches right off my bottom," he cried

"I told you don't sit across the table from her," Jay Gould the tycoon laughed. "She had me wrapped around that sexy voice of hers. Spit me out for breakfast. My ass is still sore." She turned most of her attention to Fred's business.

"I can't believe this," Dorothy gushed upon seeing the revamped parlor. Clara said, " Mrs. Thomas has given me complete authority to run the shop, Mary." She still hadn't gotten used to it.

"I was so nervous yesterday I almost peed my dress," she said. "Half of the staff has gone with her to run the company. I get to hire my own people," she said.

"I love her," said Blanche. Another woman given huge responsibility. "I'll never let her down.

Never," she said. "I'd work here for free. I love this job."

"Mrs. Jo Ann, is going up against the biggest names in America and holding her own. She is amazing," said Edith.

Clara Downs not only was in charge of the shop, she was a black woman in charge. In bidding wars Jo Ann had undercut Vanderbilt twice and won railway right of ways that added to the company's bottom line and would provide a nice return on investment.

CHAPTER SIXTY FIVE

Terrell Thomas was born May 14, 1875 in Washington General.

"Come on Jo Ann, come on, that's right push," said the doctor.

"Ahh, my God, what is it, a whale," Jo Ann screamed.

"Oh no, nothing is that big," she yelled. "It hurts. I'm going to die. Both of will pass!"

"One more push," the doctor instructed. "Come on Jo Ann, once more." She arched her back, grunted, and a baby boy slid into Dr. Dolan's hands.

"It's a boy. My goodness, look at that head," doc said.

Jo Ann was troubled with a lot of bleeding during this pregnancy. But in 6 day's she was back to work. She walked tenderly, and nick named Terrell "Tough man." Willies widow, Bertha had taken over the raising of the children. She was a God send. Jo Ann was a TENDER MOTHER THAT LOVED HER CHILDREN DEARLY. But Jonathan was lurking in the background. He was not gone. There were times when he was right there, ready to spring out.

Jonathan reared his ugly head just once during this time. He caught A Klu Klux Klan officer in town for a convention of law enforcement officers from different parts of the country. He was from Tennessee, Nashville. He tarred and feathered a young Negro boy, and hung him by the neck until dead, one night, for the offense of drinking from the white man's water trough, in town on a Saturday morning. He was arrested, convicted, and lynched. Jethro Hopkins boasted of his exploits to the local newspaper reporter, who snapped his picture, and put it on the front page of the paper.

Jo Ann, rather Jonathan took care to torture him slowly. It took four hours before this white supremacy passed on to his marker. The manner of his death, too gruesome to recount. He was beaten and tortured until death was a welcomed relief.

"Good riddance you sadist," Jo Ann bidded him in death, his body still twitching.

"Your right ear took two slices and your eyeball would not come out. I'll have to get new tools," she said. "Your tongue was a tough one, and your pathetic little dick took two whacks. I will fix that the next time. The work was quite sloppy," with that she departed, and let the ants and snakes finish their jobs. Blood was everywhere, and she was quite exhausted.

IN THE MEANTIME O'CONNELL WAS PERSISTANT...

"I know I need to go back to the alley. I missed something there, and I know it is right under my nose," O'Connell tracked the trail left by the arson, and kept coming up with nothing. But there was something there that kept bringing him back.

One day he ran into Willie, the bum in the alley that kept jogging his memory. Willie told him again that he knew something about the lady. Something about the lady that owned the store that burned down. O'Connell started to go back to the beginning. "Let me dig up the facts about Jo Ann Douglass Thomas. Let's start with my friend Allen Pinkerton. He can find out about this mysterious woman who is talking the business world by storm. Who is she? Where does she come from? What makes her tick?"

O'Connell just let Willie walk with him through Baptist alley and talk while he recounted the evening of the fire. Baptist Alley is where the assassin of President Lincoln made his famous escape from Fords Theater after shooting President Lincoln in the head with a 44 caliber derringer. He escaped from 10th street, to F Street and made it to the Potomac, (now the Anacostia River Crossing). The now famous 11th street bridge. Back then the Navy Yard Bridge into Maryland. It was so named because a church used to occupy the spot in the alley.

While O'Connell and Willie went back over the historic event, O'Connell remembered one important detail. The man that was said to have been holding the horse for Booth when he burst out of the back door of Fords and limped to the horse waiting to carry him to safety was not interviewed for over 3 months. He asked Willie about that man. Willie was intrigued. He was hooked. He thought hard this time, and finally it clicked.

"You going to think I'm crazy," he said to O'Connell.

"Listen boy, I'm not daft. Just listen. I am that man," Willie told him.

He recounted the story about the shooting of President Lincoln. He remembered every last detail. Then he hit the nail on the head.

"It was the same person as this lady," he said. "I swear before Jesus. He damn near broke my skull. It was the same person I'll never forget those eyes. They blazed like a fire! Her scar on her cheek is still there," Willie said.

O'Connell looked at Willie like he was out of his mind. But something rang true. Those eyes. "They blaze just like fire," said O'Connell. "So does Mrs. Thomas eyes," he said aloud. "So does Mrs. Thomas!" He said it slowly, and softly.

CHAPTER SIXTY SIX

Allen Pinkerton had the best detective agency in the United States. His tentacles reached into the gutters of New York, and the heights of Paris, France. The Lady known as one of the wealthiest in America certainly had not started out this way. So O'Connell asked Pinkerton to dig. Dig he did. But a wall of silence kept popping up. Somehow the trail kept ending at Fort McNair. There was a missing piece of time that would not come together.

'I can't find her family," said Pinkerton. "I can't account for her prior to McNair," He explained to O'Connell. "Do you want me to send my men in a search? It is not going to be cheap O'Connell, and it may draw a blank. Tell me what you want. I'll do it." Determined to solve the mystery, O'Connell gave the go ahead and paid Pinkerton. Dispatching 3 men, Pinkerton sat back and waited. For the next 30 days the mission was find Jo Ann Douglass Thomas beginnings.

Last Tuesday, Willie waited outside of the shop being rebuilt for the lady named Mrs. Thomas, as she came hurrying out of the shop and prepared to board her carriage to leave, Willie asked, “May I speak to you for a minute.”

She paused, “What is it sir?” She asked. “I'm in a bit of a hurry.”

“I know,” Willie whispered. ‘I know who you are,” Willie told her.

Her face turned as red as a Beet. Willie said, “She recovered quite nicely, but the damage was done. She got right up in my face. We were nose to nose.”

“Sir, I don't know who you are. I don't know what you think you know. I will tell you this,” she warned. “Accidents seem to happen, around here all the time. You don't seem like a man who is prepared for tragic circumstances,” she said. “People fall, people are stabbed, knives end up in the wrong place, bullets seem to fly into the back of unfortunate folks too often, and too deeply. Some bridges are just too high to peer over. There are many ways to have an accident,” she said. “Let's not look for tragedy “she promised.” Before I go down, you be very, very careful with false accusations."

"I understand my lady," Willie replied. "Perhaps I was mistaken," I said to the lady. "Her eyes, they blazed brightly. She is a killer, no doubt," he said. "For all the gold in the Yukon. I would not sell out this demon. She is Satan's sister for sure," he mumbled and started walking away.

Jo Ann's eyes burned a hole in Willies back. He was deathly rattled. Never had he seen such deadliness in a person's demeanor. He would have bet his last money that not only was Jo Ann lethal, but that she would strike like a rattler in a heartbeat.

In this town where the war had pushed Willie into contact with many killers, con men, robbers and others, he had never felt such lethal energy, such enmity as in Jo Ann Douglass Thomas. Conveyed with her eyes, she was not a woman to trifle with.

Man plans. God laughs.

The weapon that Tycoons of the 1870's armed themselves with was foresight. An uncanny ability to see into the future what technology was coming and cash in. Railroads, oil, and communications were industries that yielded fortunes. The northern citizens used these weapons to dominate U.S. Finance. Southern people formerly wealthy because of the value of their slaves were left to struggle and falter. The citizens of the Border States were caught off guard and flat footed. The politicians in Washington were engaged in corruption and bribery. It was the only way they survived.

In the meantime.....O'Connell fought his own demons, while hunting for a killer.

CHAPTER SIXTY SEVEN

The major figures of the war by now had begun to fall on different kinds of adversity. President Lincoln's assassination started the snowball rolling. By 1870 Robert E. Lee was dead. Jefferson Davis had done a prison term, and was almost destitute. Bedford Forrest, the great general, was dying from diabetes. Braxton Bragg had dropped dead on the street. Joe Johnston would accuse Jefferson Davis of stealing some 2/1-2 million dollars worth of confederate gold. U.S. Grant, President, sometime later would die of cancer of the throat from his cigar addiction. So many of our war heroes from the North and South ended up either destitute, disease ridden or ill Fortuned. Jo Ann/Jonathan was a beneficial exception. A hero, who made good in her civilian persona.

It is the first Saturday in December and Jo Ann watches Mosby emerge from his hotel (the Mayflower) it is 7:00 A.M and a bitter cold, gloomy day is in store for the city. Dressed in a black, thick fur coat, heavy dark brown hunting boots, leather gloves, fur hat, and a thick black wool scarf, Mosby ambles in the direction of the Lays Hotel, one block east on mud encrusted Connecticut Ave. His bodyguard was not with him this morning. He wanted no one to know who he was meeting this morning.

"Ah, there she is", he says to himself. He meets his mistress, Margie Houston, every weekend at this time. She is the South Carolina bred wife of Senator Richard Houston, a wealthy plantation owner that grows cotton and corn. How the civil war did not ruin him is a question still not answered to anyone's satisfaction.

"Such a fine piece of booty", says Mosby. "Her blond hair and blue eyes are perfect," he laughs. "She sucks the life back in a dead body," he sighs. "Oh, what a freak."

Aside from her sexual exploits, they share the same perverted views about blacks being the Inferior race. Also a bitterness about losing the war. They support their local Klu Klux Klan, the terrorist group. Forever stuck in 1850 southern principles, they are both forty five year old bigots.

Half way to the hotel, Margie joins Mosby. Jo Ann follows discreetly from across the street. Jo Ann, disguised as a man, crosses the streets behind the couple, pushes a revolver in Mosby's back, and says "I will kill you both unless you follow my directions, Margie." His use of her first name startles them both. The shock convinces them both to follow orders as given. "I know you don't want this to become a public display. Neither one of you can afford to be found out. Let's just stroll and smile shall we," she says. "Just a short walk up the street", she said.

The building reads Holidays Washing & Cleaning. The door is unlocked. "In here," she says. "That's right" she says. "See it is nice and warm in here." A glow from a wood burning stove is toasty warm. Preparation is obvious. Someone has planned this with a lot of thought.

"To what do we owe this warm, cozy room, sir?" Asks Mosby. For an answer he takes the butt of a gun square on his head.

"I ask the questions," says the voice behind him. "You shut your mouth."

The Sherman rubs the Chloradan filled cloth across both of their faces. Both Mosby and Houston fall out. Straw mattresses await both of them. She binds their arms and legs tightly. "Now I got to work," Jo Ann thinks to herself. And work she does. She stripped both naked and now the fun will begin for both Mosby and Houston.

"You wanted to kill my friend, you bastard. You wanted to rob a nation of our leaders. Well here's what we'll do," she roars.

"Wake up, goddamn you, wake up bastard," she shouts.

Groggy, shaky, half conscious, they both slowly come to. Margie is first to panic. She sees the pliers, the branding iron, the razor, and a bag of salt. Minutes later the senator is fully awoke. His eyes jump wide as saucers as he surveys the equipment.

"This promises to be grueling, a man needs his nourishment," Jo Ann/No Jonathan/No Jo Ann finally says. "A snack is nearby."

BACK AT THE OFFICE O'CONNELL IS BEGINNING TO GET INFORMATION COMING IN. IT IS FAST AND FURIOUS.

Jo Ann has been traced back to Philadelphia. From the Alcott's, to Grand Harvest, to Master John it is all there. "Rumor has it Harriet Tubman, the famous Moses of her people, got her away, and to freedom. From the bounty hunters, to the link to the brothers, it is all there. From there it gets cloudy, but this is quite enough. A rumor of service as a nurse in the Union Army is there. I'll see what they have. This woman may be Negro. My God this is strange," thinks O'Connell. A Jonathan Douglass from NY is listed as enlisting around the same time in 78th. Couldn't be.

"A war hero," says O'Connell. "The medal of valor. A man who is a symbol for this country to follow. Couldn't have a link," he thinks. "Impossible, isn't it?" Says O'Connell. But to O'Connell nothing is impossible. This is a man who has many dark sides to him. "I killed my father," he whispered. "I have tortured suspects. I have hung a man in his cell," he remembered. "I have taken pliers and squeezed a man's balls until they burst, when he raped his 7 year old sister," he admitted. "I have done things I am ashamed of, in the name of justice," he thought out loud.

'The final straw' he thought, was his drowning of his mother when the cancer was eating her body away. "The pain is too much" she said. "Please stop the pain Michael," she begged. 'And I did' he cried silently. "I did," he said, shame faced and muttering.

So he understood something's are perverted. Some things people don't understand.

"The army records show nothing," he said. "I'll find you Jo Ann, I'll find you somewhere." O'Connell searched on relentlessly.

CHAPTER
SIXTY EIGHT

The Reconstruction era was fast coming to a close in the United States. There was a financial panic in 1873. Political Corruption, and continued graft in the middle, 1870's. Reestablishment, of the home rule, the throwing off of the federal Yoke in the south. The concentration of the Government on Indians, basically we used armed force to take their land. Establishment of new technology like sewing machines, telegraphs, Phonograph machines, telephone messages. And our first national celebrity, Mark Twain. Simply because the railroads made it possible for him to travel in a matter of days, all across the country. We have become the major industrial power in the world. So now we can concentrate on other things.

BACK AT THE TORTURE SPOT ....

So as Jo Ann is winding up with Mr. Mosby and Mrs. Houston, she has begun to get ready for an end to the killing and revenge that she has been meting out. "This must end after this one," Jo Ann thinks. "I'm sick and tired of killing. I'm going to stop this payback. I've got to raise my family now, but first things first," says Jo Ann.

"Mosby, time to pay the piper. Time for you to pass on," she said. "The devils in the details," she smiles. She started with the finger nails. With the pliers doing the work, she removes them.

"Oh no" Mosby yells. "Aah" as the blood streams from his fingers.

"No", Margie yells. 'please, no." "I don't have anything to do with this sir," she pleads. She is a couple of minutes from passing out. Jo Ann stops.

"You're right," she says. "We will let you off easy," she says.

"Oh thank you sir. Thank God. I'll pay you. I have money!" Mrs. Houston shouts. At that Jo Ann removes her left shoe.

"We'll let your fingers rest. We will start with your toes," Jo Ann replied with a hiss. With that pliers start the painful nerve racking, horrifying, work. The blood and tissue spilling everywhere. The screams from Mrs. Houston, coupled with the howls from Mr. Mosby, singing a chorus of pain. Smelling salts kept them from passing out when they are right on the edge. Torture, applied with extreme malice when fingers and toes are stripped of their nails, Balpine Hammer finishes this work. Four blows a piece smashes fingers and toes, and assures both victims that they will walk limping forever. They will never hold a glass, nor a cup again.

In the meantime in another part of town O'Connell, his mind pulled back to the present by his trusted assistant, is studying the information that he has set in front of him. "Are you sure O'Hara?" Asked O'Connell. "Has this been double checked? Do you realize what this report means man?" He wondered.

Jo Ann has been traced back to Philadelphia. It is said the famous Harriet Tubman bought her to freedom. It is almost certain she is of mixed race. She came from Grand Harvest Plantation in Dorchester Country, M.D. The rest of the report appears to be a miracle, starting from a raid with some bounty hunters and ending with the possibility that she fought, and fought valiantly and heroically, in the War Between the States! It is a strong possibility that she did so as a man!

O'Connell is flabbergasted. To say this is astounding does not give this revelation enough credit.

His mind just won't wrap around this. This just won't compute.

Not five miles from O'Connell Office an operation is in the second phase that would make a grown man's bowels break, and his stomach turn in disgust. Jo Ann Douglass Thomas is in Jonathan mode. The results are horrifying.

"My favorite utensil," Jo Ann says, as she looks lovingly at the red hot branding iron. The sight of it causes Mrs. Houston to vomit.

"Smell this," Jo Ann states as the iron touches Mosby's feet on the soles.

"Oh Lord." They both bellow. "It hurts, my God, please no!!!" Mosby begs.

Urine and feces has let off a stench. Jo Ann seems not to notice. She got used to far worse under surveillance in combat. "It won't be long now" Jo Ann promises. "Feel this," she says." "A cigar burn is healthy," she laughed and giggled. "Would you like to die now or die later?" She asked. She plunged the hot Branding iron in the rectum of both captives. In less than five minutes they were gone and Jonathan was no more. His fury was sated.

CHAPTER
SIXTY NINE

As O'Connell pondered the evidence and put it together to act on, all the things that together had brought America to this point, also had shaped O'Connell's new attitude toward this case. Just like this was a new America that we lived in, so was the evil that lurked in the hearts of men and women.

O'Connell had to see for himself. He took the reports, put all the information that he had accumulated and set out to finish his investigation the old fashion way, legwork. Destination Harrisburg PA.

He got lucky in an attempt to locate someone who had served in the 78th volunteer during the war; he was directed to SGT. Luther Johnson. He knew SGT. Jonathan Douglas personally. After talking to SGT. Johnson, he was directed to two more of Jonathan's unit team. Show me what you got, Detective O'Connell. "How good are you sir?" his alter ego asked.

Three weeks later, and six interviews down the line Detective O'Connell was rudely interrupted by a knock on his door. "Sir", said CPL. King of the homicide squad. "We have a bad one. I think you need to see this one yourself," he said. The Senator that has been missing, we found him. What's left of him anyway? A more gruesome way to pack it in, I can't imagine. You have got to come see."

Swollen, buck naked, bowels burst, and almost unrecognizable, Senator Mosby and some female, were all but burned inside out. Maggots and flies, along with rats, and a stray dog or two, had destroyed the two corpses.

"My Goodness", said O'Connell. "You have to have a good mind for torture to think this one up", he said. "The .Devil couldn't have thought up a more bitter end," he said. "A jealous husband?" "A cuekheaded wife?" "A contract killing?" "Must be someone berserk." He asked. "My Goodness he crushed both of his testicles!" replied the Cpl. "I have never seen such cruelty," he muttered. "This trip to hells gate was long and slow and personal," said O'Connell. "In the end it must have been the straight razor," said the cpl "It is our friend again, isn't it?" he asked.

O'Connell, stomach queasy replied. "The dogs didn't leave much. They ate much of the man's face, but the wallet clearly lets us know this is Senator Mosby. Looks like our friend, it sure looks like our friend." he questioned. "This time it looks personal. This is overkill."

CHAPTER SEVENTY

Mosby and his mistress was an item for a couple of weeks. The Washington Post milked it for all that it could.

New Years 1876 brought in the Centennial. America was 100 years old. There was a moral hole in the country the size of a mountain. God was on the money that was printed, big and bold. God was less in the hearts and souls of Americans, especially in everyday life.

Around March 1876, when the twins were two years old, the Thomas household got a big surprise. Fred started to get some feeling back in his legs and toes. He was starting to make a partial recovery. The doctor wanted him to ease back into his business duties very slowly, but Fred was impatient.

During this time he got to know, and really love, his children dearly. His relationships were now up close and personal. He laughed and rolled around, frolicked and were wrestled with them. He learned their favorite food and colors. He knew which ones liked to run and throw snowballs. Which ones liked to read stories and do schoolwork, and they worshipped him back. Diamond became the little boss of the household. But she always checked with Fred before she issued her orders for the day. They adored their dad, and poppa loved thru ground his children walked on. Even Asa, who was now eleven, called Fred poppa and meant it. May and June kept their grades high in school, and started to notice the boys now. Fred even talked to them about boys and sex. He talked about other things a poppa was suppose to, with his children. The only enigma was Donald.

He was a loner, and didn't socialize a lot with other children. He would rather play his harmonica, and whittle wood with his pocket knife. He was tall and thin. His hair was short, brown, and his eyes were rather crossed. He had a cleft in his chin, and a thin pair of lips. He favored flannel shirts, cowboy boots and denim jeans. He could handle himself in a scuffle, but was not aggressive or a bully. He also had a secret crush on Jane, who was five years older than him.

Jane was now 18 and would be married in two months. 5'3, 115lbs, ebony skin, and short cut brown hair. She had large brown eyes, and a luscious full round mouth. She had very good legs, and large 36D breast. Her husband to be, Gerald Armstrong owned a café right outside Fort Stevens. He was 26 years old. He worked hard, and was ambitious to boot.

Gerald felt uncomfortable around Fred and Jo Ann because of the lightness of their skin. That was not a factor in their minds, Gerald thought that it was. They admired his mind and his attitude and just wanted the best for her sister. She planned the wedding and spared no expense. This would be the wedding Jo Ann never had,

In the meantime Jo Ann was getting closer to a meeting with O'Connell. He was working hard. He left no stone unturned. He had come to a conclusion. He did not know how, but somehow Jo Ann and Jonathan Douglas were the same person. It was out of this world crazy. It seemed all but impossible. What convinced him, was the four men that had disappeared from the platoon. All had some type of association with Jo Ann. Everyone said Jo Ann/Jonathan was a killing machine, that had no peer. He was to be feared if you got on his wrong side. His exploits in battle were the stuff legends were made of.

There was no doubt he was a killer extraordinaire and his relationship with Corporal Kelly, and the dog Buster was not just an ordinary friendship. Suppose Jonathan didn't die in the stable fire. Suppose people that died or disappeared from the 78th were related to people that are missing or dead in Washington? Could it be possible to pull off that feat during an entire war? How could you pass for a man? How in the hell could you pass for a white man?

John Dobb's was the lead that sealed it. His death was a revenge killing. The reporter from the Washington Post that broke the story of Jo Ann's mixed heritage, then ended up dead. He was the victim of heinous torture.

What you know and what you can prove are two different things. As the big boys say, PROVE IT!

CHAPTER
SEVENTY ONE

The complex puzzle that was Jo Ann Douglas Thomas was never more evident than events that happened in July 1876. The nation celebrated 100 years old, with a festive day in Philadelphia. Jane was back from her honeymoon.

She a Gerald settled into running their eatery. The local extortion gang that collected their bribery tax with brutal intensity went to work. The first payment due was $2,000.00 and due in one week. Not knowing what to do and scared to get the police involved, Gerald told Jo Ann about the threat. Jo Ann calmly told Gerald to tell the leader of the gang, Roland "Big Tiny" Wright, that the payment would be made at the Lays Hotel, 3rd floor and that she would talk some sense into the gangster.

"Mr. Tiny I'm so nervous inside meeting you," Jo tilted her head slightly an sighed.

"You oughta be bitch," he roared. "Got me up here in this damn mouse trap.. Hurry up, fore I snap yo neck. You are a pretty ole gal. I should take me some fore I go," he said. Jo Ann batted her eyes, played with Tiny's hand for a second.

"Well big boy, let me give you what you came for."

She pulled him forward, swift knee to the groin. Two flicks, left, right. Blood spurted like a water pump,splattering the jet black outfit she wore.

"Goddam!" Tiny cried.

"Take these to Hell with you," Jo Ann said

Two bullets from a .44 Deringer lodged in his dented skull.

"I gotta go," said Jo ann. She opened the room door. She stepped quickly inside. She threw on her Blue Robe, stepped over tiny and flew down the steps.

"Nobody," she said as she hurried down the alley. She threw the gun in the trash, threw the dress in the gutter and stepped into the street to wait for her ride. Game, set, match.

Frustration setting in the chase of Jo Ann was entering year two. O'Connell decided to strike. Afraid that the body count would go higher, O'Connell hatched a plan. One of his most cowardly and no account informants, Chester Robins, would sell his mother for five dollars. O'Connell talked Chester into letting him beat him up, one broken leg, a swollen eye, some broken ribs, and a pair of swollen lips. He plants some evidence that has been accumulated over the years, in a barn in the Foggy Bottom.

O'Connell claims he has followed Jo Ann to her estate from this barn. Supposedly some bloody clothes, some weapons and some gloves are found in a basement room during a search. Along with the clothes is a razor. It is enough. With Robins in Washington General giving an eyewitness account, a warrant is secured, which leads to an arrest.

Jo Ann's arrest leads to shock. From Fred to the children, from the children to brother and sisters, and from brother and sisters to society and neighbors, no one believes it. At the Arraignment, no bond was granted. James Wood III, the best attorney is hired.

"This trial will have everything", says the Washington Star Newspaper.

"Serial killings, famous defendant war hero, and famous victims," the newsboy hollered.

"The trial of the century," the prosecutor promises.

"She's innocent," Fred yells.

"Two weeks, and I'm so weak I can't walk," Jo Ann tells willow and Jane on a visit.

"Just a few hours more sis," pleads June.

"This jail is terrible," Jo Ann complains. "Rats, bugs, roaches in my food," she cried out. I can't take it. I have got to get free. I've got to get out!"

As they start to leave, Willow looks over her shoulder "see you soon baby, see you soon," she reassured her.

CHAPTER
SEVENTY TWO

"Mighty white of you Leroy," said Jo Ann. He helped her into the sealed wagon that would take her to the court house.

"I must be important, four men riding with us." The men glancing around, lumps in throat, butterflies in their stomach, pistols with their fingers wrapped around the triggers, took off beside the wagon.

The sky dark and angry, the breeze calm and cool, the wagon slowly ambled down the pitted muddy road. Jo Ann spits the handcuff key out her mouth. Leroy is 500.00 dollars to the good and a drama unfolds. The air is filled with four perfectly aimed arrows. They find their marks and three guards fall silently, but violently. The remaining guard opens the door and Jo Ann scampers down the steps, and runs to a waiting horse with an escort.

Harvey of course is wounded; an arrow finding its mark in his arm and leg. Four men rush in to lead Jo Ann to freedom. The Washington, DC jails first ever escape is a success.

"My God I'm free," Jo Ann exclaims. "Let's run men, lets run," she yells. By the time she mounted the brown chestnut mare, there is no one to stop her. She looks back and yells, "This way boys. Get me to freedom." Her heart beating like a drum, sweat rolling down her brow, mouth dry, and hair filled with the wind, she runs for her freedom. She rounds the corner, and sprints for the Navy Yard Bridge and across into Maryland and down route 5, she headed for Charles County. She is reminded that J.W> Booth ran for his life after killing father Abraham, our leader, and president, this same route.

CHAPTER SEVENTY THREE

Having left behind an entire dumbfounded city, Jo Ann was now a wanted fugitive. Fred was not going to take this laying down. A rich powerful man, he reached into the DA's office, and the chief of police office.

"Mr. Thomas, it looks like a frame up," says the police chief. "It was a frame up from the word go. I don't know how much of this case is lies and fabricated evidence, but I do know this case is an illusion and O'Connell will pay dearly," he says.

"There are people that want to see Jo Ann swinging," says Fred and Bertha."

"People that can't wait for her to be dead."

"They will dance on her grave marker. They will smile at her tombstone," says Mr. Wood, Her attorney.

"The Mellon's, the Vanderbilt's, the Rockefellers would all love to see her swing," says Zack.

Now onto the hair raising part of this escape. Time is now the enemy. The telegraph, the mail, the systems that now traveled faster than ever are the enemy. Stealth, now Jo Ann's partner. In a matter of hours everyone on the east coast will know of Jo Ann's escape. They will shake every tree and stop every wagon. But Zack, Willow and June have together worked out a plan to save their "sister." They have put into action their vow to save Jo Ann. She is Douglass blood and a miracle is what they have planned!

Three hours after the daring escape from the jail transport wagon, Jo Ann has rumbled onto the first stop on another underground railroad, the Baltimore estates of Junes millionaires husband, Thomas Hardy. The effort to free Jo Ann has reached phase II intact. The sun is setting and the city will rest, now so will Jo Ann. After resting for a day, and waiting until the night of November 22, 1876, an adventure was now in store.

"I'm glad to be spending the holiday with you June. I've missed you so much baby sis," Zack said.

"It was so kind of you to invite my crew to a thanksgiving feast. Most of them are quite far from home."

Zack, one of the Navy's true civil war hero's, was a welcome visitor at his sisters estate. "I'm honored to meet your mayor," Zack said. "And two state senators to go with him," Zack crowed. "The chief of police is the icing on the cake."

"I hope every one of you enjoyed dinner," June said. "Next year we will do it again."

“The music is superb,” said the mayor. “You are a lovely host, my dear.”

“The security is a joy to behold, sir. No one would dare try anything crazy with all of the city’s top officials here,” Zack assured them.

At 9:00pm exactly, after expressing his pleasure with the wine, Zack bided everyone farewell. He had to set sail in the morning for New York Harbor. With the chief of police offering a helping hand, the four deputies brought down stairs a large trunk filled with heirlooms to be donated to The Museum of Natural Art, in New York City. The Admiral in charge of the US Naval Ships anchored in New York had offered his ship as transport, using Zack in command. Carefully they transported the trunk down to Zack’s ship, anchored in Baltimore Harbor. The men saluted Zack and made their way back to June’s massive estate.

“Alright men, please be careful when you take it aboard. There is a special room in the bowels that will be the resting place for the trunk,” Zack said. “Thank you and good night,” Zack left them alone.

A half hour later the lid lifted in darkness on the trunk. “I think I am safe,” Jo Ann said. Exhaling a deep sigh of relief, she pushed open the lid, and stretched her legs as she did. “This was a stroke of genius,” Jo Ann said. “While the world looks for me on the road, I sail past everyone on my brother's ship." She shook her head in wonder. "Zack is quite the genius. His plan is inspired," Jo Ann whispered.

CHAPTER SEVENTY FOUR

"I hope you are finding the food to be enough," Zack said to Jo Ann. Every evening after dinner he took leftovers to Jo Ann in the bowels of the ship. The hiding place was almost perfect.

"In two more days we should be in New York," he said.

"I'm fine my dear brother. You make me feel like I'm in a hotel," she said with a smile.

"Stop girl," Zack cautioned. "There are rats down here as big as some dogs. I know you here them at night," replied Zack. "Just don't get bit down here, and don't wonder around," he cautioned. She had enough fresh water, and a place to empty her bladder and bowels. But the cold air at night was not comfortable. You could see your breath in the air.

Though most of Zack's men were loyal to him, this was the US Navy and some of these men were patriots first. A fugitive on the ship could cause a man to turn to the police if he desired. So only three of Zack's officer's knew Jo Ann was aboard. Among them, gentle man James Corbett, whose grandson would become the heavyweight boxing champion of the world one day.

Every four or five days, Jo Ann would walk the length of the boat for exercise, at 2:00 or 3:00am when everyone was asleep. “Who are you sir?” Jo Ann asked the sailor she bumped into one night while stretching her legs

“Why I’m Borders miss, he said. “Who in the hell are you? What are you doing down here?” Surprised by a woman on board, he started to think about how long it had been since he had been with a woman. Too long he reasoned. TOO LONG.

Jo Ann let herself be carried to a small storage area in the back of the ships dark rooms. As she let herself be pushed back on the table to be ravished, she turned the tables on the poor man. Minutes later it was over.

“I think he is dead,” she mumbled to herself. He was dead before he hit the ground. Neck snapped, arm broken, ribs bruised, spine twisted, death was less than two minutes incoming! Jonathan had reared his ugly head. “I’ll put him behind these crates and barrels,” Jo Ann murmured.

After stashing the dead sailor, Jo Ann was exhausted. Phase III will be harder than Jo Ann thought. Jo Ann has to kill Jonathan! “How will I do that?” she wondered. “How will I do that?”

THE NEXT DAY....

"Jack is missing, captain Douglass. No one has seen him since yesterday." The ensign reported. "Where could he possibly be?" he asked. "Where in hell's bell's is he?" Zack was scared stiff to the answer.

CHAPTER SEVENTY FIVE

They found the sailors body and landed at the New York Harbor on the same day. Since land was ahoy, the murder was second in importance to the end of the trip.

"I'm glad this trip is over. I'm happy it's payday and leave day," the sailor said.

"They found Jack in the store room. He was dead as a door knob," the ensign announced.

"To bad but accidents do happen," said the sailor. "How long before pay hour? I need me a woman," He complained.

"I said Jack was found dead. Can you hear?" said the ensign.

"Well I didn't kill him. How long to my money?" the sailor asked again.

"Line up at the window. You will get paid right away. Tell everyone to line up." And with that Jack's death was forgotten.

Most of the men were illiterate and the majority never bothered to read the newspaper. They were unaware of a fugitive, and unaware of a serial killers' arrest or escape.

Zack was the only one that felt uncomfortable. He knew he had a killer among his crew. He just prayed it wasn't his sister. It would not be the first time he had a murder on his ship. It would probably not be the last time. He just hoped that the truth did not lye in a trunk that he had smuggled on board. For that he would have to choose between his sister, and his men. He did not want to do that. He was not ready for that one. He pondered. He sailed on. In an hour he was docked. "I love you Jo Ann," he thought. "I love you dear sister. I hope I made the right choice; he prayed and got a little scarder. "God help me," he thought.

Thomas Food and Grain Inc. was part of the Thomas Empire of companies. It was located on Manhattan Island, and was where Jo Ann, lieing in the oversized trunk was carried by wagon.

"Careful James," demanded Zack. "Don't be too rough with the wagon. I'd hate to get this far only to break my sister's neck on the way in." They had reached phase III of the escape plan and Zack was quite nervous. He was almost done with his part.

Jo Ann had given a lot of thought to her next destination. She had decided not only a new place to live, but a new way of life would be next. It was now December 21, 1876. A new year right around the corner.

CHAPTER
SEVENTY SIX

Now it was Willow's turn to help her sister. Hers was the most dangerous part of the journey. This part meant a life in the future or death coming up shortly. "It is what it is', Jo Ann thought. While hiding out in the daytime and venturing out some nights on the streets that never seemed to take a nap, Jo Ann used the time to ponder what to do with the rest of her life.

"I've got to change my lifestyle," Jo Ann said to herself. "Why?" her alter ego questioned. "I have killed. I have sinned. I have lied, cheated, and spent more time away from the children than with them, she admitted. "God will punish me if I don't change," she sobbed. "Hells gates will open up and swallow me whole," she acknowledged. "My life's been a mess. A ball of sin and confusion," she whispered. Truthfully, the youngest kids barely knew her. Bertha was more mom to them than she was. Jo Ann felt guilt ridden.

She came to a dramatic decision. She would turn her life over to the lord. She would repent for her sins and then raise her kids in Gods light. She would renew her soul as a minister, and give him her life as a reverend. She would found her own church. She knew just the right place.

AT THE MEETING WITH HER HUSBAND...

"Are you crazy Jo Ann?" Fred bellowed. "You have lost your mind woman," he yelled.

Jo Ann had summoned Fred to New York. It had been thirty days since she came ashore from the harbor. Fred had waited patiently for Jo Ann's message to meet her. He wanted to see her so bad. He never told the kids if their mother was safe or even alive. It was killing him to watch them wonder and worry. Finally word came. Meet me in New York. He confided in Asa.

Asa said, "I will die before I tell mama's secret." And he was good as his word. He went with his father to meet Jo Ann.

"Mom, you can't do this," he cried. "You can't turn to a preacher. What will we tell the children? They won't understand," he whined.

"I have made up my mind," she said. "God has led me this way." "Fred, my soul is at stake," she said. "God has commanded me," she argued. "Please understand."

Back and forth they went for three hours. Finally, Fred exhausted to the bone said, "Okay, let's just try for a month."

"I love you so much," Jo Ann sang out. "God will bless us and keep us." Jo Ann already knew where she would settle. Three days later, she was on her way to Auburn, N.Y. That was the home of Harriet Tubman, her hero.

Nine days later, a tired Jo Ann knocked on the door of a bungalow house on the out skirts of town. It was a home for the elderly Negro residents of the town. Mrs. Tubman and her husband, Mr. Davis, 24 years her junior, had dedicated their lives to taking care of the aged. That included her "Niece," Margaret, who moved in with her.

"I have money Mrs. Tubman, I will never forget what you did for me," Jo Ann said. "We will build you another home and I will build us a new church. People from all over will come to our refuge," Jo Ann said.

"Child, God has blessed me with this name," Harriet replied. "I'm so happy to just be alive. These times are not good ones for our people you know," she explained. "We fought a civil war to be equal, and white folks still won't let us be free. You build your church," she said. "I'll keep your secret, I promise," she said, once more. "The Reverend Martha Miller will be the angel rose from the ashes," Harriet (minty) exclaimed. Reverend Miller was born that very day.

CHAPTER SEVENTY SEVEN

In the meantime back at the homicide squad in Washington, detective O'Connell was frantic. He kept going over to Baltimore to June's estates spying on her, and trying to catch Jo Ann bringing herself in secret to the Hardy Estate. She finally caught O'Connell spying on her, and sicked her dogs and houseman on him. They tussled until the houseman fired his shotgun in the air, and they broke up the fight. He cleaned up his busted lips and bleeding nose, and he was nursing a sore groin from a kick. O'Connell tried to bluff his way onto the property to search, but June was not intimidated, and would not let him.

She then made a fatal mistake. In her hurry to let Jo Ann know that the hated detective was still hunting her, June was tailed to the station by O'Connell. He found out that June's ticket was to New York City. He was on the same train to New York that June caught. Now he had a solid lead. O'Connell's investigation, and the extensive research done by Allen Pinkerton gave O'Connell encouragement to aggressively continue his pursuit.

"What is in New York City?" He wondered. "Why is she in such a hurry?" He questioned. "I wonder if Jo Ann could be somewhere in the largest city in the United States?" He pondered. Is this my break to solve this case for sure?" Head spinning.

As he rode in the rear passenger car, O'Connell's heart beat fast and furious. After he followed June to the Carriage rental stable, and inquired as to her destination for the next day, O'Connell finally wore a smile. His destination for tomorrow would be Auburn, N.Y. His journey and his meeting with destiny would be finally at the end. "Tomorrow, Jo Ann, tomorrow!" he said to himself.

CHAPTER SEVENTY EIGHT

He smiled to himself as he trailed June to her destination. Not to close, but close enough not to lose her, O'Connell was on horseback. "I don't want her dead. I just want to bring her in," he thought.

Jo Ann has accomplished a lot in three weeks since she had established her small church. "I welcome everybody to my church," she said. She had rented a small house, and workmen gut it and put in some seating. A small altar was built out of raw cedar. It was the beginning of a small Baptist church. This Sunday would mark the reverend Miller's first sermon.

"My God June, what are you doing here?" A surprised Jo Ann asked June after a short kiss and hug.

"The detective, that O'Connell, he has been spying on me. I caught him hanging around sniffing and sneaking. He is still on you Jo. He is still hawking you like a vulture smells death. What do you think I should do honey? Should I have him put down?" said June.

"I have no desire for violence June," replied Jo Ann. "God knows I need piece," she said quietly. Jo Ann looked at her sister. "You wouldn't understand June. I need piece in my life," she said. "Just watch what he does and be careful. Just let me know if you sense danger to me or the kids," a tear rolled slowly down her cheek.

They embraced and June said, "I'll come back tomorrow Jo Ann. We will spend some time together and I will go home. I love you sis, I'll always love you," she said. "Before I go Jo Ann, I've just got to know. Those things that they say," she said. "Those things that they say that you've done. Those awful things people claim that you did. Look me in my eyes darling. Did you do any of those things? If you are responsible for those things, just tell me the truth," June pleaded.

Jo Ann looked June right in the eyes. She grabbed her shoulders and looked. "I swear, as God is my witness," she said. "I have done none of those things. I am innocent my sister. I've done none of those things." She smiled and crossed her heart as she did it. June smiled back, turned and walked away.

CHAPTER SEVENTY NINE

O'Connell watched as June goes into the small house on the hill. He knew from the population the preacher was suppose to be reverend Miller from N.Y.C. The woman had to be Jo Ann. The broken down 7 year old horse that brought O'Connell up here was tired and hungry. "Be careful O'Connell. This woman is dangerous," he said to out loud to himself. The last ¼ mile, he dismounted and crawled. "These field glasses are no good to me," O'Connell thinks.

As he looks toward the building, June exits. She gets into her carriage and slowly drives down the lane. O'Connell waits on his chance. Finally he walks up to the front door and knocks. A plain faced, short haired woman, no rouge or lip-gloss, no dimples or earrings, wearing a plain white clerical collar under a plain black dress, answers the door. She shows no recognition of her visitor.

"Yes. I help you sir?"She asks. Her plain black framed glasses seem to go right with her. The disappointment in O'Connell's face is visible. He does not recognize this plain faced, middle aged woman in front of him.

"Excuse me ma'am," he says. "I was looking for someone, and I was told that they lived here. It seems I have made a mistake."

"It is okay my son," says Reverend Miller. "Perhaps I can help you. I am Reverend Martha Miller. I have only recently occupied this church. Maybe you need to find the previous occupant. What is it you need to know?" she asks.

"My name is detective Michael O'Connell from Washington, DC. I am a homicide detective reverend. The person that I am looking for has escaped from my jail, and was reported to have been seen in this town. Perhaps I've been mislead."

"My goodness, you mean you have come all the way from Washington?" says the reverend. "There are no fugitives here my son. But you are welcome to a cup of coffee."

"Thank you, I am kind of tired. It's been a long trip," O'Connell answered. The sweat ran slowly down Jo Ann's forehead. Her throat itched like sand. The palms of her hands were slick and sweaty, and her heart was thumping rapidly. Jo Ann's mind was racing. Her face however, was calm as an ice blue lake in the summer time.

CHAPTER EIGHTY

The coffee, hot, black and delicious was served in the rather plain kitchen. A small round wood table, a butcher block with two knives with 8 inch blades, three small wooden cabinets, recently painted sunrise yellow, adorned the small area used as the eating area. A green table cloth and two wooden chairs now occupied by O'Connell and reverend Miller were opposite each other at the table. A small plate of homemade Ginger Snap Cookies, were in front of O'Connell. Though Jo Ann knew right away who O'Connell was, she did not act like it, or show any signs of recognition to O'Connell. She acted so demure that O'Connell was caught completely off guard.

"Tell me about this man you are chasing," Jo Ann asked. O'Connell was puzzled. He thought he might catch Reverend Miller off guard. The idea that she assumed he was after a man almost cemented the matter.

"Oh no, Reverend Miller, It is a woman I'm after," he admitted. She is quite dangerous," warned. He decided to play all or nothing. "This woman has money, and plenty of help. Her sisters from Baltimore and I tracked her to New

York. In fact the trail has led me this way," he said. "She is a lovely woman. Her name is June Hardy. Her husband is wealthy. She was seen around these parts recently. She's riding a buggy with a dray pulling it. Her nose is spotted and there is a white star on her forehead. Have you seen such an animal in these parts or a woman that looks like this?" He showed her Junes pictures.

Joann hesitated just a second, but that was enough. "No, I don't think I have seen such an animal. The woman is very handsome," she replied. As she bent over to hand the picture back to O'Connell a pearl handle could be seen peeking out from her frumpy black sweater. "Reverend Miller has a weapon?" Michael asks himself. As the Reverend inquires, "More cookies or more coffee, kind sir?" Before O'Connell can say no thank you Joanne makes her move!

First she grabbed him by the head and twisted. Failing to snap O'Connell's neck she delivered a sharp right hand to the jaw. O'Connell, caught off guard grabbed Jo Ann in desperation, and they rolled to the floor. The coffee cup saved him. He grabbed it and hit her. It punctured her skin.

"My Arm," he shouts. "Aagh, my damn arm," it is broken and limp. Joann follows with a kick to the kneecap. "Yes!" She hollers loudly, "take that!" Yes you scum. "I'll kill you right now!" Adrenaline is flowing, the sweat running down her face. O'Connell has collapsed like a ragdoll. Five minutes of stomping and kicking brings blood, and bruises turn red and purple. O'Connell is on the on the verge of passing out from pain. Desperate and scared stiff, he grabs Jo Ann's ankle and twist. “Damn it!" she slips on the blood that has spilled on the floor. O'Connell grabs for her face and pokes her eyeballs as he continues to grab at her face, he feels for soft tissue.

“My eyes, not my eye,” Jo Ann screams in pain. He catches her high on the temple with a piece of broken saucer.

“Noo,” Jo Ann yells, the blood spurting from the cut. It blinded her vision and she lunged from the chair. She tried swinging it wildly and caught O’Connell low on the mouth. Teeth flew like broken glass. “Oh no, oh hell,” O’Connell cursed from the blow. The pain was too much. He faltered and fell. He glimpsed the pearl handle as he fell to the floor. On the way down, he grabbed at the razor and caught it strictly by luck. Aiming at nothing, he swung it blindly and slashed the web of Jo Ann’s left hand. “Shit, my damn hand, you cut my damn hand,” she shouted. Blood spurted like a water fountain. Dishes tumbled and broke. O'Connell and Jo Ann slipped in the blood. Both were hurt and scared shitless. Jo Ann’s hand was now almost numb. The feeling was quickly leaving. The slashes from the razor had Jo Ann and O'Connell dancing a ballet with death. Jo Ann's slipping and crawling and O'Connell out of breath and injured badly.

“Aah,” O’Connell kept yelling. “Oh my God, oh my hand. I can't feel my hand,” Jo Ann kept bellowing. Crimson blood, bright red, flooded the floor, pouring from both of them. "I'm so damn dizzy," Jo Ann desperately whispered. She fell to the floor any heap. O Connell was still close to vomiting. The coffee and cookies with spilled everywhere. Jo Ann was at the end. She breathed deeply twice and stopped, her heart slowing down. Suddenly she was still. Her clothes soaked with red liquid.

“I can breathe, I'm not dying,” O’Connell said to himself. He finally got some air in his lungs. “My lungs are on fire,” he was holding his chest. He looked down at the lump of flesh that was Jo Ann. She was still, and not moving. “The devil is dead,” he pronounced. “I can't believe she fought that hard. I got to get to a doctor.” He knew he was hurt badly. It was over at last. “Let me make sure this demon is gone,” O’Connell said out loud. He bent his head down to Jo Ann's chest.

“Ahh you mother ....,” Jo Ann shouted.

"I'll kill you, you bastard! I'll kill you for sure,” she shouted as she grabbed hold of his neck, and latched on with a bite. O’Connell twisted and squirmed. He rattled and rolled. Jo Ann held on for dear life. Her teeth sunk in his neck. Jo Anne clamped her legs around his body. The blood on the floor made O'Connell slip and fall again. “Oh no, oh God, I hurt man. It hurts O'Connell thought he was yelling. Instead just gurgles came out. Just sounds, not a word. He tried punching her face. He tried banging her head on the floor. “Backwards, fallbacks,” he thinks’, as they struggle. As he falls backwards, his hands grab a piece of the saucer. They roll back and forth. He jabs backward and down. “Oh hell that's my eye,” Jo Ann shouts from the floor. The saucer has struck home. The eyeball has burst. Blood and soft-tissue explodes on Jo Ann's face. She grabs at her eye socket. It's too late for that. O’Connell flips over and keeps stabbing the eyes and the throat. Jo Ann's artery is sliced. She now chokes on her blood. O'Connell takes his right elbow and leans on Jo Ann's throat. “Die Dammit” he yells. “Bitch die, don't you get up.” Vomit and blood combine for a stinking mess. The smell of death is among them. He does not stop until Jo Ann is blue. Finally it’s over. Jo Ann is quite dead. For 10 minutes he keeps pressing, scared she won't die right now. Finally, his strength is gone, he can't kill her again. “It’s over” he cries. “It's over, she’s gone.”

Epilogue....

Joanne was laid to rest in a beautiful ceremony held at the plot of land set aside for her by Zack and the rest of the Douglas family. Scanning the members of the family at the gravesite we can't help but ponder their fate in the future, and the Civil War error that spawn them. Fred remained confined to a wheelchair. At the time of his passing he was still president and chief officer of Thomas enterprises in 1885. Asa, "Blue" Douglas graduated from Harvard University and assumed the chief officers title at Thomas enterprises. Diamond Douglas Thomas, married, bore four children after graduating from Vassar College for Women. As a sign of the times she never worked or voted before her passing in 1894 from smallpox. Zack Douglas became a naval hero a senator from the state of Maryland and suffered a tragic accident some years later. Willow ran the grand harvest plantation until her passing in 1900, and June bore 3 children and was never discovered as she maintained her lesbian relationship with her childhood friend Sadie Mae. She passed in 1888. The Douglas family went on to become one of the most famous spawn in the Civil War era. Their legacy runs on, and Donald? We will see. That is another story.

A $500.00 award was granted along with his promotion to lieutenant. Mr. O'Connell was severely wounded during the capture of this notorious killer. "God be with him," it says.

As the man in the deli walks outside the eatery, he opens up his umbrella and steps into the rainstorm. In the back of the deli a man steps out of the abandoned building. He is facing the building as he clamps a padlock shut. His pearl handled razor he is holding is snapped shut, and he walks quickly away. He looks up to the clouds. He smiles into the rainstorm. He utters these words, they are etched in his mind, "someone has got to pay", he boast. "Someone has got to pay." He slows down his walk. He is safe for tonight. For Donald Douglass Thomas the war must go on. It is July 4th, let the fireworks begin. THE END

Recommended Reading for all Ages, Colors and Intellect

Foundation Builders in a bookstore near you.

"The truth shall not only set you free, it gives you power over your surroundings!"

Black Robes White Justice *by:*	***Bruce Wright***
Illusions of Justice *by:*	***Lenox Hinds*** *(Iowa University)*
The Browder Files *by:*	***Anthony T. Browder***
Bad Blood *(The Tuskegee Experiment) by:*	***James H. Jones***
From Superman to Man *by:*	***J. A. Rogers***
Assata Shakur *by:*	***Assata Shakur***
Stolen Legacy *by:*	***George M.G. James***
Miseducation of the Negro *by:*	***Carter G. Woodson***
They Stole It but You Must Return It *by:*	***Richard Brown***
The Isis Papers *by:*	***Dr. Frances C. Wesling***
The Gnostic Gospels *by:*	***Elaine Pagels***
Possessing the Secrets of Joy *by:*	***Alice Walker***
The Conspiracy To Destroy Black Boys *by:*	***Jwanza Kujufi***
Before Columbus *by:*	***Ivan Van Sertima***
Christianity, Islam and the Negro Race *by:*	***Blyden***
Glory of The Black Race *by:*	***El Jahees***
7 African Arabian Wonders of the World *by:*	***Khalid Mansour***
Blood In My Eye *by:*	***George Jackson***
The Autobiography of Malcolm X *by:*	***Alex Haley & Malcolm X***
The Holy Quran translated *by:*	***Yusuf Ali***

HOOD WARS by ESCO
ISBN# 978-0-9844071-4-9
Page count: **401** Price Book **$16.99**
Prison order price: **$11.00**

Nina and Toast are two disheartened enemies who vowed to "WARN AND PROTECT" each other over the course of an impending war. Soon, Nina feels betrayed after a rush of slugs nearly claimed her life. She next goes on a manhunt tracking down Toast, revealing her own treacherous behavior to her circle that soon may get her killed!

Toast has too much to worry about than explaining his innocence to Nina. At the moment, he and his "FLUNKIES" are having a transformation of power. Toast must find ways to keep him and his underlings safe from the most monstrous gang in the city. Plus the risk of death ten folds when Toast soldiers have a clash of ideas and a division of loyalty. Plunged into a world were HONOR and RESPECT is cut paper thin, Toast is not going to know who to trust.

Who will be left standing when the smoke clears at the end of this bloody tale of deception, betrayal and survival of the fittest? Will Nina be able to eliminate Toast before her own treacherous past catches up with her? Will toast find sanctuary away from the madness; or will he walk right into the line of fire set up by either friend or foe?

D.D. Ellis explosive novel HOOD WARS is non-stop action, filled with larger than life characters, and will keep you asking "What will happen next?" It's a must read!!!

FIVE STAR REVIEW

Esco you got one. HOOD WARS truly a great read.
Finally a representation of a writer from Allah Born.
Very entertaining. Keep pushing, we're moving......

GOAT
Albany, New York

E-Books $8.99

FALLEN ANGEL by FruitQuan
ISBN# 978-0-9844071-3-2
Page Count **333** Price Book **$15.99**
Prison order price: **$11.00**

From the Brownsville slums of Brooklyn, New York and Los Angeles, California all the way to the Federal Penitentiary, the hourglass is ticking, the streets are watching, and Gangstaz gotta KEEP IT GULLY!

With Albert Anastasia roots and links to the Biggie Smalls vs Tupac rival, Brooklyn's home of the legendary Mike Tyson is saturated with history...... Brownsville has a story to tell.

FIVE STAR REVIEW

Fallen Angel is a story of the games that are played on the streets; some people's reality. The characters in the book remind me of actual people that live & hang in the street of the five boroughs (NYC). I found myself constantly picking up the book to read at every opportunity that I could.

FruitQuan did an excellent job characterizing Hurricane, the main character as well as the others (Mama Maxie, Pale Face etc). Hurricane reminds me of "Midnight" from Sistah Souljah's book "A Coldest Winter Ever". The story is written whereas you know Hurricanes every thought, whether you agree with those thoughts or not. So if you like a book with lots of family love, street hustle, action & fast money this is the book for you."

Crystal
Brooklyn, NY

E-Books $7.99 www.kobo.com

WHAT'S NEXT by Courtney B. Walker
Drama, Pain, Heartache & Betrayal
ISBN# 978-0-9844071-2-5
Page Count **257** Price Book **$12.99**
Prison order price: **$9.00**

The author weaves a dynamic plot showing how one young woman's life undergoes drastic changes with each situation she faces, much of which leads to more pain and heartbreak. The character, Angel Reneé Walker, is unlike other people in the world. She can tell what lies ahead 惘 all the drama, pain, heartache, and betrayal. It all began on the first day of her senior year when her mother's life was taken in a car accident. Since then, her world has turned upside down.

Angel finds herself in difficult situations, while her relationship with her father is at its breaking point. It seems that nothing can go right. She starts to give up on life, on everything. When she meets someone who makes her believe there is still a chance, she feels hopeful again. But like everything else in her life, will this love be destroyed? Angel will be tested when a dark secret shocks her and she finds out that the one person she trusted most in the world was involved in the tragic accident that took her mother's life. Is she destined for a life of despair and betrayal? What's Next reveals all.

FIVE STAR REVIEW

"I recently read "What's Next," and I was amazed. I thought that this book would be a self-help book to help young people deal with the trails of growing up. But I was wrong. It was real talk from the beginning to the end. The young Angel Reneé Walker goes through things that a lot of adults can't handle. She lives, learns and falls down. But most of all, she had to find a way out of the place where people hide to get away. I find that this book is inspirational and just what is needed in today's world for our young people, both guys and girls. Grief comes to us all, but not all of us make it through. The aspect I admire is how she maintains her social standing among her peers."

KAY JOHNSON
Brooklyn, NY

E-Books $7.99

BROOKLYN ICE by Anthony Brewer
ISBN# 978-0-9844071-0-1
Page Count **308** Price Book **$14.99**
Prison order price: **$11.00**

Brooklyn Ice follows its main character Theresa Jones. A Financial Consultant and Attorney; known through academic, corporate and judiciary realms as Ms. Jones. She is known on the streets and by friends as B.G. (short for BabyGirl), and there is only one thing she loves more than her desire to acquire money or her zeal for drama - and that's Joseph Cohen.

Joseph who is cut from the old school cloth of stick up kids use to rob banks, drug dealers and payrolls. He started investing money early on and sent his virgin love to school while he styled under the guise of a Real Estate Agent. That was back in the day, but now, the laid back, more reserved J.C. comes to find his BabyGirl has adopted his old gun slinging ways and combined them with her education and unrelenting Brooklyn ways.

Tempted by millions in diamonds, Joseph has decisions to make. In a time of recession, the Brooklyn bad boys are coming out with hopes Joseph will let Brooklyn do what it has always done - get money. Ride with J.C. or BG; she will not only get you money, but she'll show you how to use it. You decidc. But whatever you do, don't get it twisted. The school girl is no longer taking lessons: she's giving them...... There's a new Brooklyn bully. Who would think it's a female?!

FIVE STAR REVIEW

"BROOKLYN ICE by Anthony Brewer is an exciting, breath-taking, fast pace novel to read. This book will have you on the edge of your seat waiting for the next piece of excitement. This book is definitely a page turner. BROOKLYN ICE is packed with plenty of action..."

Barbara Morgan
ATL, Georgia

E-Books $7.99

TERRORIST IN BROOKLYN by Anthony Brewer
Revolutionary or Conspirator
ISBN# 978-0-9844071-1-8
Page Count **272** Price Book **$14.99**
Prison order price: **$11.00**

Terrorism activity has picked up on American soil as a result of the construction of an 80 billion dollar American oil project in Iraq, leaving the Federal Bureau of Investigation with work to do. With Corporate buildings getting blown up, dead bodies appearing out of thin air and the Bureau short on answers all fingers point to Special Agent Black of CTU.

No one ever thought terrorism would be on the door step of Brooklyn residents as victims or practitioners, but what is discover will change Brooklyn forever.

It doesn't help matters when Sheppard's Private Contracting Security Agency (Mercenaries) who served in the Iraq, Afghanistan and Saudi Arabia killing with impunity, have come to America after MOST WANTED terrorist that fled from Iraq seeking refuge in Brooklyn.

Equally alarming are the African American faces with international ties that are popping up as suspects of terrorism. In the midst of Agent Black's investigation, he connects Muslim residents from local Mosques supporting none terrorist. What's worse he finds he is not only a suspect, but a MOST WANTED.

With all eyes on Special Agent Black, he will have to choose between clearing his name when suspected of terrorism activity or making a name for himself by standing for justice against terrorist no matter who the perpetrators......

E-Books $7.99 www.kobo.com

SHOESHINE BOY by Charles Belim
ISBN# **978-0-9844071-6-3**
Page count **271** Price Book **$14.99**
Prison order price: **$11.00**

The "Shoeshine Boy" saga chronicles events in the life of a young kid growing up in Boston, Massachusetts. At age ten he's given an opportunity to shine shoes in a shine parlor deep within the "Mob" controlled section of Boston's notorious 'North End'. Unbeknownst to him, the shine parlor is a front for illegal betting from horses to the local 'nigga number' in his community of Roxbury.

The experiences and exposure of that Summer will catapult the Shoeshine Boy into being dubbed one of Boston's most infamous 'Common Known and Notorious Thieves.' The Shoeshine Boy story is about his beginning.

"Payin' My Dues", **"Plastic Money"**, and **"Paper Money"** by the same author, will chronicle his rise, fall, and resurrection. Mr. Belim's resurrection as a new urban writer has given his readers a glimpse into the Black Underworld of trickery and deception.

E-Books $9.99

LOYALTY REIGNS by Japlin Cureton
ISBN # **978-0-9844071-8-7**
Page Count **413** Price Book **$17.99**
Prison order price: **$11.00**

“Loyalty Reigns" exposes the raw and often ugly truth about survival in a world tainted by jealousy, rivalry, violence, drama and mayhem; disagreements settled only by bullets and blood. The question whose answer determines who lives or dies that day is, "Will Loyalty Reign or will the storms of betrayal make it hail?" Be for warned, it's not a fairy tale or a story for the squeamish or the faint-hearted, but if you’re unafraid to be inoculated with a dose of reality, jump into a Destinations Cab and join Jap Cureton for an "adults-only" tour through the unforgiving world where only "Loyalty Reigns," and honor rules.

This story chronicles the act of deception where there are no honor amongst thieves. Where mayhem thrives in a sinful world of MONEY, SEX, and POWER. Decrypt coincidences, coordinated murders, set-ups, perpetrated by Blueberry, and dishonest Agents will test ones quest of LOYALTY REIGNS!

Jap Cureton is presently at work on the second book of the "Loyalty Reigns" trilogy.

E-Books $9.99 www.kobo.com

INDICTED by Lamont Christian
ISBN# **978-0-98440071-7-0**
Page Count **341** Price Book **$16.99**
Prison order price: **$11.00**

They say that there are two sides to every story and to every coin, but what most don't know is that there are two sides to a small section of the city's world renown Island "MANHATTAN". And it all Depends on which side you are on. Harlem always rung louder and there is only one thing that mattered above all and it's that "paper".

In this story of East meets West, the traditional fashion of how the sedative that is excreted from a syringe, through the eye of a needle and finally into the blood stream of heroin hungry veins, causes sides to clash. This eventually places the "self proclaimed king of Harlem" Lavell Collins in direct opposition with the eastside and that inadvertently puts Yvonne, Lavell's girlfriend in a freedom compromising, life altering situation.

INDICTED is a story that illustrates love, lost and the desperation that often justifies the behavior of those residing in Harlem and the various communities that mirror it. Places where addiction consumes the home, demoralizes the people and erodes the spirit. Like the many that came before it, INDICTED gives readers a unique and in depth look at a world where the social, economic mechanics, that has for generations plagued our culture, could be unfair and outright discriminative.

This goes beyond the 2014 version of Romeo & Juliet because it takes place in HARLEM where Lavell and Yvonne have to fight for everything, including the basic liberties such as life and love while fending for one another, even if it's by their own set of rules.

E-Books **$10.99**

www.kobo.com

FANTASY BALL by ADENA

ISBN#**978-0-9844071-9-4**

Page Count **437** Book Price **$17.99**

Prison order price: **$11.00**

ABANDONED 310 MILLION YEARS AGO, IN WHAT IS NOW SOUTHWESTERN PENNSYLVANIA, A GROUP OF BALLS ARE SLOWLY UNEARTHED DEEP IN A FAMILY COAL MINE. THE FIRST TO BE DISCOVERED IS A NINE FOOT TALL YELLOW FANTASY BALL. NEITHER, NASA OR OTHER SCIENTIST CAN IDENTIFY WHAT THE IMPENETRABLE SPHERE IS MADE OF.

WITH NO APPARENT USE OR VALUE, THE OWNER OF THE COAL MINE PLOPS THE BALL DOWN IN HIS BACK YARD FOR HIS 13 YEAR OLD SON TO PLAY ON. YET IT IS THE AUTISTIC NEIGHBOR GIRL WHO USES HER GIFT OF MENTAL TELEPATHY TO OPERATE THE YELLOW SPHERE. SO JOIN CHAD AND VENUS ON THEIR SOMETIMES DANGEROUS, YET ALWAYS THRILLING, ADVENTURES THROUGH TIME AND SPACE IN THE FANTASY BALL. THE FIRST BOOK IN THE SERIES.

ORDER FORM

Name:____________________

Address:____________________

State:____________________

Phone# ____________________

Send Mail :

New Era Books

2569 Pitkin Ave

Brooklyn, New York 11208

Title(s) purchased:

____

______________________________ Ship: $2.50

______________________________ Total $______

Purchase on line: www.newerabooks.net or call 347-651-6366

Always include alternative book selection for unavailable books

Book Submissions & Inquiries: newerapublication@aol.com

Free shipping with the purchase of any two books.

PRISON DIRECT

Prison Direct: Family and friends can send New Era books, posters, greeting cards directly to any inmate in State/Federal prison. New Era Books promotes education for this reason we sell books to the prison population at a discounted price. Order Prison Direct through newerabooks.com

Rehabilitation Begins With Education……